AGRUSHELL

MARTIN MORRIS

SEVERED PRESS
HOBART TASMANIA

AGRUSHELL

WWW.SEVEREDPRESS.COM

ISBN: 978-1-925493-53-5

AGRUSHELL

Beneath the ocean's glimmering waves, beyond the reflections and early light-shafted shallows.

Outside the commercial shipping lanes, far from the breakers of land's shores, in a place where the sunlight fails to reach.

In the deepest subterranean currents, the deepest abyssal trenches of the seabed, there in the darkest of endless nights, the Agrumen seek and hunt with ancient cunning and skilled lore.

Born of the deep, hunters of old, in the cold dark waters of the fathomless ocean's floors, the Agrumen kill and feed.

The masters of their world, unfettered by its pressured depths, they have adapted to the harshest of environments on the planet we inhabit.

In waters barely glimpsed by the dark eye of the blue whale or suggested in fanciful stories of deep-sea divers of our kind, in these waters, creatures with alien emotions and dark passions rule supreme.

They are homed in a deep water world of dark pressure and cold, honed by nature's extremity to a sharp and deadly edge.

CHAPTER 1 — DAWN

The merchant ship Evectoria, *chartered by Flomax PLC, a civil oil company, dropped its undersea seismic charges in grid reference 33445-55. This returned geological data of anti-syncline of a magnitude with a high chance of oil. The owners of the company were very pleased. The seabed where the seismic charges fell was made into a wilderness.*

Neither the stillness of the sea, nor the mirror of its silver surface could hide the Atlantic Ocean's immensity, nor conceal the knowledge of abundant life within its infinite and unseen depths.

The edges of retreating storm clouds glowed with honey and intricately bright straw yellows with the new day's light. The dawn reflected across the ocean to point at silhouetted box shapes, a towering derrick, and the dark metal shapes of cranes.

The North Sea oil platform Danson, field3 was an alien construction of man in a world of ocean, crisscrossed metalwork that stood impervious to the battering white-tipped waves from which it sprang, on vast grey-painted steel columns.

The changing wonder of the dawn, however, escaped 'Mud Engineer' Steve Staples completely; he observed the growing light with a hangover-aggrieved squint.

He was leaning over the helipad railings and shivering. His black half-length coat and jeans were failing to keep out the dawn's early chill. Long brown hair fell away from his face as he drank coffee from a polystyrene cup. Then, as he hung his head over the rails again, his hair fell to cover his red-rimmed eyes.

A tight knot of worry was clenched in his belly as he worked his thoughts around the events of last night, causing anxiety to creep like sickness up his throat.

He rubbed his eyes and cursed his aching head and roiling stomach, which had turned to bile at the taste of last night's copiously, consumed lager.

He spat weakly over the side of the oil rig's helipad railings and raised the cup of black bitter coffee that 'Gerald the cook' had pushed into his hands, probably just to escape his stale beer breath.

Steve was sure the tub of lard hadn't washed his own hands since he got on this trip. How dare he look down his sweaty nose at him, hangover or not? Although, he knew from vast experience that his hangovers were not a pretty sight.

He took a moment to visualize himself pouring his coffee over 'le fat chef' but soon lost the mental energy. Instead, he was left feeling weak and generally sorry for himself, with only the ghosts of a self-confident identity for company.

As he pondered his self-inflicted sickness and the consternation caused by last night's card game, a voice disturbed his inner thoughts.

"Hi there, Mr. Staples!"

It was Dan Giles, the ship's resident junior geologist and generally happy bugger, calling out to him as he walked across the helipad.

"Are you enjoying the dawn?" he asked, his face already lit with a ready smile. "It's quite something, don't you think?"

Dan was blue-eyed, well-spoken, and big enough to give you pause for thought. All topped off with a modest and easy manner. A man whom Steve wanted to resent for his good fortune but couldn't. He could see the man's genuine warmth in a soft, almost imperceptible, amber radiance. Dan's head and shoulders were shrouded in a delicate vivacity of light, which Steve had seen and trusted before.

The subtle radiance reminded him of his aunt in her purple dress, imbued with the none-too-subtle aroma of joss sticks and that warm glow. She was the one who'd first mentioned the word 'aura' to him, like a shared secret wisdom, in a room filled with glass and pottery angels, and who'd shared the same gentle luminosity of colors that Dan emanated. Perhaps, despite his customary aloofness , it was why Steve had begun talking to the man so soon after they'd met.

He was instantly drawn to the genuine friendliness he saw and the easy companionship on offer. It left him torn between the inner distance he tried to keep from people and his own desperate need for friendship, all of which only seemed to increase his inner confusion.

Waiting briefly for an answer that didn't follow, Dan continued talking.

"It's strange, the change between the dark of night and the dawn of the day," he mused aloud and then looked earnestly into Steve's eyes.

"The time when one changes to the other, it's primal, like we're at the beginning of everything, feeling the world begin again all around us. Or maybe we realize the fragile nature of our existence, having survived the cold of the night, shivering in the dark and waiting for the dawn?"

With the delicate state of his stomach and the ache behind his eyes, Steve certainly felt fragile.

"I don't know," Steve said. "It's bloody cold enough, though." And Dan laughed as if they had shared a great joke together.

Bemused and strangely unsettled by Dan's words, as if they were a warning or explanation of something he couldn't quite understand, he wanted to ask for an explanation, to try and share in this revelation, but that something inside him like a barrier in his chest held him back as it always did.

The long-distant sound of his mother's voice was wise and patient in his memory. "The sensible voice is the one that listens before it speaks."

He remembered her soft voice and kind smile, and for a moment his defenses were down as the memory of her kindheartedness flooded him; tears sprang to his eyes, and he clung desperately to the railing. Then, the rawness of another memory of his mother, this one painfully dark, sprung up, and his emotional shutters slammed shut. He glanced quickly to see if Dan had caught his momentary weakness, but Dan's eyes were out to sea, on the rising dawn.

"It's just another crappy day in paradise, Dan, and this coffee proves it," he managed weakly.

He raised his half-empty cup, grimaced, and mimed a gag, hoping his voice was steady.

Dan smiled a golden-brown gentleness, and Steve's inner barrier was again shaken.

"Well, Steve, we may not have great coffee, but we have some view," Dan mused, returning his gaze to the sunrise.

Steve was suddenly saddened by the feeling he was missing a connection, a sharing of something important, and he understood that the failure was in him. He brooded on his hangover again and wished that he had the courage to open up his feelings, to finally share his inner thoughts with his companion. But all he could do was watch Dan from the corner of his eye, searching for (and not finding) a way past the silence of his solitude to share his well of emotions with the other man.

He heard a familiar childhood chant in his mind: 'Freaky weirdo, with a strange hairdo.'

Still unanswered, Dan gently shrugged off the quiet and said in a benevolent voice, as if he were accepting Steve's failings, "Perhaps, it is that the dawn's fragile light gives us hope, after the fears of the dark night."

Quickly brightening, he said, "Well, enjoy the new sun and a beautiful day. I will see you later, Steve. I've got to make a call home to say goodnight to the kids."

Steve watched him leave with sleep-grimed eyes that unexpectedly seemed a little blurry. "Yeah, I will see you later ..."

And Dan strode away.

"Oh, marvelous," he admonished himself about his useless interaction with his friendly conversationalist. "Very well done."

The undemanding and friendly Dan had left him feeling aggravated and remote. He was a little disappointed that Dan hadn't the time to reverentially talk about his family; he enjoyed the feeling he got when Dan described them, a tingle of gladness, as if the children were laughing somewhere close by.

He kept seeking the man's presence—he desired the warmth he felt in Dan's company—but like a wise old moth he feared the flame. In his heart he envied the easy nature of the man, and it left his inability to risk exposing his secret a nagging irritation.

He looked down over the walkway bars again, to the water's surface beneath him, and in a fit of annoyance dropped the half-full polystyrene cup of 'le fat chef' coffee. The cup smacked against a pipe, spraying its contents out over the oil rig's inner framework. The random act of vandalism dismissed his thoughts of Dan but opened the doorway for his trepidation about last night to return. He kicked a walkway post with a steel-toe-capped rigger boot for good measure and was pleased by the solid thud and subsequent thrumming vibration, but his physical display was also rewarded by a sudden wave of nausea.

He quickly went down two levels, nervously looking around the accommodation levels, white corrugated metal rectangles piled like huge Lego bricks on one side of the platform. With the operations and science blocks they were piled the same, but in red and green on two of the sides. The last side of the rig's metal-framed square held the cranes and helipad substructure.

Jogging up the walkway toward his cabin, he began to feel relief loosen his knotted insides. He'd made it without running into the source of his anxiety, but when he turned the last corner to his cabin, he found it waiting for him with a stomach-turning grin.

The large beefy frame of Lee Jones turned toward him with a fake welcome on his large fleshy face. Behind him like a smirking wolf was Brainy Michaels, who was the rangy opposite of the big, brawny Lee Jones. Brainy radiated oddly mixed yellows and reds in his aura, shades too confusing for him to interpret, unlike those of Lee Jones.

"Hello, Stevie, mate. Was just coming to check how you were feeling. Just wanted to make sure you hadn't forgotten about the money you owe me from last night."

He drawled around a replay of his toothy grin, while putting a chunky hand on Steve's shoulder in an uncomfortable imitation of friendship.

Steve sensed a void of compassion that hovered in Lee's aura, like a black lake of spite behind his façade of charm; it leaked a radiance of dark, gangrenous greens.

"Mind you, you could always try and win again tonight, if you feel a bit luckier?" Lee continued with his act of good-natured banter, but it was colorless and without friendship.

Steve's stomach dropped, and his mouth went dry. He had lost every penny he had to Lee last night.

He'd always been good at cards, had always seen in the shifts of their surrounding radiance when the other players had strong or weak cards, when someone else wasn't confident in the card they played or was just plain bluffing. But last evening in the hot and oppressive atmosphere of the canteen, when he was faced with Lee's smiling antipathy, he needed lager just to get through the experience, and his gambling edge had vanished in its haze.

He was caught as always between his need for acceptance and being the person he felt himself to be inside, while never finding a place of contentment between the two.

"Er, yeah, sure, Lee, of course I can ... You can give me a chance to win it all back, mate?" he asked, his voice sounding too high and anxious.

Lee's grin became even wider.

"No problem, Stevie. I wouldn't want you to go ashore with nothing. Or without feeling you'd paid your debts, mate." His tone was jovial, but a cutting edge hid beneath his easy tone.

Lee laughed and Brainy joined in. Steve felt a wave of cold wash through his bowels that settled like ice in his stomach. When they had left, he went to a metal toilet cubicle, locked himself in and waited till his guts unclenched and the shaking in his legs subsided. The worst was his knowing that he'd have to try and win tonight, or he would be broke and would have only his home, his mother's old flat, left to pay off his debt.

Dan retreated from yet another perplexing conversation with the enigmatic and dark Steve Staples that left him frustrated. They had been coming across each other on the helideck since Dan first arrived six weeks ago. He felt that the roughneck man, though mostly quiet, was more than he seemed to be. In between silences he let slip moments of humour and intelligent insight that tantalized Dan's interest. Unlike the man on deck today, Steve usually seemed to have an innate ability to catch whatever mood Dan was in.

It may be that he wanted to see more in Steve than was there, because of his lack of common ground with his management colleagues. Dan had expected, with his university background, to be welcomed as one of their own, but the management had turned out to be a mixture of arrogance, ignorance, and overbearing self-importance.

Maybe he just missed the camaraderie of student life. He'd not located one person with a shared interest or a desire to discuss anything beyond the work the rig carried out, football, cards, and TV and action films.

He arrived at his cabin still pondering the strange yet enigmatic character he had begun to think of as a companion and went straight to his desk, picking up where he had left off in his latest letter to his wife. Due to his boredom and social seclusion, the letter was reaching epic proportions.

He told her more stories of his boss and head of geology, John Lawson, or 'School Bully' as he nicknamed him, trying to imagine her smile as he wrote about the man's 'egg in a nest' balding head.

He found himself telling her about the 'Mud Engineer' Steve and one of his acerbic one-liners about the roughneck crew all being *Planet of the Apes* extras. He chuckled a little to himself as he wrote.

He described their conversations quite often, and he hoped his latest descriptions of everything and everyone on the platform would not make her as bemused or perplexed as he felt.

He turned to look at the picture on the wall of his kids and his wife, Lilly; her delicate features lit by the brilliant perfection of her smile stopped him in his tracks and made his chest ache, as he wondered for the millionth time why someone so beautiful and amazing would love somebody as average as himself.

He sat on the edge of his bunk looking at the clock, knowing it would be an hour till he could call and say good night to the kids, as he waited on this heap of metal in the middle of the ocean, missing everything that mattered to him. He wondered again if the money was worth what he'd left behind.

Thinking once more of the kids, he set about drawing another picture for Arron, who shared his love of drawing. He fancied himself a half-decent artist, and he started a picture of a wild-haired man standing on a raised metal area, gripping a railing with one hand and pointing out to sea with the other; behind him a storm was coming in.

Hundreds of miles away and as deep as seven Grand Canyons, in the Puerto Rico Trench, at the edge of the Atlantic Ocean's reach, a being the length of a blue whale and twice its width rose like an ethereal shadow from the pitch black deep.

Its upper surface the dark of night, its underside lightened like the sunlit shallows far above, its colouring camouflaged it from above and below.

It stretched its senses wide, seeking for prey and danger alike, till its awareness covered miles of open ocean water, all monitored by its cold, calculating intelligence.

A being with a name that we would understand as Agrushell *accelerated effortlessly while water surged over his outer shell, flowing with frictionless ease around the fractal perfection of his shape. Thrusting like a spearhead through the water toward an unsuspecting giant squid, Agrushell was a dark disguised shape with infinite power and the prowess for fatality.*

Before his prey had opportunity to evade, a dull electrical thud resonated through the water, leaving the squid stunned. Suctioned coils gripped and newly formed blades entered like a clamp, till blackness was all that remained of the squid's final moments.

When the pleasure of the kill had been savoured, and his hunger sated, Agrushell began to feel a different kind of hunger, a yearning toward the cold waters of the north—the calling to where the females of his kind lay on the seabed in ancient hibernation, waiting for the time of awakening, breeding, death, and renewal.

Streamlining his shape to maximize his speed, he began accelerating like an underwater jet to the north east, toward the oil fields of the North Sea.

CHAPTER 2 — DEFEAT

Steve paused outside the canteen door and inhaled and then blew out his cheeks in a slow, ragged breath that shuddered with the nerves writhing in his stomach; his mouth was dry, and his mind whirled with different plans and scenarios— what he should do when he went in, or whether he should go in the room at all.

The first plan that struck him was that he should go back to his cabin, lock the door, and not come out till it was time to go ashore on the next resupply ship.

He could refuse to play cards with Lee Jones and his cronies, get his dinner and find a table as far away from them as possible.

But the weight of worry in his belly was caused by the knowledge he'd have to play and could not afford to lose. He couldn't lose the only thing his mum had had in the world to leave him when she'd died; it was the only place that he'd truly belonged in his life. It was all he had.

Against his own will he pulled down the cold metal handle, stepped through the iron doorway, and was met by a blast of warmth. He closed the door behind him, keeping his back to the room as he took off his coat and hung it with the line of others on the rack alongside the door, all the while avoiding the faces behind him.

He paused, listening to the hubbub of voices and the odd, raucous laughter that were the colour of butterscotch and gold in his mind. Then, with a sigh and a dash of motion, he turned and hurried toward the canteen kitchen serving plates, trying to focus only on his intended destination.

He arrived to the aroma of tonight's 'toad in the hole' dinner, and he quickly picked up a hard brown plastic tray like a shield. As he turned slightly sideways with a glance, his eyes caught the faces at the closest table, and he saw Jones's sidekick, Brainy, and his group of mates. They seemed oblivious to his arrival, wrapped up in their own discussions over their meals, and his hopes rose. He was about to turn back to the glass-fronted serving plates, when, at the end of the table, he caught Lee's face; Lee looked straight at him with that familiar grin, and Steve's heart sank.

Jones waved him over, pointing to the empty seat in front of him, and suddenly the temperature in the room seemed to be rising. A movement of the air made him aware of the sweat forming on his brow.

He turned back to the hot plates and was looking straight at Gerald, the overweight and resident 'le fat chef.' The man's large face was red and slick with a sheen of sweat from the heat of the stainless-steel serving dishes in front of him; he exuded thin yellows shot through with a grey radiance of indifference. Each of the trays before him was heaped with the individual steaming elements that made up tonight's dinner.

"So, what'll it be?" the man asked disinterestedly as he brandished a stainless-steel serving spatula over a steel tray of toad-in-the-hole.

Steve felt his stomach seesaw and couldn't imagine anything he wanted less than something to eat. He pointed without any real desire at the tray that the big chef stood in front of and watched without appetite as food was loaded onto his plate. They followed this formula till his plate was covered in a full meal that he couldn't imagine eating a mouthful of.

The chef waddled back to the start of the line to serve the next person, while Steve picked up a knife and fork and surveyed the selection of condiments and sauces, trying to desperately delay the moment he had to turn around.

"Are you going to use any of those?"

He was shocked by a voice right next to him that made him jump. He turned with his heart in his throat to look into the quizzical face of Dan.

"You okay there, Steve? Or is it your intention to hold the tomato sauce hostage?" he asked with curiosity and humour in his tone.

Steve was suddenly dumbstruck with the shock of the unexpected interaction, and, unable to find a response to the quip, he just glanced hesitantly past Dan to the patiently waiting grin of Lee Jones.

Dan followed his gaze, and his tone became more serious.

"Is everything alright, my friend? You look a bit out of sorts."

Dan radiated a warm pink threaded with the gold of concern, and it calmed him.

"No, Dan, I'm fine, thanks." He paused; the visceral nature of his apprehension made him want to speak out, but at the same time he didn't want getting Dan getting involved in his troubles or complicating his circumstances. Maybe he just didn't want to admit what an idiot he was to Dan.

"Must not be a fan of amphibians in my hole, I guess," he managed feebly.

Dan gave him a smile and moved to secure a glass bottle of Heinz ketchup.

"To be fair, you're probably right. Nothing worse than a frog in the throat. It could get serious, and they'd have to hop-erate."

He smiled again and left Steve with a wink.

The ridiculous repartee left Steve feeling momentarily cheery, but as Dan walked away Steve's eyes were drawn back to Lee and the lead in his abdomen returned.

With a slow, resigned pace, he drifted slowly over to Lee's table and the waiting chair and sat in front of the big man and his wide unforgiving grin.

"Well, Steve, old mate, get that scran down your throat, and we can break out the cribbage board for the night, what do you say?"

He spoke sociably, but his eyes were like a predatory bird's, and the black lake behind them was chilling. Steve almost got up and left. But he must keep his nerve and make back at least some of the money he'd lost.

Most of the others at the table were already playing over the rectangular cribbage boards. They were perforated in two parallel lines that went up and arced around their outside edge, which the men were moving matchstick pegs along to indicate their scores, then onto the next end, back up the middle to stop near where they had begun, with two coloured holes for a finish line.

Each set of two players was fixed on the cards and moving their pegs while maintaining a level of chitchat, banter, and discussion about their ongoing games. Their auras were coloured in reds and ambers; depending on who was the more successful, they had more warmth in their shades of yellow. As he watched, Brainy flicked him a calculating glance. Brainy was an odd mix of darker scarlet and honey colours, both threatening and warm, that oddly drew Steve to the unnerving man. Snatching his gaze away, Steve refocused on the food he was pushing around his plate while avoiding the eyes of the man in front of him.

"Well, Steve, you don't seem to have much of an appetite, mate. Shall we get on the game?" Lee's voice, though pitched in a friendly tone, was underlined with impatience.

Resigned to the inescapable necessity of what was about to happen, Steve managed to force a forkful of sausage into his mouth as if he'd been making a real attempt to eat, then he put his cutlery together and pushed the tray away.

"Whitehead, me old mucker, would you take this tray away for us, my friend? Me and Steve got some serious man cards to play," Jones said, fixing Steve with an unforgiving scrutiny.

He spoke with cheerful good humour to the man next to him, while never turning away his blue-eyed, black gleaming gaze from Steve.

"Yeah, sure, Lee, I'll just finish this hand," Whitehead said, leaning intently over his own cards.

Lee's smile disappeared, and he turned his frigid gaze onto Whitehead, who managed, with obvious difficulty, to hold his nerve under the weight of Lee's stony look for several seconds, until finally the pressure told and forced him to put down his cards.

"Right, let me grab that for you now, guys." Whitehead attempted to sound happy to help, but a flick of his eyes toward Lee gave away his irritation.

He leaned over and picked up the tray, then struggled to climb out of the seat with a man on either side of him. Lee watched with an emotionless face until the man stood and began to walk away.

"While you're up, mate, why don't you do a beer run for us all?" Lee asked with a flat tone, which was as much a demand as a request.

Whitehead pulled up short as he walked away, his shoulders bunched as if he were trying to master his emotions, which flared in a crackling red and scarlet corona around him.

"Sure, Lee, why not, eh?" he said in through clenched teeth, continuing on with a now slightly angrier stomp to the canteen serving counter.

Lee turned back with a contented grin again on his face, but his eyes glittered with satisfaction that seemed to leak black emptiness around their edges. He produced a board and cards from the jacket on the back of his chair, and they began setting up the cribbage board to begin the game.

"Shall we start at a pound a point, Stevie boy?" Lee asked happily around his fake cheerful smile.

Steve knew that cribbage was, on the face of it, a simple game of making cards add up to fifteen, with runs of cards to score points, and that there was a large element of luck in the hand that was dealt you. The secret skill in winning over a long period, without luck, lay in the pegging (each player must lay down one of their four cards in turn) to score points, before the score in the hand you'd been dealt could be added up.

By estimating how your opponent played, whether the first card they laid could be paired or whether the player would want you to pair, so they could lay a third card of the same to triple their score, or whether laying an eight, was a gambit that could create runs or a seven could be laid to score fifteen. There were multiple ways of upping your score even with a poor hand; the box (two cards from each person's hand to make an extra hand of four for the player on his turn) could also be made rich pickings for points or, on your opponent's turn, a barren resource.

All of these options were improved if you had a feeling for which options your opponent was taking, say because of a shift in the shimmering colours he exuded. So it went with the early games as Steve read Lee's shifting crown of light and scored heavily off him. And, with a decent run of luck in the cards he was dealt, Steve quickly amassed about seventy-four pounds, and Lee's false smile began to fade.

"Let's make this interesting, shall we, Steve? How about we do ten pounds a point and see if we can get you back in the black, eh?"

Though he tried to sound as if he were attempting to be encouraging and benign, Lee's tone was one of truculent condescension, the faint shimmering eddies of light around him dark and shot with reds.

"Sure, Lee, that's mighty kind of you," he said, trying to keep his tone even and free of sarcasm.

Lee eyed him darkly for a moment as if trying to find insult in his words, then, as if deciding that Steve's words were immaterial, continued setting up the board. He followed this with shaking an empty beer can at Whitehead, who, with his own fabricated smile of compliance, grudgingly went for more lagers.

The games continued, and Steve continued winning, reading shifts in Lee's emotional reactions. His emotions shifted from shades of pink shot through with orange that turned to scarlet reds of anger as his traps and pairing guesses failed. But all the time the well of black malice behind the man's eyes built, till it seemed to fill his eyes like a black mist of spite.

As Steve amassed about a thousand pounds, some nine thousand short of what he owed, Lee's veneer of affability was quickly disappearing. It was replaced by grumbling against Steve's outrageous good fortune and a baleful black glare that seemed to be gradually injecting the man's bile into Steve's subconscious. The weight caused by Lee's outpouring of disgruntlement and rage felt like pressure building inside Steve's skull. The man's growing anger appeared to break the dam holding back the black malice behind his eyes, and it poured out in vaporous black streams, cascading over Steve like cold air from a freezer, invisible to everyone else around him.

His mouth dry, his insides turning to knots with a fevered oppression, Steve began gulping lager in an attempt to dissipate the malign mist that pervaded his senses, and for a short while, though less successful, he continued to win.

As his winnings amassed, the outpouring of Lee's malign fury increased till Steve found himself encircled by its cold loathing and a growing collection of squashed lager tins. Almost as if this sudden recognition of his surroundings triggered a change in his fortunes, Steve lost any insight or intuition he had previously had—it seemed to evaporate in his drunken state—and from then on, he began losing steadily.

Dan had kept an eye on Steve since he'd sat down to eat; he

watched him sit across from Lee Jones, and it raised hackles of concern, as Steve seemed bowed by the big man's presence. He looked forlorn and fearful in his company, and it seemed impossible that he would have sought it unless under some form of duress. It would explain Steve's quiet introverted behaviour earlier today, he thought.

He'd come across Lee Jones only infrequently, but the man's perpetual over-easy grin seemed more like a mask to him, and he'd heard odd comments that suggested the bloke was something of a bully, at best. So, with unease he watched them as the evening progressed and as the large thick-necked man became more angry and aggressive.

He had no difficulty observing the card game on the other table; none of the other management team members seemed interested in engaging him in conversation. The senior management only wanted to hear what Storrel, the rig's 'Company Man' who'd arrived only two weeks prior as a replacement, had to say. He was something of a company celebrity, Dan had been told, a major player in the company's activities.

Since he'd arrived, to Dan's sinking disappointment, the rotund black-shirted Texan had led most conversations with the management, which seemed to consist of his holiday memories, work triumphs, and the general trappings of his success. The others interjected small, related holiday tales or their own work victories (probably overinflated, he thought) that might up Storrel's opinion of them, as they jockeyed for the approval of the man in charge. To Dan's frustration, they never asked why Storrel had come or what the necessity was for a high-ranking official on this rig, and Dan felt far too lowly to ask.

Chief Johnson seemed particularly eager to push his own obvious agenda for a land-bound promotion.

"Yes, the wife and I found a lovely cottage. Not an hour's drive from the company headquarters in Paisley."

Then, again, later: "Yes, sir, with my thirty years' experience with the company and my spotless record, I'm hoping to soon find a company position ashore."

And so the evening continued; Dan's only interest was in how long Storrel would stomach the ongoing barrage of hinted requests and comments aimed at securing his good opinion.

Tonight Dan had zoned out from the repetitive conversations and sucking up early and wished that, like Jenkins, the gregarious 'Barge Engineer,' he could join whatever company he chose. He enviously glanced at the table Jenkins was sitting at, a table that seemed to be sharing jokes and lively conversation the likes of which Dan's companions had never dreamt of.

He flicked his eyes away, back to Steve and his card game, to see the man slumped in his seat, his head weaving and his gaze bleary. It reminded him of a man at their church who'd gambled away his car, house, and life. All the while continuing to gamble in an insane attempt to win back what he'd lost. He recognized that particular look of free-fall insanity.

Lee Jones's face was once again lit up with his trademark grin, but this one seemed to have a malicious pleasure in its making. Suddenly, concern drove Dan to his feet, and he walked briskly around the room to reach the table on the opposite side of the canteen.

"How you doing over here Steve? Having a good game?" He ignored the sudden bristling annoyance that radiated from Jones, which was soon followed by Jones's and his hostile glare. This, too, Dan ignored.

Steve's head remained down as if he'd lost the strength or will to lift it or to make the effort to answer Dan's question; it just hung in the silence between them.

"Steve …" he tried again. But Jones quickly interrupted him.

"We're having a nice friendly game and a few beers, but many thanks for your concern. Steve's fine. Aren't you, mate?" Lee said without hesitation and an edge of aggression in his tone.

The repeating of his name seemed to rouse Steve, and he looked indecisively between them with alcohol-bloodshot eyes, which Dan could see were filled with misery and loss.

"Looks to me like he's had enough," Dan said, ignoring Jones and lifting Steve to his feet. "I'll get him back to his cabin."

He finished pulling Steve up and got his arm over Steve's shoulder.

Jones stood as well; his eyes had gone flat, and any pretence of friendliness had disappeared.

"I think he's fine just where he is. It's no business of yours. It's not like he's your girlfriend, is it?" Lee's chin jutted with challenge, but he glanced nervously at the management table Dan had just left, and it was obvious that his bluster was a bluff.

"If you gentlemen will excuse us, I think it's time I get my other half home."

He smiled at the table, which was made up of slightly bemused faces; with the exception of the roughneck he'd met called Brainy, who had a happy grin on his face.

With a last look into Jones's eyes, Dan dared him to do more before he turned to leave with the dead weight of Steve. The big man seemed to master himself, however, and, with feigned disinterest, sat back down.

Dan took his opportunity and made for the exit.

CHAPTER 3 — CONFUSION

Steve fled the other roughnecks when the flat harmonica note of the siren signaled lunch; he was hungover, dirty, and in need of fresh air. He felt as if he had been washed in sour-alcohol-laden sweat from his hangover, until its stink had permeated into his flesh.

His day so far had been one of degradation and humiliation.

He had undergone a tirade of ridicule from his coworkers, along with a casual splashing and splattering with anything sea-wet or oil-filthy.

Chief architect of his belittling was Lee Jones. The hulking roughneck supervisor wore a grin that failed to conceal his hard nature as he watched the others taunt Steve, behavior that Jones had orchestrated, no doubt.

"Jones tells us you don't stand up like a man when you have a gamble. That true?"

"Don't pay yer debts? What are you, some sort of thief?"

"Where do you get off trying to rob our mate? You loser!"

On the occasions that Jones's eyes met Steve's, the black and emerald vapor of his look was of hard-hearted contempt; it was enough to put ice in his veins.

The message was clear: pay up, or else.

Jones led the others by the force of his hostile will, and the eight other roughnecks all had auras of a similar green, mixed with cold yellows. They were arranged in a pecking order below Jones, and Steve didn't make a rank of importance, so he was just pecked.

He was like the other men, in that he shared their work, but essentially he was different. He'd always found it difficult to deal with others' emotions—they were too intense, too unnervingly personal—and his avoidance marked him apart.

The cold hostility and comments had continued all morning, till it seemed he was being hollowed out and his mind was being shrunk within his skull. Only his anger at his own weakness kept him going.

But his desperation and inner ire always led him back to the same place, his mother screaming on the other side of a white-paneled door.

Lee Jones seemed to share the same ability as Steve's father—just the memory of him gave Steve an emotional stomach cramp—they both seemed able to drown him with the force of their cold emotive supremacy.

His card gambling debts had grown beyond his ability to repay them, and despite his offering his parents' home as collateral, Jones was not satisfied; he seemed to smell his deceit, as if he knew the tired old flat would not cover the size of what he was owed. His questioning was becoming more intense, and the large man's aggressiveness had grown each time that Steve failed to convince him of his honesty. He knew it was only a matter of time till Jones would want to beat the truth from him, and the dread made his stomach writhe and acid rise in his throat.

Tired and soul-sick with desperate anger, he sought the safety and escape of the helipad. Subconsciously, he probably sought the earnest companionship of Dan, whom he often found there; maybe he could get his help.

He stalked toward the metal-fenced edge, weakly cursing Lee Jones and his band of apes in a litany of angry impotence.

He waited for Dan to magically appear in answer to his need, he desperately wanted the man's friendship, but at the same time he was afraid that Dan would simply reject him. His need brought out his rage; it was the only way he could find past the eye of his inner fear. He began cursing more angrily.

So, he waited alone on the pad, with only the far cry of seagulls on the wing, the smell of sun-heated tarmac, and the taste of salt in the sea breeze for company. Feeling weak-kneed, he rested his arms on the cold tubular metal railings, trying to gather the will to go back and finish his shift.

It was then he felt the vibrations for the first time.

In the cool, air-conditioned operations room, the data on the incoming vibrations had caused a heated debate. Johnson, the Chief of Operations, was watching the young geologist Dan being berated by Lawson, the rig's head geologist, while he felt a growing band of anxiety tighten around his head.

Lawson was insisting the oil rig pipeline had been impacted by a moving surface incident (an earthquake). Johnson couldn't think of anything in his experience to equal such a threat, and the arrival of Storrel seemed to hover in his thoughts like an impending flood.

Taking Johnson's silence as a lack of understanding, Lawson began, with annoyingly exaggerated patience, explaining his theory to him again.

"It is geological movement in the earth's plates, like an underwater earthquake, pushing against the drill line, sir; I expect that the vibrations will soon fade. After all, there hasn't been any major tectonic movement in the North Sea for thousands of years," he said with self-importance, giving Dan a look of disdain.

"Sorry, but I don't think so," Dan interrupted. "We have no prior or ongoing seismic readings to support an earth tremor; I strongly believe something else is going on, sir."

Before either Johnson or Lawson could interrupt, he quickly continued, "These vibrations are regular and have not affected the platform's positioning, the anchoring, or the drill readings. These vibrations are not originating from the seabed." Then, belatedly trying to soothe over his disagreement with his boss's conclusion, he added, "In my opinion, that is, sir."

Lawson blushed red with embarrassment and then purple with anger as his theory was shot down by his new junior.

"Yes, well, luckily your minimal experience does not influence this rig's operations, young man," Lawson snapped. "This is obviously a pipeline problem! Pipe meets shaking seabed, causing this irregularity."

Under the stress and annoyance caused by their bickering, Chief Johnson's patience ran out.

"The question, gentlemen, is no longer of diagnosis. What do we need to do to cure this?"

He heard the snap in his voice and felt the flesh of his face wobble as he shook his head. He was aggravated by the wrangling between the pair of geologists; he needed a smooth-running and problem-free rig. The arrival of 'Company Man' Storrel on the oil platform could have deep implications. The man was a big hitter in the company, sent where there were problems and opportunities, and this could affect his bonus, share options, and promotion opportunities. More importantly, it could affect his and Rosie's plans for the future, and his failure to get a move ashore would find him on the wrong end of her fiery displeasure.

"Alright, I have listened to both your hypotheses and need to consider the best strategic way forward based on the knowledge I depend on from my valuable scientific crew," he said, trying to appease both men after momentarily losing his temper. Really, though, he was considering on whom it would be best to hang the burden of responsibility.

He'd not worked himself up through the company to chief of an oil rig without learning to make sure his decisions were always covered and that someone else would be in the firing line. His determination, with Storrel on board, was to keep his record flawless, and this was not about to be tested by any minor inconveniences created by this pair or a lack of leadership.

Johnson stood up from his chair, trying to put himself in an authoritative position above the two seated men. Smoothing down his blue pilot shirt over his ample stomach, he adopted a serious tone.

"Alright, then, gentlemen, I have heard enough. We will take decisive action to ensure the continued safe and productive running of this semi-submersible platform from the potential danger of seismic activity. To protect production, we will suspend operations pending a report."

He turned to the seated Jenkins, the rig's 'Barge Engineer,' who was bent over a laptop studying the latest data on the mooring anchors and positioning system. Johnson suspected that Jenkins's turned back and the movement of his shoulders meant he was laughing at the ongoing argument between the geologists.

Jenkins was an ex-naval man, a highly skilled merchant navy man with a large disinterest in the oil company's chain of command.

Johnson was anxious to get this situation resolved quickly and be rid of this inconvenience. "Do you agree that the chief geologist's assessment and concerns are enough to allow his suggestion for action, Mr. Jenkins?"

Jenkins swiveled around in his chair, his face a somber mask of concern.

"Yes, sir, I think you are obligated to follow his suggested course of action."

Johnson knew that when he reported to Hank Storrel later that any fallout from his decision would land on the chief geologist's shoulders, exonerating Johnson from any responsibility in the temporary closing down of production.

The young geologist, Dan Giles, was red faced and looked about to jump up and protest; Johnson gave him a hard stare, and the boy slumped back into his chair.

"Okay, Mr. Lawson," he said, "your call—what do we need to do to ensure this operation and its safety?" He had little interest in safety, but promotion and meeting his targets were at the top of his list of priorities.

John Lawson suddenly sounded as if he was preening as he rattled off his ideas.

"I suggest we get a diver down to check the rig's pipe entry into the ocean bed. I can call the oceanographic institute for updates on seismic activity, and Mr. Giles," he said sneeringly, "can monitor for activity from his geological station. That should show us the true state of affairs."

Johnson looked at Dan, who was still angry and defiant, and then at Lawson. Even though Lawson's whining upper-class voice was annoying, one look at the bald pate and the white lab coat of his head geologist were credentials enough to swing this vote, he thought. He probably had a working rig in his bathtub at home, the sweaty old geek.

"Okay, let's get Jock and Oxo down in the water," he said, picking up and clicking the handset to the rig tannoy. "Diver, to dive bay! Repeat, diver to dive bay!"

He paused and then clicked again.

"Jock Williams to the operations room, Jock Williams to the operations room," he announced over the intercom and turned back to the geologists. "Right, gentlemen, let's get on with this."

"But, sir!" Dan started.

"Shut it, junior," said the chief.

Dan looked shocked and aggrieved by his quick dismissal.

"I want answers and results, not a debate. Lawson, get down to diving bay five, and tell that diver where you want him to go and what to look for."

Lawson nodded, squared his shoulders, and shot Dan a look of malice and, fueled by his own self-righteous fury, stalked out through the operations room door.

"Alright, Mr. Giles, you know what you should be doing. Let's get to it," Johnson ordered, eager to get rid of the next irritating but necessary scientific ego.

After the peeved young geologist had left red-faced and angry, he leaned back in his chair, running his hands through the sparse grey remnants of his hair and sighed.

"Well, Jenkins, what do you think?"

Jenkins, an immense man in all proportions, of which weight was king, turned his cropped black-haired head around to face him and offered him a look of serious intent. His opinion would as always be honest; he was merchant navy and not directly a Flomax employee.

"Well, the earthquake theory sounds like a sack of crap, so the kid is probably right." He smiled, obviously enjoying the fact that old Lawson was wrong.

"So, something else is causing these vibrations. But Oxo is a good man, he'll find out what's causing it and report back what we need to know, then we can act on his information from there," the big man offered self-confidently, down turning the sides of his mouth with an expression of 'no problem.'

"Okay, and good, but what do you think it is? What's causing this damn shaking, and should I be concerned?"

Jenkins, with a glint in his eye and the flicker of a smile, replied, "My theory is, we have snagged a flock of mermaids, and they are really, really angry about it."

Johnson laughed out loud; it felt like his chest was

decompressing. Looking at Jenkins's grinning face, he felt some of the mounting pressure melt away. Though he was still tense about reporting to 'Company Man' Storrel, the moment of humor seemed to put things in perspective.

"Well, we are going to have to get some answers quick," he said, leaning on the deck table and looking down at his hands. "I can feel this damn vibration through my teeth."

When Phil Roberts, the rig's 'Driller,' interrupted the platform's day shift and told them work was suspended for the day, it started an air of mutiny lead by, to no surprise to Phil Roberts, Lee Jones.

"What do you mean, 'just stop,' with no explanation whatsoever? What are you trying to hide? If there's any danger, you have to tell us." Jones leaned his angry face close up to his.

With a sinking feeling in his stomach, Roberts replied, "We have some unwanted vibrations that we are looking into, and, just as a precaution, we are stopping for the day to get it sorted. Simple and no drama, Mr. Jones."

He tried to reinforce his words with authority, but it was a confidence he didn't feel; everybody knew these big companies only cared about the production quotas and profit margins.

"If it's nothing to worry about, why can't you tell us anything about what the problem is?" Jones closed in as if smelling his lack of assurance. The other two roughnecks with him looked suddenly menacing, with their dirty faces and fierce, white-surrounded eyes.

As if to back Jones's argument, a big shudder ran through the rig, making them all misstep slightly. It ran a lightning shock though Roberts, who tried to gather himself to do his job and explain away this new phenomenon.

But instead of the shuddering increasing the mutiny, fear and doubt appeared on Jones's face, and Roberts was determined to make the most of the opportunity.

"Right, lads, let's get shut down and cleaned up. I will get a report on the situation and buy you a beer in the canteen," he said with brisk finality, as he intended a quick exit.

Steve Staples returned from his lunch break at the precise moment that Roberts wanted to make his escape.

"Right, Staples, I want you to make sure that these boys get this mess tidied away and this deck washed down. Make sure they do a good job, or I might have to chuck you off this rig," he laughed without any real humour.

Steve Staples blanched noticeably, shooting a fearful glance at the other roughnecks, and Roberts felt a twinge of guilt; he had obviously stuck the man in a difficult position by misdirecting the men's anxiety. One look at Jones's face and he saw that the man's momentary fear had turned to anger and that Staples was now the focus. An instant passed while he considered what to do, but his body was already ahead of him and was turning away from whatever situation he had created behind him.

In the operations room, Johnson could feel his blood pressure going up.

"Well? Was it a blow out?" he asked Jenkins urgently.

"Subsea engineer Patrick says not. He says he is compensating against extra motion from the rig. He thinks that we might have lost our forward anchoring point."

"What effect will that have on the rig's production abilities?!" Johnson could feel himself being close to shrieking.

Jenkins was impassively calm. "The effect can be compensated by the rig's internal positioning engines till the anchor can be reaffixed, and it should offer no safety concerns." There was an edge of reproach in Jenkins's voice, that safety hadn't been the first order of business.

"So, no. The platform's production shouldn't be affected by the recent incident, but we still don't know the nature of the underlying problem."

Jenkins's curt summary of the situation took the edge off his immediate apprehension, but still felt as if events were getting out of his control, and he couldn't afford for it to be seen that he wasn't capable of dealing with any emergency, not with Storrel monitoring his every decision.

"Right. Once Oxo has discovered the source of our vibration

problem, we can get that sorted, and when the support boat returns tomorrow, we can get that anchoring point fixed. Does that meet with your approval, Mr. Jenkins?"

"Yes, sir, that should deal with things, alright. I will radio the boat for its return time and confirm it has a new anchor point on board, so we can make good those repairs."

Jenkins spoke in a professional monotone voice, which he couldn't read for condescension or mockery. But Jenkins's back seemed to radiate how little he thought of the orders he'd received and the person who had given them.

Before Johnson could think of a reasonable thing to say in return, the American Hank Storrel strode into the operations room.

He wore a Dolphins team baseball cap at odds with the navy jacket and white shirt that was stretched and hung over his low-slung khaki chinos. But with one look at the gathering storm clouds on his wide face, Johnson forgot about his wardrobe.

"Well, gentlemen," Storrel drawled in a southern American accent, "what kind of a shit-storm have we kicked up here?"

Steve Staples stumbled away from the sharp blow he had received; the thumping pain in his now-bleeding nose sent him reeling against a metal stairwell. Hanging onto the metal bannister, he turned back to look into Lee Jones's flushed fat face, but he was transfixed by the malevolent pleasure in the bright blue eyes as Jones closed in again with a rolling swagger.

"You play cards with me, fucker, and you had better pay me what you owe me," Lee spat at Steve in an angry rasp.

Lee deliberately clenched a fist for Steve to see, the pink fleshy hands belying the size and power behind them, size and power of which Steve's ringing skull was now suddenly and all-too-acutely aware. He could feel the man's rage radiating off him like an emotional bonfire of scarlet and black; the man's enmity seemed to twist inside Steve's mind, his rational thought fleeing in the face of the haze of hatred.

Lee's cronies stood behind him in the doorway, blocking any escape and enjoying the entertainment.

Jones and Whitehead had dragged him into the tool store and

out of sight as soon as Roberts was gone.

Steve began to panic, his guts loosened, and he suddenly felt a desperate urge to piss. Words spilled from his lips in an incoherent burst, without a drawn breath till his chest felt like it would collapse in upon itself.

"You'll get your money. I got it landside, mate, and I'll double your cash, honest. My mum's place will cover everything, honest. You'll get every penny. I wouldn't lie to you, mate. I wouldn't. I fucking wouldn't. I would … not," he gasped out.

He was beginning to lose control; it wouldn't be long till he was weeping for pity. Breathless and beaten, he slid to his knees and hung his head, trapped in the misery of his desperation.

Lee was smiling, a thin sneering smile.

"Double, you say?" he paused, as if considering the generosity of the offer, then snarled and wrenched Steve's head up by his hair, till they were face to face.

"You know what, mate? I reckon you'll get to land, and you'll vanish, just like that." He snapped his fingers in Steve's face.

Steve felt nausea rise, and he realized that he had instinctively meant to do that very thing. He was frantic with the need to escape at any cost, to escape the fear, to not be caught again with his father's empty-eyed rage in a blood-spattered kitchen.

His face must have betrayed him; his mouth had no more words, his face felt numb, and his eyes were watering. He saw only black violence in the eyes of the man who held him.

"That's what I thought, you little bastard." Lee seemed to swell with his own righteous rage. "Don't worry, we'll make sure you can't run away … not with a broken fucking leg."

Before his threat could be initiated, a massive shock ran through the metal, and a shimmering blue wave of force blasted him into blackness.

CHAPTER 4 — A REASON FOR VENGEANCE

Agrushell had thrust through the dark water of the North Sea, leaving an ephemeral trail of light in his wake. He had traveled the massive distance without stopping, without feeding. He would not, could not stop. The calling was a consuming desire that drove out all other needs.

As he cut through the ocean like a massive arrowhead, past memories flashed through his mind ... the streamers of light as the males trailed their shimmering azure mating colours in a phosphorescent challenge to the females, who enacted almost impossible hurtling maneuvers to avoid their pursuit and the almost impossible hurtling maneuvers of the small females.

He replayed their vicious changes of direction and their glorious sleek torpedo shapes as they rocketed through the water. Their beauty in motion opened and heightened his senses and raised levels of awareness within him.

He remembered the emotional interplay of flashing light signals and color, the language of shape and movement expressing the poetry of his kind. The rising spiral of his emotional force unbound his hunter's nature, and he began to connect again with his emotive being. He was burning with the inner ache to begin anew, his awoken passion driven by its new desire.

He burst onto the breeding grounds, radiating his modulated sonar call to awake the females that hibernated in the seabed below him.

But no answering resonance rebounded to him, no call of pleasure as the females awoke, only an empty silence.

He coasted close to the seafloor, throwing up rock and spirals of sand in his wake until he came across the broken casing of a female's cocoon, the fragile coral-like structure cracked along its lozenge-shaped edge. He nudged it across the sand, and a hard-shelled scavenger sped sideways from inside; the bright light of the creature he sought had long been extinguished.

He faltered in the water, unable to react to the loss of his kind, till the clouds of sand he had created drifted away, and he perceived the wreckage of other female shells, spilled and splintered across the sandy seafloor.

The shock and hurt at his kind's desolation left him floundering in emotions beyond his range of understanding, with a cold storm of rage building in his core. The fire of an unfamiliar fury and sickening anguish ran through his system, till with an immolation of emotive pain, his core state changed. Like the passing from the heavy pressure of the deep to the light-water shallows, his passion passed from the emotional fire of mating to the passionless patience of the hunter. Only the cold rage survived his altered behavioral imperative.

Suspended in the tidal flow of the current, he slowly shut out the processes of his body, seeking connection and alignment with the endless volume of sea, seeking the vibrations and echoes of life.

Agrushell's search bore quick results; the sound imagery of the deep that registered in his long perception reflected a shape in his mind. It was odd and angular, with peculiar coral shapes. This coral structure was built of precise straight lines; it screamed of an unnatural intelligence. Images and lore of the creatures in this structure had been shared in the deep.

Power flared in him, and he jetted strongly toward the creature-made reef, keeping low to the ocean bed and skimming the tops of sandbanks, leaving swirling vortexes of silt behind him. His color merged with that of the light sands below him, his senses ranging ahead, collecting sonar vision of the structure that floated part below and part above the sea surface, with long anchor lines that stretched to the seafloor.

He ghosted up to the nearest securing line and investigated its nature; the corded metal was large and encrusted. He peeled away the encrusted covering from the metal core and then peeled each individual metal strand apart, gripping each individual strand with adroit tentacles and began clenching the filaments in his reaching tentacles, closing around them and squeezing out power from deep inside himself. A pale blue energy was slowly released, thrumming up through the inside of the cable in waves.

He watched for a long time as the energy resonations returned, bringing back images in blue pulses, slowly revealing the construction's mechanical and electrical nature. Meanwhile, in another mind, he observed each and every life form through the eye of his abhorrence.

He'd seen the drowned corpses of the light-water beings he saw above, had seen them in flash-imaged memories from the elders; they were weak and ill-adapted organisms.

Enlightened about the enemy above, he snapped the heat-weakened metal. It released the taut pressure of the line and let go its potential energy, resulting in a massive jolt. He spread himself into a defensive pose, with every sense and weapon ready for an attack from above.

He waited in expanded time, but no response came.

Jetting cautiously to one of the large air-filled containers submerged at the base of the made reef, he examined their function. These long cavities appeared to keep the structure above balanced and afloat.

Here he began to make his plans to bring his enemies down to meet him in the sea.

He glided to settle upon the underside of the encrusted iron planes of the container and began to build the blue potency in the chamber inside him, starting a swirl of power that he gripped and felt condense inside him, gradually squeezing the torrent tighter, until the burning inside became like the molten fire he'd seen pour from the deep-sea rock, its painful potency demanding release.

Before the moment of discharge, he sensed danger above, a vibration like the stone-grinding surfaces in the deep; he released the puissance inside him into a bolt of blue energy that rent a large jagged hole in the metal below, sending a detonation of blue power surging up and through the metal of the structure above. Then he sped at the shadow moving on the surface overhead.

The Danson rig's serving diver, Jon Cuber, or 'Oxo' as he was popularly nicknamed, jumped into the water, feeling the familiar icy surge of the North Sea enter his wetsuit.

He'd been briefed on the vibration issue by Lawson, the lanky bald geologist, and despite having little time for the man, he had listened conscientiously as he was lectured on what he was to do and be looking for. But as always when he entered the water, he felt released. The banal, the irrelevant and endless chatter of his species that saturated him on the surface, ceased to be. Here was the peace many found in spirituality and places like his parents' Catholic church. The ocean was his angel of solitude and communion.

He was from Portugal and had been brought up with the notions of God and religious belief from childhood, but had never found any kind of comfort in them. Only the echoing silence of the sea made him feel like he was part of something greater.

He quickly located the direction of the vibration, deep and to his left, like the thrumming of a bass drum being played in a rolling beat. He followed its direction and was surprised that it did not originate from the drill site, but from the northeast side of the rig. He radioed his change of direction to Jock in the RIB (Rigid-Inflatable Boat) above, knowing that the boat would be positioned as close to above him as possible, in case of emergency. He smiled behind his mask; there was no getting away from his diving mate, Jock, who was probably already fretting and tutting at his watch with impatience. With a tight smile he kicked on toward the rig leg and the vibration's source.

He kicked his flippered feet to a faster rhythm as he felt the current push him a little off course; adjusting his direction, he glided through soft light beams dancing in the green water around him, and he followed the light down, where he caught the outline of the oil platform's leg, with the submersible pontoon at the base of it.

The thrumming was now insistent; he felt it through his wetsuit, skin, and teeth, making it difficult to focus. He blinked and squinted, trying to clear his vision from the ripples that seemed to be being born in the water before him. The dark silhouette of the underwater structure below was hazy, but there in his distorted sight loomed something large, an impossible dark shape at the edge of his unfocused vision. The terrible manifestation surged toward him, and a blue-white flash of detonation wiped his senses out in an instant.

Concussion…

He became aware again, feeling warm and comfortable; he was in his bed at home. He felt the gentle pressure of his wife lying against his side. He could tell it was morning; the light made his eyelids translucent orange.

The kids would appear soon, excited but afraid to wake him too early, their voices shy and quiet, but soon they would raise their volume in their desire to have him come and play.

His eyes opened, and the fantasy was chased away. He was on his back, looking up through water to the surface—pink: red folds of diaphanous color, like drips of tea in hot water, floated past the mist-edged view of his face mask. He was aware of an uncomfortable silence pressing against his inner ears, like the pressure of depth or after one of his wife's nights out to a pub gig. He could see the surface only fifteen meters above. He fumbled groggily for the pressure gauge against his side…

Concussion—

Light … jolt … light, then dark … He found a confused consciousness; his vision was blurred, light to his left, dark to his right. He realized he was now on his side.

With a jerk he attempted to angle his body upward to try to dig his hands for the surface. But his body was lethargic and seemed to be responding to his commands in slow motion; he could see the surface closer now, only four or five meters away.

The long shadow to his right was the rig, its outline strangely angled across the water; the platform seemed much closer than it could possibly be. As this information reached his brain through a fog of torpor, he was suddenly and acutely aware of objects floating around him.

Surely only a little time had passed, where had all these things come from? He slowly reached out to one of the unknown shapes, and it came sharply into focus, the consistency and color. He knew it to be the debris of Jock's boat, black rubber and plastic from the oil rig's RIB, shredded into fragments. He looked left. He could see a rose-tinted mangled shape hanging only yards away in the water ... Jock.

Fear stuck in his throat as he watched the remains of Jock turn in the current, a face like white wax, with unseeing dark eyes and an open, hanging mouth. A sound like high choral voices surrounded him—he could hear his children singing in the sound; he could see their soft fragile upturned faces singing Christmas carols last year at his parents' church nativity. It was his last thought before blades entered him with a sharp lancing pain, then a final blackness.

CHAPTER 5 — SINKING

Janice Strong connected the radio call from Barge Engineer Jenkins on the Danson oil rig to the bridge speakers of the oil platform support vessel 'Halia.' His static-distorted voice came over the radio speakers communicating the rig's requirements and his humor.

The big engineer's voice boomed and was just as unmistakably large as his physical proportions, even from over a hundred miles away.

During his initial contact with her, he'd spared the time to ask her to marry him (as per usual) and told her how she was missing out on a real red-blooded monster of a man. After she rebuffed him heartlessly for a hundredth time and he admitted defeat, he finally asked with a hound-dog tone of disappointment to speak to the captain. She was still laughing as she connected him to the speakerphone.

He precisely laid out the problems they had suffered on the rig and what they needed from the support vessel.

"We need chain and equipment to re-anchor one of the rig's mooring lines," he reported.

He then informed Captain Rodriguez "to stop fishing for cod out there and to pull his finger out" and added "and bring some decent whisky back here with you, too."

The dark eyes of the captain found hers, and he flashed a wide grin, his teeth white against the perfect coffee cream shade of his skin.

"Apologies, oil platform Danson 3, but this vessel only

supplies essential company items, over," the captain deadpanned back to the barge engineer in his lightly-Spanish-laced accent that gave her a tingle.

"I bet you've drunk it all with the rest of your rum pirates," Jenkins came back. "And tell that ship rat Janice that she still owes me a back rub. Travel swift and safe, Captain, and we will check your inventory together when you arrive, over."

Jenkins's outrageous flirting always put a smile on her face. They were all aware of his lovely wife and the fact that the big man loved her immensely.

Her smile faltered when she caught the brown eyes of Captain Rodriguez regarding her and she remembered that hot stare from last night. She suddenly felt a little too warm and decided to bury her face in the clipboard she held while scribbling nothing in particular on her log, hoping no one could see the red glow heating her face.

She flicked her eyes over the board and as always she found him watching her. She smiled and quickly hid her face again, feeling the familiar prickling of passion in her belly.

They had been grabbing spare moments together since last week after giving in to his subtly sexual suggestions and to her desires, while trying not to let the rest of the crew know about their affair. His cabin, her cabin, and unused storage areas gave them privacy for releasing their passions. She burned to see her pale flesh against the dark of his, to feel his strong weathered hands stroke, cup, and touch her skin. She loved getting lost in the taste of his kisses and of him tasting her. One more week and she could find a hotel on land and have him all to herself, without constantly looking over her shoulder for curious crew members.

She bit her lip against a wave of desire and wondered if it was just his wonderfully exotic nature and foreign tongue that attracted her, or if it was a part of her ongoing rebellion against the drab family home she left ashore, filled with her mother's limiting expectations.

Thinking of her mother quickly cooled the warmth from her face. The two of them always seemed to be in 'different ports' after her father had died, or perhaps she'd just never noticed how different they were while he'd been alive. Her mother had always been on land, grounded in a world of the considerations of 'society' and restrictions of the feminine sex that hailed from the 50s.

Women did not go to sea with ships full of men.

Her mother's shrewish disapproval of her 'unfeminine clothing' and her even worse crime of 'hacking off' her wonderfully long red hair was another familiar shore-leave refrain.

Her dad had been the one who had taken her to sea on all of the many vessels he had captained or on one of the many sailing boats that he'd borrowed.

Just the thought of her father brought to mind his thin grey hair sticking out from under his rumpled navy captain's hat and the cheeky grin on his weathered face. He had patiently shown her knots or how to trim a sail or any of a million things that she had wanted to know as a child, all while sharing his wonder of the sea. She'd missed him desperately when he went away for weeks at a time with the merchant navy. It left her to the monotony of school, to the unwanted ministrations of her mother and her attempts to turn her into a 'dignified young lady,' which had only reinforced her desire to be set free from the shackles of life on the land.

She leaned into the radio cubby as the ship changed its course toward the Danson 3 rig, glancing around to make sure that nobody was paying her any attention and then she found the dark eyes of her captain and gave him her best smoldering gaze. She knew that it wouldn't be till early the next day before they reached the oil platform and that both of their shifts finished in an hour; she wanted him thinking about it, too. Putting thoughts of her mother aside, she started to daydream of her and the captain alone together in his cabin.

She was shaken from a languorous sleep by a rapid knocking on the cabin door, and groggily, with a content smile, she remembered whose warm arm was across her belly and whose cabin she was in.

Another knock and she began gently shaking the arm of the

slumbering captain.

"What?!" Rodriguez exclaimed next to her, thrusting himself up on his elbows. "What the hell is it?"

Obviously thinking that the question was aimed at him, the person behind the door replied.

"Sorry to disturb you, sir, but we seem to have a problem contacting the rig, and we were ready to prepare the anchoring line on deck ... Er, we need an estimate of length and loading." It was Alan Frey, the ship's assistant captain, trying to whisper loudly through the door.

"Shit, Al, what time is it?"

"Erm, 4:30, sir. We wondered if, er, if you might know where Janice was? Y'know, to help us with the, erm, the radio, sir?"

"I see. Right. I will be on deck within five minutes, and I will see if I can rustle up our missing communications expert. Thanks, Al. I'll be right with you!"

"Ahem, yes, sir," said the uncomfortable voice from behind the door.

Captain Rodriguez waited till the sound of Alan's footsteps disappeared and then fumbled the light on and looked at her. They both began laughing. He stroked her face gently with his fingertips. There was a smile on his lips.

"You, my beautiful Chiquita, are going to get me into trouble."

"Do you think I am too much trouble for you to handle, for an old man like yourself?" she asked, snuggling against him.

His eyes narrowed, and he pulled her slight frame against him and kissed her with heat, causing a rush of desire. He stroked his hand down her side to the firm flesh of her rump, caressing, gripping, and then pinching firmly.

As she yelped, he quickly jumped up, attempting to avoid her fury.

She prepared to launch into an attack with a pillow, but found him struggling into his pants while trying to escape off the end of the bed, which made her burst out laughing again.

"I think this old sea dog can teach you a few tricks, my little siren," he chuckled.

He managed to duck the first pillow as he dragged a shirt on, but didn't evade the second, which hit him full in the face as he struggled to pull on a sock.

"I think you will need to be quicker on your feet than that, shipmate," she crowed, satisfied with her direct hit to the face and enjoying watching his agile figure flex and bend. Though she felt a little disappointed that clothes were going on and not off his muscular Spanish bum.

"Ha ha, young Chiquita, I will find the time to punish you for your mutiny later, for now I must leave. I can only hope that I may find a lost radio operator at such short notice," he said with a wink, and slipped behind the cabin door, just as another pillow hit it. He reappeared back around the door with a grin on his face.

"You had better run out the door, señor, or I will have to put you in your place when we get back in this bed," she mocked. "If your aging heart can take it!"

She stuck out her tongue as he saluted, winked, and then disappeared.

She collapsed back onto the bed with a contented sigh, and after an indulgent minute of recollection, she began feeling in the bed for her knickers.

With Frey's obvious knowledge of their liaison, she began to wonder how many of the crew knew about their relationship and what Frey would be thinking.

Giving herself a fierce shake, she told herself to stop worrying, that she would easily face them down if they all thought she was a tramp. She could be twice as foul-mouthed and ten times more cutting if they started. It was amazing how easy it was to back a male down by insulting the size of his manly masterpiece or by suggesting his inability to use it.

With a sigh she set about throwing on a T-shirt and her slightly oversized sweatshirt and slacks. She had realized early onboard that if men couldn't see a few curves then they'd pay much less attention to her femaleness. With her slender figure and unflattering choice of clothes, she attained more of a teenage-boy look and, happily, got treated more like one of the boys by the ship's crew.

She looked at her face in the mirror and saw a happy grin and blue, far-too-pleased-with-themselves eyes. She had a slight flush around her freckles from her banter with the Spanish tease-master.

Finding herself thinking back to last night again, she gave a throaty groan of disappointment and dragged herself off to the bridge.

Alan Frey pulled Janice away from the digital transmission information on her screen by gently touching her shoulder and wafting a steaming mug of coffee under her nose. With a grateful smile she took off her radio headset and rubbed her eyes.

"Is there anything yet?" Captain Rodriguez asked.

"No, it's weird. It's kind of like the rig has disappeared or something."

She stretched and swung around to face him. His face was eerily lit up by the thin blue light from the navigation screens in front of him and beyond him Chief Officer Barret looked even more ghostly. She felt a chill and gave a little shudder.

"You okay over there, Janice?" said Rodriguez. He looked concerned, and she felt herself melt a little; as usual, he missed nothing.

"Someone just walked over my grave, I think," she said with a smile. "Still, it's pretty strange ... no radio response at all. But odder still, no mobiles or internet connection. I can't even poke anyone over there."

She grinned as the bridge crew cracked up. It was moments like this that she loved her life the most, sharing daily banter with a family of people whose work and lives she shared.

"We will be there in an hour, and the sun will be up. You can stand on deck and poke your finger at them," Barret said in an uncharacteristically cheerful fashion, which set her off in gales again. Normally, Barret was a bit of a dour practical man.

"Keep trying, Janice," Rodriguez ordered, returning a serious tone to the bridge. "I am not pleased with this situation. Any ideas as to what kind of problems they might be experiencing?"

"As I said, Captain, it's very strange. If they had had an electrical fire, it might have taken out most communications, but I would be surprised if the damage stretched to mobiles and the internet. I wouldn't want to speculate further, but I think the sooner we are there to help the better," she replied.

He frowned and nodded, and for a moment she had an irrational urge to go and throw her arms around him for a comforting hug.

The faint light of dawn was appearing off to starboard, and the thin light began to invade the darkness ahead. Instinctively, she looked toward the horizon for the rig, but the wavering black line in the distance revealed no structure, only the growing definition of the oily black waves directly ahead of them.

"Right. Mr. Barret, Mr. Frey and I are going to take binoculars and see if we can get an early heads up on what we are approaching. Keep us on course and let me know if anything unusual shows up or if Janice gets any kind of message back."

"Yes, sir, Captain," Barret affirmed.

She watched them put on waterproofs and life jackets, feeling irrationally resentful that he didn't want her to go. Maybe feeling her eyes, he turned back before he left the bridge and flashed her that smile. He opened the bridge door into the noisy roar of the sea outside and let in a spray of seawater, which cut off suddenly when the door closed behind them.

"What do you think they will see this early, Mr. Barret? We won't see the rig for a while yet, will we?" Janice asked.

"No, Janice, we won't. But the captain will be looking for a glow on the horizon or smoke, if there's been a fire or such like. He will want to assess how close he thinks we can safely get the ship and if he should radio for an accident response team. Either way, I'd be ready for the worst … I can't see a happy outcome here. So, I'd be prepared to radio for assistance as soon as we know," Barret said gruffly.

Turning back to her station, she saw the forgotten coffee and suddenly realized that she didn't have the stomach to drink another mouthful.

Donning her headset, she tried again to communicate with the silent oil platform, all the while her gaze drawn back to the foredeck and the two men silhouetted in the pale dawn light.

Time passed as she listened to the hissing static in one ear and the silence on the bridge in the other, till they seemed to merge in the front of her mind.

When she next glanced out to the deck, she took a moment to

see that the two figures outside were suddenly animated and pointing to the horizon in front of them, and she thought she caught a glimpse of a distant shape. Her heart leapt; there was no smoke to be seen, and she turned to Barret with a smile. He simply looked and nodded brusquely. But she felt suddenly buoyant and gave a massive sigh of relief, as the tension seemed to flood out of her bones.

Her good cheer was interrupted by Barret's sour tone of worry.

"Something isn't right with that rig."

Looking hard out through the glass of the ship's bridge, she could just make out the rig as it dipped in and out of view, and then she saw it.

"It looks like it's leaning!"

Before the words were out of her mouth, the door crashed open and Frey entered the room, dripping water off his waterproofs across the floor.

"Janice, call into base. Tell them we have an emergency. It looks like one of the rig's flotation pontoons is damaged and has become flooded; they will need to get people off that rig ASAP and get an underwater engineering crew on-site, today."

Before he could finish, a large shock ran through the ship, knocking Frey clean off his feet to land with a meaty thump on the deck, while she was jerked off her seat and sent sprawling to the floor.

Only Barret remained standing, holding fiercely onto the ship's controls and cursing out loud.

"What the fuck was that? We must have hit something … There was nothing on the fucking sonar. What in the name of bastard Christ was that?"

She managed to get to her knees, still slightly shocked and winded. She was surprised to find that the deck seemed to be vibrating.

"What's causing that, Mr. Barret?" she asked, hearing the surprise in her voice.

"Prop damage, maybe, or something in the engines has blown. I'd better cut power till we find out what it is, or we might need sailing practice. Janice, see if Frey is okay, will you?"

She crawled across the floor on hands and knees to Frey's side.

He was moaning quietly. She touched him gently on his arm.

"Are you alright, mate?"

"Bugger it, Janice, I think I broke my arm. It hurts like a bitch."

One stomach-churning glance at his bent forearm confirmed his diagnosis.

"Alright, let's try and get you sat up, and we'll see if we can get you some painkillers and get old Francis Cooper to come and splint that up for you. I reckon it won't be too long before you're trying to put that arm around me."

Frey let out a muffled 'ha' which she hoped was a laugh.

"Right, then. We are going to roll you up and over, away from your bad arm, okay? Then we can get you sat up from there. So on three. One … two … th …"

Blue energy pulsed up from the deck and snuffed out her awareness.

She had no idea of time passing. Nothing entered the black abyss she floated in. Eventually, the surrounding blackness was punctured by the nagging sensation of being shaken. A persistent voice finally penetrated her mind's insensibility.

"Janice! You must wake up! Please, my lady, wake up!"

She heard his voice like she was waking from a dream and began to reach up for him as if he were just leaning over her in bed.

"Janice, you have to take my hand, Chiquita. We have to get you up."

The urgency in his voice made her crack her eyes open, and she saw his blood-caked face as it came sharply into view.

"Oh, shit! What happened to you, Rodriguez?"

The shock of seeing the bloody gash above his eye seemed to make her chest ache and her senses spin.

"It's just a bang in the head, Janice. It is nothing to worry about," he spoke reassuringly as he pulled her up from the deck, but stress showed around his eyes. "A few stitches and I will have a good story and a cool scar." He managed a thin smile, which was close to a grimace.

Sitting up, she put her hand against the other side of his face. His perfect skin seemed suddenly pale, and his brow was knotted.

"We have to get you up on your feet, my lady." He was struggling to stay calm, and his clenched jaw was crying out pain and urgency.

As he hauled her to her feet, she stumbled on the oddly sloping and rolling deck, which sent a jolt of fear through her that made her grab onto his arm with shock.

"It's okay, Chiquita. We have hit something and are taking on water, but we should have plenty of time to get to the escape boats and clear out. We need to get you on a boat quickly, though, just in case."

He was squinting at her as if she were shining a bright light in his eyes, while his attitude spoke of an underlying need to hurry.

"We need to get you medical help, Rodriguez. Let me get on the radio and get you a medevac out of here," she said, trying to gather her wits.

"Janice, the radio gear is out. Everything electrical is out." He paused as if searching for the energy to go on. "We are slowly sinking, and I want every member of crew on one of the inflatable RIBs and off this ship, now. And that, lady, is an order from the captain."

He attempted to soften his demand with a smile, but pain and effort made his sweat-beaded face frown with strain.

"Okay, okay! Get me to a boat, sir," she said, trying to offer her support to him.

They struggled across the inclined deck and staggered through the hatchway, where they were given assistance by Barret, who helped them to the port side where the waterproof-swaddled medic Francis Cooper waited.

"Right, Janice, get this on," Barret said, handing her the thin nylon package of a life jacket. She looped it over her head and tied off the familiar straps.

"Get yourself down the ladder, Janice, hang on tight, and be careful of the swell." Barret was as resolute as always but patted her arm with gentleness and afforded her a rare smile.

As she put her leg over the port rail, he steadied her arm, and Rodriguez came and held the other.

"You are in the first boat, Chiquita; I will be along in the second, once we have everyone else off the ship. You will be fine. Now, if you could just look after Mr. Frey, as he is feeling a bit sorry for himself," Rodriguez said, pointing into the boat.

She looked down at the small group of yellow waterproofed figures in the orange RIB below, and she could make out the gangly form and yellow bushy hair of Frey, who was gripping his damaged arm across his stomach as if it might fall off.

"I will be a great nurse, but you hurry along straight after me, Captain. Don't you stay a minute too long? I am not drying you off if you get all wet."

Despite everyone around them, she kissed him fiercely and started down the ladder.

When she got into the rocking boat below, she quickly squeezed past four of the yellow waterproofed crew to wedge in next to Frey in the bow of the boat and looked back up into the face of her captain.

John Armstrong, one of the ship's engineers, fired up the small two-stroke outboard, and he began forcing the RIB through the swell toward the slanted rig only a mile or so distant.

As she kept looking back between the peaks and troughs of waves, she saw small yellow-clad figures climbing down the side of the improbably angled Halia and after some minutes the orange flashes of the second emergency RIB as it bobbed above wave tops. She found herself biting her lip as she concentrated intently on trying to identify Rodriguez in the small group of yellow-clad figures in the far-off boat.

A groan from next to her, Frey, snapped her out of her distant focus.

"It's okay, mate," she said, suddenly guilty for forgetting her charge, "won't be long now, and we can get you into the warm, with some painkillers and a big glass of something strong."

Frey didn't open his eyes, just nodded, his face pasty and drawn. The bouncing boat was obviously taking a painful toll on him. She looked forward again to see that the rig had become much larger before them; she was now able to take in its detail, and she thought she could see tiny black figures moving on the walkways.

"See, we're nearly there, mate. We will soon get you shipshape and in a drunken state."

She squeezed his shoulder, wishing that it could help ease his pain, and she wished her ever-positive captain was here to help. Involuntarily, she looked back—the ship had begun listing to port as the stern disappeared from view, and she was shocked at the speed it was sinking. She began scanning the distant wave tops again for the other RIB. Despite straining her eyes, she could see nothing, till a black speck seemed to crest a distant wave.

Was that a raised arm? She thought.

"John, I can't see the other boat!" she shouted down the length of the RIB, trying to get her voice heard over the noise of the outboard. Anxiety suddenly gripped her; she strained to see above the upsurge of waves behind them.

"We have to go back. They must have gone over," she yelled.

At the back of the boat, Armstrong turned and stared toward their sinking ship; impatience gripped her as he did nothing but stare at the sight.

"John, they may be in trouble. We have to turn around and go back now!" She almost screamed, letting frustration take over her voice.

"Alright, Janice, alright, I am. Stop bloody nagging, woman," he grumbled.

He finally pushed the tiller to one side and began turning the boat, which rocked alarmingly as the waves caught the boat in a wallowing turn.

She held on tightly to a rubber handle as the boat pitched, while still trying to catch a glimpse of the other RIB across the sea rollers.

The boat began to power forward again, and she anxiously searched till she thought she saw a shape ahead in the water. She was just about to call out to John to see if he'd seen it, when the words died in her throat.

There was a shadow among the waves, something surging toward them under the water. It was moving fast, much, much too fast. It was tearing toward them like a torpedo, with its own bow wave on the surface, which was cutting across the direction of the ocean swell.

Time seemed to slow down into blurred moments as they moved too fast for her to comprehend. Then, as the impact came, everything was crystal clear for a frozen moment.

For the blink of an eye she could see definition in the dark shadow in the sea—a monstrous shape surrounded by… an electric blue… radiance…power… Her mind stumbled at the incomprehensible vision, and in the next instant she was suspended in the air.

It seemed for an endless second in time that she levitated. Then the air was abruptly shocked from her lungs as she hit the cold water. She found herself scrambling to get the right way up underwater and to get to the surface to ease the burning in her chest.

She broke the surface coughing and urgently kicking her legs, trying to keep her face out of the waves. She inflated her life jacket, frantically spinning around and looking for the dark shape beneath her, till she saw the overturned RIB.

Hanging onto the boat with one arm was a yellow waterproofed figure.

Was that a flash of Frey's blond hair?

Before she could swim closer or shout to attract his attention and too quickly for her to follow, Frey was snatched below the surface. It was so fast that it barely left a splash or any sign that he had ever been there.

Panic grabbed her around the chest and seemed to shoot its iciness into every one of her limbs, paralyzing her and leaving her panting.

"Oh shit, please no, oh fucking shit, oh shit, please no," she begged like a mantra.

The bubble of her terror burst when something brushed against her leg, and with a massive spurt of adrenaline, she screamed and began swimming desperately toward the oil rig.

CHAPTER 6 — A NEW PERSPECTIVE

Dan was intent on his computer monitor, analyzing the latest 'geosteering' data as they prepared to reset the new drill head after the damage caused by the rig's unanticipated movement, when the blue shock of energy surged through his workstation and up into his chest, exploding behind his eyes like a firework night sparkler and resulting in him completely blacking out.

When he came to, he was amongst a snowfall of paper and office equipment that was strewn around him on the cold metal floor where he had landed.

Pushing off the general office scree, he managed to sit up and found himself jammed against the wall. And was it his imagination, or was the deck now canted?

His mind swam at the sudden change of angle and the complete devastation of the small office around him. Computer equipment and all manner of stationery had rolled against the wall he was against, as if attracted by some giant magnet. Only the floor-mounted desks and a large desk lamp remained in place. The lamp was aimed directly at him, only held back by its taut electrical cord as it seemed to strain toward him with malign intent. He edged away to his left, out of its direct path and toward the now oddly angled door. He struggled to make sense of the new perspectives and planes in this newly skewed world.

The thought struck him that he was back in the crooked house he'd been to as a boy. Memories came flooding back: he and his brother laughing as they ran, being thrown off balance by the sloping floors, which made them collide with the walls and each other with screams of delight. He began to smile at the memory, when a piercing shockwave ran through him. The nearby computer monitors imploded with a flash of heat and sparks, his vision blurred blue, and he was falling into darkness again …

Time passed. Moments, seconds, or minutes he could not tell

one length of time from the next. His vision went from blurred to sharp with the instant rush of his returning senses. The acrid smell of burnt ozone and electrical wiring struck his nostrils, making his eyes water and his vision swim, all of which seemed to add to the confusion in his seasick stomach.

It occurred to him that he might have been electrocuted, and he looked numbly at his hands for burns. As soon as he attempted to move he comprehended that he was now face down on the cold metal deck. He snatched his head up away from the floor, which proved a poor decision. His head rang with firecracker splinters of pain, like the worst-ever red wine hangover he'd ever had, and he let out a heartfelt groan.

As the clamor in his head faded a little, he began to take in the new office surroundings. The room was only thinly lit by the dawn light coming through the small window above him, and he knew that the rig's electricity must be out. He was just beginning to consider what could have happened when his consciousness was extinguished again by a blue surge sweeping through every part of his body … Darkness.

Steve Staples came too quickly after the first pulse of blue energy had snatched his senses away, unaware of his good fortune at landing on the bodies of his assailants. They padded him from direct contact with the deck, minimizing the second blast of blue puissance that hit the structure.

As he struggled with his befuddlement and untangling himself from the unconscious embrace of the men piled around him, the third shock vibrated through the rig. Again the mass of the bodies around him shielded him from the full force of the blue energy, and he was left only partially stunned.

His fear had him up and quickly on his feet, adrenaline getting him moving before his mind caught up with the new angle of the deck beneath his feet, which caused him to stumble and desperately reach out to catch his balance on a hatch door.

Panting for breath, he looked frantically behind him for the mob of his former pursuers but found them still heaped around the far wall of the stairwell where they had had him cornered. With no small amount of shocked wonder, he breathed a sigh of relief.

He felt his nose, which suddenly hurt, and his hand came back from his face smeared with his blood; he could taste the metallic flavor in his damaged mouth. A rush of rage suffused him, and he wanted to go back for justice, to repay them for his pain, to make them afraid like he had been. But in the same instant came the fear that they would wake up and come for him. The unreality of the situation and the split in his emotions left him gasping.

In the end, his cowardice won out, and nursing his bruises, he made for the main outer decking. He would need someone, anyone, to protect him; he went looking for Dan.

As he went out into the near dark of the early morning, his mind refused to accept the new tilting surfaces of the rig, which only added to the increased desperation that filled him. He needed something, someone to hold onto while his mind whirled in anxiety and shock.

He moved along the railings that now leaned over the ocean, clinging to the metal without looking down. Steve urgently pulled himself along the new upward gradient of the walkway, which would lead him to the operations block and comparative safety. He could see the operations block rising up in front of him, atop a new and impossible hill.

As he pulled himself along, he looked down to the sea's surface, and highlighted below in an unnatural faint blue glow subtly tinged with purple was the shape of something unreal, like a terror born into life. There, suspended just below the surface, was a creature that seemed born of every dark nightmare he could imagine, bringing a wave of fear that felt like it would suffocate him. He gripped the railing as if its solidity would keep him upright as his legs quivered beneath his weight.

For a minute they regarded each other, one in frozen terror and the other with the disinterest of a satiated great cat. Beneath its hunter's indifference, he felt a cold purple-lined lethality, a promise of death that soaked his consciousness. As he stared so hard that he felt his eyes water, he sensed at the edge of his awareness some kind of icy touch that was clawing at a deep part of him. As it seeped into his mind, he felt as if his own thoughts were slipping away, dissolving under the weight of the mightier organism's mental domination.

Then the creature seemed to accelerate away in an instant, disappearing into the murky water as though it had never been near. As he followed the nightmare apparition's course outward, he saw a distant ship's lights on the dark horizon.

Dan came around feeling like he had road works going on in his brain. He was still sprawled across the deck of his office with the cold metal pressed hard against the left side of his face. He staggered to his feet and was met with a wash of pain and nausea, causing him to lean on the slanted wall for support. Driven by some half-thought idea of finding assistance, he painstakingly made his way up to the door that led out to the walkway outside the office block and felt the salt and cold morning air blowing in, which heightened his queasiness.

"Oh crap!" he groaned as he leaned out of the door, seeing the deck fall away before him. The view seemed to exacerbate the rolling of his stomach and the thumping in his head. "Bad mistake."

He looked across the upper level of the rig, taking in the new aspect of the shapes and perspectives around him in confusion; he was appalled by the strangeness of the positions of the once-familiar surfaces of his home. Staring down across the new angles below, he took in the white-painted crew levels and the skewed outlook to sea, which made him feel as seasick as he had felt as a child on the ferry to the Isle of Wight.

One memory led to another, and he recalled his father overdoing the sympathy, shaking his head while holding back a grin, when he was a seasick twelve-year-old boy. He remembered squeezing his eyes shut and trying to be brave, wanting desperately not to let his dad down by throwing up on his feet, but failing upon a second bout of nausea.

Dan turned away from the ocean that was making his stomach roil to look down through the confusion of metal lines and framework into the drilling platform at the heart of the rig.

On the lower levels he saw men laid flat on the drilling deck, and the sight of their motionless bodies goaded him into sudden action. He began to make his way down the walkway toward them, but when he turned the first corner, he was confronted by the very angry chief of operations.

"What the hell is going on here, junior?" the disheveled, frizzy-haired Johnson demanded. "Have we had some kind of a gas blowout? How badly is the platform damaged? I need answers, and quickly, mister," the short, rotund man demanded shrilly.

Dan found himself caught between shock and a wild sense of unreality. Suddenly, the whole thing seemed completely crazy, and for no reason he could understand, he started laughing at 'gas blowout.' Maybe it was just because he was trying to imagine a giant fart causing all this damage, but, anyway, he couldn't seem to stop himself.

Johnson was furious. Since Dan had landed on the rig two months ago, Johnson had always been officious and serious. Somehow, this just seemed to make Johnson's words funnier and made Dan laugh all the more.

"Wipe that idiot grin off your face, Mr. Giles," Johnson barked. "Or you will find yourself in a heap of trouble here … I want answers. NOW!"

"S-s-sir," Dan stammered, suddenly snapped back to himself. "We seem to have suffered a massive electric surge." Growing more confident as he spoke, "Perhaps fusing the lines from the generator due to …"

"Are we in fanciful land again?" Lawson, the head geologist, interrupted, coming from the research block Dan had just exited, with a bloodied white hand towel held against his head.

"Obviously, the seismic activity has triggered a subterraneous gas pocket or some such, causing an explosion. We are just feeling the aftereffects of the detonation," Lawson said, showing them his bloodied towel as if it were evidence enough of his words.

"I'm sure that the electrical damage is caused by the blast, like an EMP effect traveling up the pipeline," he said imperiously, his face a mask of bloated conceit. Dan could see he was childishly hiding his fear behind a display of arrogance and self-importance.

"I think you should leave thinking to the grown-ups, Dan," he mocked, while making it sound like a hopeful question at the same time.

Lawson suddenly seemed transparent to Dan, like one of his kids fighting for attention by being overdramatic and insistent. Though Lawson tried to hide his petty nature with a disguise of importance and knowledge, Dan could see the panic in his wide eyes. Looking at his sweaty and blood-smeared face, he felt a deep pity and sudden desire to help the man.

"Yes, Mr. Lawson could be correct," he said, dropping his head as if in submission.

"All well and good, gentlemen. Let's sort the problems out in order and get things in focus." Johnson was attempting to sound authoritative, but instead he came across as hollow and unconvincing.

They were distracted by loud grunting and the purposeful but overlarge, lumbering form of Jenkins appearing. Jenkins arrived sweaty and grim, having struggled up the precarious walkway.

"Mr. Jenkins, can you give us any information on damage we have sustained to the oil platform?" Johnson began.

Jenkins fixed him with a fierce stare. "I have come across one man with a possible concussion, one man with a broken leg and several men with bad cuts, sir."

"Umm, yes. Well, of course, the health of the men is of, ah, of paramount, er, importance," Johnson spluttered.

"Firstly, we need to check the condition of the crew. Then, we need to assess the damage to communications to get the injured ashore, sir." The big man was implacable, and Johnson seemed to shrink beneath his gaze.

"Of course, yes, if I could get you to organize the well-being of the men, while I, er, organize some feedback on the rig's damage, and you can keep me apprised of the shape of the crew. See all resources are engaged to, erm, facilitate and ensure the crew's, erm, health," Johnson stuttered.

Jenkins deliberately turned his large back on Johnson and regarded Dan and Lawson as if measuring their worth.

"You blokes ready to help?" He was intense with determination and resolve.

Lawson and Dan stood ready, happy to have someone tell them how to deal with the alarming circumstances they found themselves in.

Dan found himself desperate to help the barge engineer; Jenkins's solidity and certainty suddenly seemed the cornerstone of courage he needed to deal with the situation. Looking at Lawson, he saw the outraged child had been replaced by a needy one, and he wondered if his own face didn't look the same.

"First priority, we must find out who is healthy, hurt, or, god forbid, missing on the rig. So you two will split up and find every able-bodied man you can to help you get the injured to the canteen. We will set up a temporary field hospital there and do a head count," Jenkins ordered tersely.

"What if the damage to the rig gets worse, shouldn't we get off it while we can?" Lawson whined in a fearful quaver. "We could all go down with it!"

"Then we'll bloody go down with it, mate. We all get off together, understand?" Jenkins barked. "Besides, if it was going to fall into the sea, I think this old collection of steel would have collapsed already. Now, you pair, get a move on. I can see some of the man up and moving around down below us."

"Yes, sir!" they both chimed.

As they turned to head down the stairwell, they looked down the platform to the drilling deck and saw Steve Staples approaching them up the walkway, gripping the metal with white, clenched hands. They could see the whites of his eyes as they seemed to roll in his sockets. Dread was etched in the lines of his face.

He approached like an abandoned dog, in slow, tentative steps while his face pleaded for succor. Dan saw that his eyes were wide and his pupils large, and for the first time in his life, in the half-light of dawn, he saw visceral fear in its most primitive form. It emanated from the taut thin man like despair.

Dan wanted to catch him in his arms, like he did with his son, but Steve stopped short of them, beyond reach. Silence met his final arrival, the very palpable nature of his terror leaving them unnerved. They waited for him to speak, watching as his tortured features struggled with whatever dismay held his tongue, while willing him to announce its name.

Steve stood in front of the rig management panting; his fear had become a cold growth which reached up from his chest into his throat and rendered him mute. Despite his desperation to tell them of the creature he had seen, to have the memory out of his mind, his tongue was stopped dry in his mouth. These people intimidated him; they were like the promise of his father's malice, and his fear stole the voice of his need. He couldn't plead, 'Save me from the nightmare!'

Sweating from every pore, he looked to Dan, desperate for his understanding. Steve looked him in the eye, pleading for the permission to speak. Oh, his father would be so proud of his futility.

Dan reached out to grip Steve's shoulder. "It's okay, mate," he said in a patiently quiet tone. "Tell me what's going on. We are here, and you're safe, Steve." He tried to look into his eyes, but Steve didn't want him to see how pathetic he had become.

But like his mother's gentle touch and patient voice, the honey-gold compassion emanating from Dan seemed to break through the cold in his chest, shattering its constriction.

"In the water ..." his voice sounded strained and quiet. "It was big, so ... bloody big ..." he panted, constantly shifting his feet. He seemed to almost shudder with each attempt to articulate the memory, and Dan's eyes reflected Steve's horror.

"Was it a whale, son?" Johnson demanded, and at once Steve was pinned through the body like a sample butterfly, caught between wanting to share his inner torment and his inability to speak. Frozen, he looked at his interrogator and gagged on his trepidation. They would be like his father, harsh and unforgiving. He looked at Dan, his eyes begging for understanding and help in giving the rising terror a name.

"A thing in th-, the water ... was a monster. It was so huge. It saw me ... I felt it. Felt it in my head." He was empty but could feel tears rolling down his cheeks.

"Oh, dear," said Lawson in his driest sarcastic tone. "Are we going to need a bigger rig?"

Johnson and Lawson laughed out their shared strain and tension.

"Oh! Yes!" said Johnson. "Maybe Moby Dick has an attitude problem."

More laughter, as Steve took in their shining red and cold yellow nimbus; as they laughed, it seemed as though each was consuming the other's venom in their pleasure of humiliating him, and he felt suddenly cut off from them, sealed in the inner cold space of his mind.

Dan looked at Steve. He seemed to have shrunk into himself. He looked for all the world like he had been abandoned, and Dan thought of his son of eight coming into the bedroom after a nightmare, and his heart went out to the man.

"I think we have some major problems to address, sir," he said, talking directly to the chief. "We need to get those communications up." He spoke quickly to divert the instigators of the attack away from the frightened man.

As he talked, he looked back at Steve, but the mud engineer was looking across the angled deck, to the ocean below. Behind Steve, the sun was passing behind the large crew and mess blocks. He saw other crew members below him staggering out of the doorway shaken and afraid. Steve's face was now to the point of being a silhouette. From his darkened visage, he spoke, "It wasn't a whale … It looked … in me. I saw it going toward the ship."

"What ship?" Johnson demanded.

Moving like an automaton, Steve turned and looked out to his left, pointing to the horizon. Dan followed the direction of his arm, and there in the distance were the grey/white flashes of a distant ship.

"Bloody hell, it's that bloody pirate Rodriguez," Jenkins said with a smile on his face. "It looks like we will all be off this rig before the afternoon is over."

"Well, Jenkins, we had better get the men together and arrange getting the wounded off the platform first, don't you think?" Johnson said with renewed importance.

"Why, yes, sir, I think we should," Jenkins sighed. "Okay, gentlemen, let's get down there and welcome our brave rescuers."

Jenkins, Lawson, and Johnson began to make their way down

the slanted walkway, leaving a disappearing chatter of excitement in the air behind them.

Dan remained behind, his concern holding him back; he ached to help the sad figure that still clutched the rail before him.

"What did you see, Steve? What was it?" His questions were met by silence, and he began to fear for the man's mind.

"We'll get you down to sick bay, get you a hot drink, okay?"

He heard shouting from below them on the rig, and looking down, he saw the men below shouting and pointing. Looking back out to the distant ship, he saw that it was in obvious distress, its bow far too prominent; it was sinking. Closer to the rig he could pick out the orange flashes of a RIB between the waves.

"What the bloody hell is going on?" he breathed, turning back to Steve.

The man's face was caught on one side with dawn light; the other side was black in shadow. The changing light seemed to contort the dimensions of distress on his face. He spoke in a flat, empty tone.

"It wants us, wants us blood and all."

Janice had spent all her strength. The spike of fear that had sent her frantically swimming for the oil rig had left her long ago; her arms ached numbly and refused to push through the waves. More and more of the saltwater seemed to be forcing its way into her mouth. Her destination looked close but was so impossibly far away; she knew if she stopped swimming the waves would gradually drive her past the rig. Her exhaustion left her gasping and spluttering water from her lips as she begged herself to keep going.

"C'mon, swim. You can make it," she panted to herself. "C'mon, don't bloody die here. Please, please, please ..." She repeated the words until they had become meaningless sounds. She seemed to be fading from herself as fatigue settled into her limbs. A grey fog of indifference passed over her—twice, with new bursts of vigor, she had pushed the feeling away, but now it seemed to have settled for good like a dreamy gauze over her mind. With a sob she realized she had stopped swimming again and was just bouncing between the peaks and troughs of waves, only her life jacket keeping her face out of the water. She had reached her limits and had no energy left to fight on. She was thirsty, cold, and lost.

At the apex of her despair, a dark-haired figure wearing high visibility waterproofs and dragging a bright orange ring appeared on the top of the next wave. He thrust powerfully down the wave toward her, and suddenly she was wrapped up in the large embrace of Jenkins, the rig's barge engineer.

"I got you, girl," he puffed. "You okay, sweet pea?"

She couldn't answer as her relief and exhaustion were replaced by tears, so she just hugged him as tightly as she could manage.

"Well, what are you swimming around out here for? Shall we get you in this life preserver and back for a drink, dear?" He whispered in her ear, gently untangling himself and bringing the ring in front of them, "Can you manage to climb in?"

She tried to grip the plastic ring, but her limbs no longer belonged to her; they had become numb attachments, and she shook her head.

"Okay. No problem." He swam behind her, and with a massive grunt of effort he thrust her up onto the plastic ring. She flopped her legs through the hole and rested her arms around it.

"Now, hold on, Janice, this is the fun bit." He waved his arm over his head, and with a jerk she began being rapidly dragged through the water, with Jenkins hanging on beside.

The attached rope traveled away and up onto the rig in front of her. As she bounced closer, she could see a group of men above hauling on the rope as she skimmed across wave tops.

Below the shadow of the leaning metalwork, she was hoisted into the air, leaving Jenkins below, part of her mind sounding a warning, but reprieve and fatigue dulled its cry. Hands lifted her onto the deck and removed the life preserver over her head. Above her, a sea of faces stared down, one attached to a hefty man with a red fleshy face who put it in front of hers with a gust of acrid breath, making her want to squirm away.

"Just remember who saved you, little lady." He winked and leered at her with a yellow-toothed grin.

"Out of the way, man," a voice barked, and she recognized the rig's chief. "Get Jenkins up here now."

Her mind seemed to be stumbling, without a coherent thought. She had already forgotten about him and something else, what had she forgotten, but a warning was ringing in her mind.

"Get him … out … of the water," her voice croaked, rasping from her dry throat. "Hurry," she managed, before the effort left her wheezing.

She was not even sure anyone heard her; she seemed to be having trouble focusing, and her eyelids felt so heavy. Before she drifted off, she heard the chief tell someone to take her to "Cooper."

Agrushell had drifted lazily beneath the pitifully slow-swimming creature. He had sensed that it was a female of the light-water creatures as soon as he had tipped over their second craft, instantly tasting her difference in the water, and a cold pleasure had touched him. The thrashing males had been quickly ended—their weak flesh penetrated and easily split apart, their fluids unpleasantly warm and metallic.

He'd followed the loud thrashing of the struggling female above, observing every action of her form through the electrical emissions of her body. They revealed the makeup of muscle, flesh, and bone in vastly quick flashes of imagery. He overlaid the sound impressions generated by her vibrations in the water, which described the prey's nature perfectly in his mind. A new desire made of emotionless ice began building in his thoughts.

He examined her and the male rescuer, feeling desire turn to design, as he weighed up the threat posed by his enemy. They were pitifully weak and ill designed for the water; they were dependent on sour-tasting shells and metal machinery. But they could attempt to call their kind over distance, with their scratchy electric voice. It was only a mockery of the authority of sound in the ocean, and they would be punished for their desecration long before more of their kind could arrive. Their female would be the beginning of their destruction, and she would bear the first price of their defilement.

CHAPTER 7 — DEFIANCE

Steve sat in the sweaty and humid canteen, which had been made into a makeshift medical bay, staring into nothingness. He was as far from the other occupants of the room as he could get, perched near the exit, on a table at the raised end of the sparsely lit interior, aloof as a cat.

Men with bandaged limbs sat talking in far-off pools of gas-powered lamplight, while drinking coffee, which the black-eyed 'le fat chef' was serving them from a large white jug, but he had not been offered a drink.

At the farthest end of the room from him, two makeshift hammocks held men with more severe injuries in drugged slumber. One was a mechanical technician; the other was Sam Dunstable, a burly roughneck who was part of Jones's gang. He should have been delighted to see Sam's pain-slackened white face in revenge for their attack, but all he felt was hollowness.

The world was moving around his vacant shell; its movement didn't stir the mist-ridden wind that whistled behind his eyes. The static of his mind was all he could bear, not the memory of the thing in the water, the thing that seemed to be trying to force itself through the cracks of his awareness and back into his mind. He couldn't stomach feeling the apparition's emotionless desire for death, for his death. It still pierced his guts like the glacial talons of trepidation.

He blankly watched people come and go. The crewmen cast furtive glances at him amid whispered discussions, which had become angry stares and mocking comments. The 'freaky weirdo' was out on show. He didn't meet their eyes; he didn't want to see his apparent lunacy written on the expressions of those around him. None of them touched him; he was shut off in the cave of his mind, with the layers of his fear hiding him deep in its darkest corner.

He could have remained locked inside himself, behind his makeshift wall of disregard forever, but his mind was rocked when the barge engineer brought her into the canteen. She looked so fragile and hurt. Her lips were tinged blue and her white skin was so perfect, despite the purple of her bruised cheek. She shined in orange lighting bursts of sun-fire.

Before he was even realized he was moving, he was following Jenkins, who gently carried her supine figure. Jenkins stopped at one of the makeshift hammocks strung between incongruously angled tables and lightly laid her into one.

"Is she okay?" he heard himself ask from a distance.

"Yes, she's fine, just cold, with a little bit of shock. We will get her warm, and she'll be fine." Jenkins looked directly at him. "Are you okay, son?"

He had no answer to such an improbable question, so he lied.

"I'm fine, sir."

"Good, mate, why don't you see if you can rustle me up a couple of blankets? We need to get her out of these wet clothes, and I'd rather not do it in front of these scabby reprobates."

Jenkins pointed a finger toward the group of injured men.

Without thought he took off instantly toward Francis Cooper, the ship's medic, who looked harried and red-eyed as he bandaged a man's arm. Several men waited, quietly enduring whatever injury they had. They watched the medic's every move, exerting a silent pressure that was obviously telling on the usually happy-go-lucky man.

Steve joined the silent watchers for a short while, before seeing a pile of blankets on one of the table-mounted chairs, and without disturbing the stressed medic, he quickly snatched two and hurried back to Janice as quickly as he could.

When he returned, Jenkins had removed her life jacket and yellow waterproofs.

"Right Steve, stand up there with your back to me and that blanket held out wide in front of you, mate."

Steve looked at the man, trying to make sense of the instructions.

"Why?"

"Because I want to get her wet clothes off, and I don't want this lot of no-goods or you watching while I do it," Jenkins said, rolling his eyes toward the group of men.

"Oh, okay. No problem." The answer seemed to give the solution to the mystery, and he felt suddenly happy at its resolution.

He raised the blanket up and at arm's length listened to the sounds of wet clothing being dragged off and dropped onto the floor with a wet slap. He imagined her pale water-softened skin and began daydreaming of holding her cold fingers and breathing warmth into them.

Jenkins's voice disturbed his inner reverie.

"Okay, mate, you can put that blanket down now."

He looked at his arms, surprised to find they ached and that he had no recollection as to how long he been standing there. He dropped his arms and turned to see that Jenkins had laid her out on the makeshift bunk with a towel wrapped around her head. She looked peacefully innocent, like the pictures of angels his aunt had plastered on the walls, with soft and beatific faces caught in enchanted thoughts. He couldn't seem to stop staring and could feel a foolish smile on his face, but inside he had an ache that was close to causing tears.

"You okay there, Steve?" Jenkins asked. His face was creased with concern, but his tone was a gentle questioning. He was warm yellows and tense reds.

"What's her name, sir?" He couldn't think of anything more important at the moment.

"Her name's Janice. She's the radio jockey from the Halia," he answered, obviously interested as to where Steve's questions were leading.

"She's looks perfect, so peaceful. Like an angel," he whispered, suddenly shy at exposing his thoughts.

Jenkins snorted a laugh. "She only looks that way when she's asleep. She is a proper little hellion when she's awake." Jenkins laughed again and gave him a cheerful slap on his shoulder that gave him a feeling of being included in the big man's humor and not, as so often with the roughnecks, the butt of it.

"I think that this is the person she really is underneath, and everything else is a performance to keep cruel people away," he wondered out loud.

He startled himself that his thoughts could escape in this way. He shot a look at the big man, who seemed not to have heard him; he was looking down on her fragile face himself, with a kind smile.

"You know what, mate? I think you are probably right," he replied with a gentle voice.

The moment was broken by shouting outside, which drew the barge engineer's attention away from the girl. Jenkins gave him a long measuring stare.

"Do you think I can trust you to guard her? Make sure no harm comes to her, while I go and sort out that bunch of troublemakers?" Jenkins asked firmly.

Steve couldn't imagine wanting anything else more.

"I promise you, no one will hurt her with me here."

The big man nodded with satisfaction. "Good man. I will be back as soon as possible. Oh! In case of emergencies, hold onto this for me."

He handed him an eight-inch length of hard wood, with a handle shape at the top.

"It's a belaying pin from an old square-rigged ship I served on once; I keep it for use when overly forceful conversations are required."

With a grin and a backward glance at Janice, Jenkins lumbered up hill to the exit.

Holding the weight of wood in his right hand, Steve calculated the effectiveness of the surprise weapon and was only disturbed when Janice moaned in her bed and awoke abruptly with a start.

His heart leapt, and the pin was slipped quickly into his pocket as he knelt by her side. Her eyes were wide and afraid. He suddenly felt like her eyes were everything in the room, soaking up reality to the point where nothing else existed.

"Don't be afraid, you are safe here. You are on the Danson 3 oil platform; your ship had some kind of a problem … I'm Steve, a mud engineer." He was suddenly nervous that he might frighten her.

"Were there others, from my ship? Are they here?" Her eyes were darting around the room, searching and filled with unease.

"No, I'm sorry, they only brought you in." He longed to give her comfort, but his words just seemed to increase her trepidation.

"No one else? Did you get a rescue boat out there? Did you search for them? They could still be alive out there." Tears were bleeding from her eyes.

"I'm sorry, really. You were the only one in the water ..."

He was silent as her tears came in full. She wept and he thought he heard her whisper 'My Captain.'

He could feel her anguish and yearned to reach out and hold her, but his own stretched nerves and inner turmoil held him back. He waited while she wept, just a detached witness to her grief, till her sobs subsided.

"What happened to this rig?" she asked, returning her full attention to his face, while probing his eyes with her red-rimmed ones.

"They think we had some kind of blow out from the pipeline being caught in an earthquake or something. And that it has damaged one of the pontoons, they reckon."

"But you don't believe them?" She seemed to be trying to penetrate his thoughts with her stare while her orange-and-gold aura was flickering blue with concern. She seemed too urgent in her effort to understand him.

"No ..." he said, but his words ran out, the memory of the creature suspended below him in the ocean paralyzing his tongue.

"You've seen it, haven't you? You've seen that fucking great thing out there, haven't you?" she hissed through her teeth.

The coldness in his mind seemed to have returned; he could hear it whistling, but her eyes and the strength of her warm emotions kept him right there with her.

"I saw it, below me in the water," Steve said. "It couldn't be real, it couldn't be, but it was. I told them, but they didn't believe me. They laughed."

"What did you see?" she whispered, so only they could hear. He felt suddenly like they were the only two people in the room.

The lamplights were a dull glow and acted like candlelight, making her eyes deeply mysterious and her skin a shadowy dance, while she crackled with a gentle orange intensity.

"It was like a mixed-up experiment with a manta ray and a giant squid, smooth and black, tentacles ... a blue glow in the water." He could feel himself stammer over the words as he brought it to life in his mind. "It had no eyes, but it knew I was there ... I could feel it, watching me."

He stopped with a shudder, made mute again by the terror in his memories.

She nodded and seemed to be lost in her own memory of fear.

"I saw it come at our RIB through the water like a torpedo-driven whale, but not round at the front, more angular, like you said, like a ray. Only big, much, much too big, and the blue glow, I saw that, too."

His heart leapt; it was not some madness that had formed like a tumor in his mind, but a real creature. She had seen it, too. She believed him and shared his fear. With a one stroke, he was out of his cave; she seemed to wipe the fear from his mind. He felt a smile on his face and couldn't stop nodding that she was right.

"Do you remember anything else, about the skin?" she whispered urgently.

He tried to examine the image in his mind again, and this time it seemed more manageable and distant, still frightening, but not overwhelming.

"It had regular shapes, like huge fifty-pence pieces laid out in a pattern over it," he suddenly remembered.

She propped herself up, holding a blanket across herself.

"That's it, the pattern! Like arranged octagons across it, like it had been stamped with a honeycomb or something. That can't be natural, not something from nature. That has to be man-made?" Her voice had risen as she became animated about the revelation.

He was about to agree with her when a voice from behind them interrupted his thoughts and sent a jolt of alarm through him.

"Well, Steve, my old mate, have you got yourself a new girlfriend?"

While they had talked, Lee Jones had soundlessly arrived behind him and stood there with a sneer on his face and a pronounced red mark on his left cheek. His voice was almost cheerful, but Steve could feel the undercurrent of anger, and he had seen the violence in his eyes before.

"No, she is not my girlfriend. This is Janice of the Halia." It occurred to him, at that moment, that he hated this man.

"Well, if you two aren't together, why don't you toddle off and let me introduce myself to our lovely visitor?" His words were sugar-coated, but his shameless leer was anything but, and the dark greens of his radiance glowed with malice.

The big man nodded his head to the side to indicate the direction he thought was best for Steve to take, and a sudden fury seemed to ignite inside Steve, boiling in his mind and overflowing with red pressure into the edges of his eyes.

"NO!" he said in a voice he barely recognized. It seemed to come from his chest and his forehead at the same time, and his vision seemed to swim with enflamed scarlet.

When his sight cleared, everything was confused. He was being wrestled. People were shouting, but the words seemed to make no sense. As the tension went out of his body, the two men who were grappling with him collapsed with him to the floor.

He lay there panting and bemused. It was like waking from a deep dream and finding it was still going on.

The two men stood up over him, with their palms outspread, now speaking calmly and pointing to his right hand. When he looked, he saw the belaying pin still gripped in his hand; the wood of the handle-shaped top now had blood on it. He registered the weapon with minor curiosity, looking around to find the answer to this new little mystery. He saw Lee Jones, with a wetly blood-stained towel held to the side of his head and a vivid welt growing in a straight line across his forehead. When Steve found the other man's eyes, he saw only a depth of venomous hate, but his green-ridden glow was now filled with shock-ridden blues.

For some reason the man's enmity and injury brought giddy warmth and he felt a smile grow on his face. For the first time in his life he could face a confrontation without being swamped and lost in the fierce emotional wash. He had always been left feeling debilitated, but for once he felt strong.

This reaction caused Jones to burst up from the floor, dragging the medic Cooper along with him. The roughnecks who had been guarding him were suddenly turned to confront another enraged madman, whom they tackled to the ground.

Steve lost interest in their struggles and turned to see if the angel was okay.

She was sat upright with blankets grasped around her and looked both bemused and worried at the ensuing struggle before her.

"Hey, Janice, you okay?"

She dragged her eyes from the confrontation and looked at him; he could feel his smile grow wider.

"Yes, Steve, I am fine. Who is that moron? Are you okay?" she spoke with a quiet astonishment.

Her concern felt like a warm balm washing over him, making his heart jump, and he felt his cheeks hurt with his smile.

"I said I wouldn't let anyone hurt you."

A massive crash, as a large hand smacked down on the surface of a table, made the metal ring like an oversized tuning fork.

"What the bloody hell is going on here?" the barge master demanded. He glared at the suddenly motionless trio on the floor. "Haven't we got enough problems, without you bloody simpletons making it worse?"

"It was that fucking nutter there; he attacked me with a bat. It was out of the blue. He's a fucking psychopath. I want him locked up," he huffed angrily.

Jones was full of angry indignation, his face sweaty and flushed.

For some reason Steve could no longer connect with the fear he would have normally felt at the man's rage or with his own usual sense of inadequacy. The threat of Lee Jones seemed to have disappeared, leaving him happily light-headed.

"Well?" Jenkins demanded of Steve, looking for the entire world like one of his teachers at school waiting for him to make up an explanation that they could use to hang him.

But he could not be intimidated; he was too blissful.

"He was bothering Janice," he said simply. "I encouraged him not to." Showing Jenkins the belaying pin, Steve gave him his best smile.

"Is that so, Janice?" he asked, his eyes still on Steve, but they seemed perplexed; his brow was pinched with confusion, as if Steve's happiness was an oddity to be suspicious of.

"Yes, Jenkins, he was just getting that ape away from me," Janice confirmed.

"I was only saying hi, and then he … He went fucking nuts. Bloody liars they are, both lying through their arses," Jones sputtered belligerently with outrage, his face sweaty and becoming redder by the moment as his indignation built.

"Enough!" Jenkins shouted. "Get your thick head fixed, and then I want you outside helping get those mobile generators on deck. The rest of you get back to your jobs, and leave this young lady in peace." He stared around balefully, and there was an abrupt flurry of activity.

Lee Jones fired a look of malice at Steve. The livid welt across his head shone whitely against the red of his face. With an angry grunt, he shoved the men that had been holding him aside and stalked to the doorway muttering darkly.

"Okay, you kids," Jenkins said calmly to Janice and Steve. "Try and keep out of trouble, while we get things up and running. Hopefully we can get the radio working soon, and we can get ourselves helicoptered off this heap of rusty scaffolding before we run into any more trouble," Jenkins said amiably, with no sign of concern for what just had passed.

"The Halia didn't just sink out there, Jenkins; something hit us and our inflatables. I saw something in the water, something big and alive." She spoke quietly but with an urgent undertone. "He saw it, too," she said, looking at Steve.

"What did you see?" he said to her in a low voice full of anxiety.

"I don't know. It wasn't metal or machine, and it was bloody big. It was a creature of some kind, but it looked like it had been made or something. You know, with markings in perfect shapes, hexagons maybe." She faltered at her lack of words to express what she had seen.

Steve nodded along with her description, happy to have someone turn the fearful image in his mind into something real and possibly understandable.

Jenkins frowned and looked uncomfortable, and then he looked at him.

"Well, what did you see, Steve?"

Suddenly, the thing was alive in his mind; he watched it in slow motion as it swam below him and felt the chill of the memory in his stomach.

"It was a monster."

"Right. Okay. Erm, look, we can't do anything about what you saw; we have to deal with getting out of here and helping the injured. Please, if you could not mention what you've seen, it will help keep a lid on things until we can look into whatever the hell is going on, when we are more secure. That be okay, sweet pea?" he asked Janice in a calm but pressing voice.

"Okay, Jenkins, but that thing might not just go away."

Jenkins nodded and turned to Steve. "That be okay with you, mate?"

Steve looked at Janice, who gave a tiny shrug, and then he met the entreaty in Jenkins's eyes. He didn't want to let the large man down; he could see the genuine concern in an amber gleam around him, and he felt suddenly close to this man.

"Yes, sir," he said. "I won't mention the monster."

CHAPTER 8 — NIGHT JUSTICE

'Brainy' Michaels hid his tall muscular frame behind a corrugated steel wall, bracing his long legs against the new slope of the rig, as he sheltered from the growing wind and rain. He was dragging on the remnants of the damp 'rollie' he was smoking.

Next to him stood his twice-as-brawny compatriot, 'Big Bill' Peters, who even at rest strained his damp orange-and-blue fire-safe overalls, which he had been wearing for the last twelve hours.

His companion was six foot four inches of pretty much solid muscle; muscle was definitely what you noticed about Big Bill. He'd been blessed in that department above all the others. Not that he was stupid; he just seemed to lack any social or common-sense smarts. And then, there was the fact that the guy wasn't exactly going to sit down and read a book.

Though wary of his gorilla-sized companion, Brainy wasn't afraid of him. He had his own whipcord strength, matched with speed and cunning skills in a fight.

Lee Jones had paired him with this oversized ape, and Lee Jones was certainly not to be messed with. That was a lesson he had learned early in their relationship. The remembering made Brainy smile tightly

They were sheltered in between the container shapes of the canteen and the operations offices, above the crew quarters. Work since the rig had tilted had gone on at a frantic pace; carbon lights had been erected, powered by emergency generators that been fired up on the main deck, creating small pools of bright light. Along with yards of wiring from the stores, the light-bearing metal tripods were dotted about the square deck, with the main illumination concentrated on the drill bay. The super bright carbon lights made the darkness outside of their beams even more impenetrable, and Brainy was glad to be out of their glare.

He and Big Bill had been working with two production techs, trying to breathe life back into the gas and electricity supply to operations and the canteen. They had discovered that they stood no chance. The electricity lines were melted and the components carbonized. The techs were still bent over the fractured gas line, which had stretched beyond its tolerance when the rig tilted. They were trying to gaffer and PTFE tape the line into a semblance of usability. He wished them luck, but his patience for the endless yanking on heavy wiring and endless 'umm-ing 'and 'ahh-ring' of the nerdy techs ... frankly, it was setting his teeth on edge, and he was thinking of more pleasurable activities.

He grinned in the darkness; the techies were unlikely to demand he and man/mountain Bill return to work. He took another drag of his fag and blew out smoke that vanished in the wind.

"Hey, Bill," he said, "shall we leave the monkeys to it?"

"You, what, Brainy ... won't we get in trouble?" the oversized roughneck said, a deep frown on his large bushy-browed face.

"Don't worry, Bill," said Brainy cheerfully. "I'll make sure all is well, my friend."

Freed from worry, Bill became excited. "What do you have in mind, Brainy?"

Grinning again, Brainy said, "Well, the canteen freezers are knackered, so we could get us a steak each, get the oxy-propane burning torch and make us a nice flame-grilled minute steak."

He waited on Bill's response with checked pleasure, his eyes fierce with the intensity of his enjoyment as he mocked his friend. He had been brought up on a housing estate, where finding entertainment was nearly always at someone else's expense.

"Sounds alright," Bill said excitedly. The thought of food always interested Big Bill.

"I'm guessing there may well be some ice cream," he said in an airy, nonchalant tone, watching Bill's reaction from the corner of his eye.

Bill almost stood to attention in his eagerness. "Oh yeah,

Brainy, some ice cream would be very good."

Brainy was pleased to see his accomplice was well on board, as Brainy knew he would be. Still, he enjoyed the giant man's simple pleasure, as it meant he would do as he was told when the need for a bit of force came along. He wanted to search the presently empty officers' rooms for money or anything of value; while everyone was busy he would need a lookout and someone who could force locks with brute strength.

He was about to suggest the possibility that chocolate chip ice cream was waiting for Bill when he heard the grinding of metal over the thrum of the generators and felt the vibration of tortured steel through the soles of his feet.

Startled, he looked back at the techies in their pool of light; they had paused and were also looking around for the cause of the noise. Another grate of metal under stress and the rig shook like a giant's foot had stamped on the deck.

Stumbling against the kitchen block's metal wall, Brainy looked toward Bill. He had been thrown out toward the metal security fencing at the edge of the main deck as the rig shook, crouching to keep his balance. He looked directly at Brainy with a confused expression, and his head cocked slightly to the side, like he was listening or waiting to be told what to do, Brainy thought.

Another fierce ear-piercing screech of metal, and then the night was suddenly silent but for the generators' thrum.

Brainy took a deep breath, feeling his heart thumping in his chest. The smell of the sea had become suddenly much stronger, with brine and an acrid something else. He balanced himself with his outstretched arms on the uneven metal walls and moved toward Bill, who was starkly lit up by the carbon lights in front of him and against the darkness behind. His face made an exaggerated 'O' of bewilderment, as the noise of stressed metal began again.

"Crapping hell," Brainy breathed. "What the fuck is happening?"

No one answered him. His words were lost in the screeches of suffering metal and the shuddering of the deck. Both techies were on their knees trying to hold on to the grated deck surface. They were looking toward him and shouting, but all sound was lost in the background din. Bill remained upright, hanging onto the fence, despite the jolts and vibrations that rocked the rig deck.

"Bill!" he yelled. "Can you see wha …" His words ran out as he could see that Bill's feet appeared to be in the air and that they were juddering. As his eyes traveled up, he saw that Bill was being held up by a dark shaft whose black-crusted and scaled end protruded through Bill's abdomen. Transfixed at the sight, it was a moment before he took in the blood spattering from the tips of Bill's shoes. He watched the flat thin plates that stood up along the length of the shaft, from the tip back into Bill's blood-darkened overalls.

Insistent animal sounds made him look up past the shuddering and spasmodically dancing legs, past the pathetically grasping hands which were desperately attempting to push the thing in him away. Bill was tearing the flesh of his hands on the raised razor plates that sheathed the creature.

Brainy Michaels was drawn inexorably to look at Bill's face. Blood leaked from his mouth, which moved as if he were speaking but made only the desperate sounds of his pointless struggle, accompanied by whining breaths. Finally, he met Bill's eyes, and he was assaulted by the man's utter pain and need; his eyes were wet and pleading.

Brainy began to reach out his hand, but as he moved toward Bill, a light from behind him illuminated the shadows and the nightmare beyond. The thing was smooth across its body, which gleamed dully at the edge of the light, like oil on water, suggesting a slick, almost dolphin-like skin. It was light enough for him to see octagonal shapes indented in the surface of the creature's skin, with thick lines running down from the large elongated tip of what seemed to be a head or the front end of a bus-sized manta ray. Brainy's mind was staggering under the weight of what he couldn't accept. In the dark he caught glimpses of motion around the immense shadow of the creature.

Nothing moved for seconds; the tableau before him seemed frozen in the moment. Then fear returned as a trickle of ice down his spine, as some instinct told him that he was being watched. He started to edge back to the safety of the dark between the office units. As he did, the thing moved toward him. It was fast; as its massive menacing shape towered above him, the thing's meaning was clear: 'Where the fuck do you think you're going?'

He froze beneath its eyeless stare; death had found him. His heart thudded in his chest, and his bladder felt urgently full, while his mind tottered with dread.

Bill's body was flung to his left and smashed against the edge of the crew quarters with a dull metallic ring, sliding down to fall heavily and unmoving at his feet.

He stared horror-struck at the wreckage of man before him, retching at the smeared features of Bill's crushed face, and in that moment he realized what the thing was waiting for—it was savoring his reactions.

In this moment of intuitive fear, he looked up in painfully slow motion and saw a blood-coated shaft, just below his eye level, waiting for him, and plates like sharp flakes of black rust rose and fell down its sticky length. He knew the creature was waiting for his most terror-filled moment to strike.

Time stood still in the eternity of the dread-filled moment, awaiting the hunter's strike. The limb drew back; he knew it was ready to strike, when it stopped. Brainy became aware of shouting, wild screaming, and the limb disappeared in a hiss of motion.

Dazed, he looked back into the lights and saw the two techs were attacking the beast with metal scaffold poles, trying to stab at the body of the creature.

The thing drew back, as if considering the threat before it; he suddenly realized that the two men were trying to draw the creature away from him.

He staggered, stepping over the wreckage of the body in front of him, and stopped for a moment to watch the ensuing battle. They were swinging their weapons and yelling incomprehensibly to scare the monster away. He suddenly thought it might work, that they might scare it off, like any animal; he looked around for some kind of weapon he could use to help. But when the creature moved, its legs moved in rapid stabbing motions, with crab-like speed, piercing into the metal surface with resounding impact as it powered toward the men. It was too big and quick. It surrounded them with a storm of flashing limbs, a multitude of shafts like the one that had threatened him.

In an instant one of the men was down and pinioned to the deck. Another limb flashed into sight, its movement blurred with its speed; it bisected the path of the other tech with a sickening thud, and he was tossed away down the deck, landing with a wet echoing clang. The crumpled body lay unmoving.

Brainy looked back to the other tech man who had tried to save his life; he couldn't put a name to either of the men. The man was obviously in shock. He just made coughing breaths, looking up at the black spear in his chest, his hands clenching. Another limb flicked into the light and poised itself over the helpless man, and as Brainy watched, the tip flattened out, its edges becoming serrated. The man below watched it with fixed horror, struggling pathetically against the limb that held him pinned. With slow fluid ease, the newly formed blade was now weaving gently above its victim. Brainy could see the man's lips moving; he could imagine the pleading, the begging for his life. He felt a hot wetness in his eyes and sick in his throat. He was unnoticed by the players of the scene being acted out in the stark pool of light before him; he was merely the audience.

Anticipation ended as the black limb flicked down; slickly smooth, it ran its flattened, serrated edge across the man's chest, leaving a thick red line behind its progress. The man's gurgling scream was cut short as, in one motion, the creature's blade reversed its path to leave another red line. It held the damp edge above the man's face momentarily and then plunged it down, embedding itself deep into his chest next to the first limb. The man convulsed, expelling one last blood-misted breath, and lay still.

The blades pulled out of his chest with a damp sucking sound, revealing the stark white bones of his ribs standing out through the mess of red clothing and flesh.

High-pitched static burst forth from the creature as it inspected its work. Now, it turned toward Brainy; he was no longer audience but wanted for the play. The monster wanted their suffering; it had come not for meat, but for pain.

He turned to run; time had become a succession of slow-motion images in fearful definition. As fear-fueled adrenaline fizzed in his veins, he stumbled across an empty plastic barrel as he ran blindly in the dark; he went over, landing face-first on the gridded metal, scrabbling to grip anything that might help him get up from his sprawled position on the metal deck.

He was left face down on the oil- and grime-coated floor. He tried to wipe the liquid off, and only succeeded in smearing the ill-smelling residue around his face, and he remembered rage. He looked for a weapon to express his anger against his humiliation; a broom came to hand, and he purposely broke the head off, leaving a sharpened spear of wood, and turned to face the dark with his rage.

Dan was in operations on the upper deck with Jonnie Smith, an electrical technician and a dry-witted Scouser. He was a practical man in his mid-fifties who sported a bald pate surrounded by cropped, grey-flecked hair and had a fleshy average face. But he was gifted with anything electrical, and hopefully, Dan thought, that included the radio he was attempting to construct virtually from scratch.

Dan was propped against the slope of the radio bench, shining a torch so Jonnie could work despite fighting the deck's new inclination, a lack of good light, and frazzled components.

Jonnie had rigged a soldering iron from a tiny generator he had adapted; it sputtered and hissed to the same random tune of Jonnie's expletives. Dan had gotten sweaty and frustrated running backward and forward to the office and seismic lab for parts and equipment; now he sweated while he tried to keep the torch light steady on the open electronics panel.

As Jonnie worked beneath the radio board, Dan began to feel vibrations and then a heart-lurching rocking. With more curses, Jonnie's head reappeared with a look of puzzled fear directed at Dan. "What was dat?"

"Stay with it. We need that radio," he told Jonnie, pointing at the so-far-inert lump of components. "I'll see what's happening out there," and he handed over the torch.

"Don't worry, I'll 'old the torch in me teeth like," Jonnie said wryly.

Dan gave the man his best wink and moved up the inclined floor to the door, looking out from the uppermost room on the top level of the vertigo-inducing tilted rig. He shielded his face from the rain and stared into the darkness at the spots of light across the deck below him, looking for the source of the upheaval.

Another large vibration and screaming of metal assaulted his hearing. Dan gripped the door frame tightly to support himself while he leaned farther out for a better view.

"What da 'ell is goin' on out dere?" Jonnie shouted distractedly from his painstaking reconstruction work.

Dan was about to tell him that he thought the rig was just shifting in rising waves or increasing winds from the front of cold pressure closing in on them, but as he was about to turn back to tell Jonnie his theory, something moved in the corner of his eye; a shadow passed across the kitchen block starkly outlined by the carbon light, something much too large. He looked some fifty meters down, straining to see, when part of it entered the pool of light. It looked like a whale-shaped manta ray, mixed by some evil art with a vast armored crab. It seemed to be articulated, with a multitude of arms, far too many for an octopus, he thought, and these arms moved with precision and in unison, not like an octopus at all.

The nightmare creature flattened the fence at the edge of the rig and bent the structure beneath its weight. Dan was transfixed in wonder till the apparition dashed forward with unwieldy speed to spear one of the figures below.

"Look out!" he screamed as the creature moved. "Somebody help them."

He gasped as someone was flattened to the deck; he was too far away to make out a face. "Look the fuck out!" His voice rose to a piercing pitch with the effort of his warning.

"Wat?" Jonnie shouted, his head arising in surprise and annoyance from the equipment before him. "Now, wat d'fuck is it? Arnt I busy enough?"

Dan heard him scrambling up beside him.

"Alright, mate, wat's goin' like?"

"Have we got a gun up here?" Dan was panting, wide-eyed like he was on drugs.

"Alright, Dan, calm down, mate. Course we don't 'ave a gun, la." He almost laughed aloud at the sudden change in Dan. "Dere arnt any post offices to rob round 'ere, mate."

Dan blinked and looked at Jonnie as if he had just fallen from a troop of flying pigs. "Look outside, down there." His voice was a monotone of insistence, his face pained as he pointed.

Jonnie was chilled by Dan's behavior; he was normally such a level-headed lad, quiet-spoken and friendly; he was probably having a breakdown due to the stress.

"Alright, me old mate, I'll take a quick look for yer," he said, nodding his head to reassure his workmate. He pantomimed leaning slowly out of the oddly angled door frame.

"Look, mate, I'm lookin' out," he said like a parent reassuring his child there wasn't a wardrobe monster. As soon as his head went beyond the door, screams met him, his eyes were drawn down, and he looked aghast at the sight before him.

It was too surreal for him to grasp, so he didn't. He was watching a film, at the cinema; the dark around him helped his mind construct the fantasy. The 'replica' screams and crashing sounds below didn't disturbed him as he watched the make-believe monster attack the small actors on the rig deck.

The moment of unreality disappeared when a massive crash sounded behind him. He turned as unsteadily as a tottering drunk; stunned, he saw Dan busily dismantling the communications room.

The electronics were Jonnie's onboard love; they made him an important person here, where no one else had his skills or abilities. He kept each tool and piece of equipment in its place; attention to detail and carefulness pleased his fastidious nature. They helped him shut off the emotions that would otherwise overwhelm him while away from home; they were his defense against loneliness. His work was his only solace from missing his wife and children, and Dan was throwing equipment left and right. He felt angry and rushed to stop Dan's wanton destruction. He grabbed Dan's arm to stop him from destroying the contents of another equipment case.

"Wat d'fuck are you doin', youse idiot!?" he shouted in Dan's face.

Dan's reaction held him in check; he was calm, the wildness of a moment before gone, and he looked determined, almost impregnably strong.

Dan gripped Jonnie's shoulders. "Listen to me." Forcing Jonnie to look straight at him, he yelled, "LISTEN!" Jonnie snapped to attention.

"Is there any kind of weapon here? Anything we can use?" His tone was firm, and each word was enunciated and precise.

Jonnie's mind was blank. Dan had him feeling uncertain, and he was still fired up.

"No, we aint got nuthin. No machine guns or rocket launchers. No fuckin' light sabers, nuthin. Nuthin that will make a difference to watever d'fuck dat ting is out dere." Shouting made him feel better. "Dis place aint no fuck-arsin military base."

Dan remained calm and took a deep breath.

"Is there anything here we can use as a weapon?" he asked again, harshly patient. "Men are dying out there, people we know."

Jonnie was dumbfounded by the question and the iron strength of Dan's calm. He shook his head slowly, without speaking, and just when silence seemed to be the only response he could find, he suddenly remembered.

"Dere are flare guns, in dat top locker."

CHAPTER 9 — A RESPONSE TO TERROR

The sound of tortured metal echoed and vibrated through the enclosed space of the canteen. Steve leapt to his feet in surprise, while everyone looked around with matching expressions of shock.

"What the hell is that, Steve?" Janice whispered between the metallic squeals and vibrations of the structure, the strikes of blue returned to her orange luminosity.

He turned and saw her wide-eyed fearful expression and felt his temper rise.

"I don't know, Janice, but I'm going to find out. You stay where you are. I'll be right back. I promise."

"Okay, but Steve, be careful of that pig-faced idiot. He might be waiting for you out there," she said with obvious concern, which made something in his chest ache.

He took his angry determination and went out into the dark; the screeching of metal, which had been loud in the damp night air, came to a sudden stop and quiet echoed. The new eerie stillness was unmoved by the wind or falling rain, until the distant sound of a whining scream floated on the breeze, and in a heartbeat he was back in the cavern of his fear. The rain-filled wind seemed to match the whistling in his mind, and something in the dark sent a wave of cold death spiralling down his spine.

He turned the corner, his eyes adjusting to the carbon light pools that were visible across the tilted deck. In one of the farthest-lit areas of the rig, he saw the oddest sight.

In the distant stark beams, he could see two technicians. They had unwieldy metal scaffold poles and appeared to be attacking the darkness; their peculiar jousting seemed to match the strangeness in his head. He felt that maybe he ought to find a pole and join in with the dance or perhaps applaud their efforts, but the grin that had formed on his face froze when he caught something moving in the darkness beyond their flailing poles.

A massive shape scuttled into the light, with metal-piercing staccato steps, brushing aside the poles with disinterested disdain. Its vast oil-slick surface was surrounded by the blurs of coiling snakelike motion and striking spear-tipped limbs. One flung one of the men aside as though he were a plastic action figure, and another pinned the second man to the ground, skewering him through his chest.

The monster had arrived, and its immensity filled him with a terror that froze his heart and slowly spread into his chest, staggering his breath. It radiated purple ruination and a desire for their complete annihilation.

His mind was empty but for the horror of the creature in the night. He began to recoil, looking for any escape from the unimaginable made real. He edged back around the corner, lurching away from the sounds of metal being stressed as the creature of his nightmare lumbered across the oil platform.

He knew what was coming; he didn't need to see it. He backed out of the light and kept backing farther away. He needed to vanish into the blackness, to escape the thing that hunted him, the living horror of his mind that had come to consume him.

He watched the people in front him, those still in the light as he retreated, their attention drawn to the horrific sounds and then to the abomination that was their cause.

He was back in the dark of his childhood bedroom, hearing his father's rage beyond the door. It was coming closer, the man's desire to harm stabbing at Steve's mind, closer with each heavy step, making his legs tremble, closer— until he was awash in dread, then light and, finally, pain.

Steve's fear dragged him away, step by step, a coward's instinctive desire to flee. His evasion was stopped when he knocked into something solid and metal. His escape was blocked by the cold wet metal rung that he was touching with his outstretched hand. He stole a glance behind him and in the dim light picked out the tube-like shapes of a ladder. He looked up and leaning over him was the giant monolith of the machine above, its black contours stark against the gloom of the clouds above.

He was up against the oil platform's crane, its ladder right in front of him in the dark. He looked up at its confused angles with cold rain spattering his face, suddenly feeling a jolt of hope, and in that moment, for the first time since he'd left the canteen, he thought of her, trapped and alone, with the creature hunting them.

He looked back the way he had come, his desires split between his heart and his fear. Another screech of metal and perhaps another scream shocked him into motion. He started up the crane's ladder, while metal screeched like the beast's fury behind him.

As he climbed higher, he stole fearful glances back down and was staggered by the fiend's impossible size, lightning-fast crab-like movements, and the numerous limbs that struck like cobras at the frail human shapes below. Its enormous weight gouged the metal of the deck with each short burst of speed; the snakes, arms, whatever the hell they were, came with it, flashing in and out of the light, appearing like dark magic from the pitch black.

Now his only thought was of escape. His body was in revolt: desperation crept from his stomach, forming a lump in his throat that made it hard to breathe; his bladder was suddenly painful with need; his heart thumped at an alarmingly rapid pace. His fear drove him up the ladder, farther from it, from the thing below. He climbed quicker and quicker, the tempo of hand and foot, hand and foot becoming synchronized; more screaming from below only increased the rhythm, and even the wet and slick metal of the rungs didn't slow him.

His weight was being thrown to his left side by the angle of the deck, which made his grip feel precarious, but he climbed steadily, his dread of what was below outweighing any fear of falling.

His breath was coming in ragged gulps by the time he fell into the crane's cab. Bracing his legs against the front window, he hung his head between them and took several slow, deep breaths. Then, resuming a normal seated position, he slammed the cab door shut with a desperate jerk.

As the burning pain in his chest eased, he gazed out the window, dreading what he would see. The bulky metal frame around the glass made it seem as if he were watching the events below on a television screen. He watched the creature in the lights, with men running around it. They seemed so tiny and far away that he felt utterly detached from the scene. The silence of the cab only increased his feeling of disassociation from what he was watching; he was discomforted only by occasional vibrations and the dull sound of the wind gusting outside. He watched engrossed by the surreal spectacle before him. As the creature stopped, intent upon a man trapped on the floor, he could see its movements in captivating detail; he began to admire the smooth motion of its flowing limbs, which seemed to spring from the back of the creature's shell.

Feeling sweat drip from his brow jolted Steve back to reality, making his heart leap into his throat and his hands shake.

Below, he could see a group of men gathered just around the corner from the creature, crowded behind the canteen block. They were armed with a collection of poles, pipes, and makeshift armaments. He saw Jenkins come out of the canteen; a man holding a weapon passed it to him on his arrival. Was that Dan, he wondered?

His heart leapt with the hope that they would protect Janice. There was deep relief in the realization, and at the same time, he felt like he could weep at his own cowardly weakness.

Jenkins was talking earnestly to the group, pointing toward the dark, and with a sweeping gesture of his arm and with his scaffold pole held high above his head, he led them around the corner. They spread out, trying to approach the creature from as many sides as possible, jabbing their weapons at the monster.

The thing was obviously not expecting a concerted defense and began to retreat.

He could see the plan from above; they were trying to drive it off the rig, herding it like a monstrous sheep. He felt a flush of excitement and a shout came from him.

"Go on! Push that bastard off!" He felt hope and excitement rise in him. They could win. It was only an animal.

The creature had backed up to the fencing it had flattened when it arrived, and then it stopped. It seemed to be coiling around itself, its arms becoming a barrier against the men's weapons.

Jenkins had gone to the front of the defenders and seemed to be urging the men to keep attacking, when in a burst of motion the monster was upon him. It tore aside his scaffold pole, and several limbs entered the defenseless man, lifting him up into the air. The speared limbs dangled him there as he writhed and beat futilely against them, his mouth agape, and Steve filled the silence of the cab with a scream of his own, until with a convulsive jerk, Jenkins was ripped apart.

Steve felt sick in his throat as the thing moved forward again, knocking weapons aside from unwilling hands. The men's defensive cordon broke. They ran, retreating in fear and desperation, vainly brandishing their remaining weapons to defend their lives.

Mocking his previous bravado, Steve's fear reappeared in the forefront of his emotions. Then he saw her, moving in the canteen doorway. Janice was edging around the corner to where the thing would soon see her. He began frantically banging on the glass and shouting warnings that she couldn't hear. He swept the sweat from his eyes and looked desperately around for some way to warn her, but there was no way to communicate that he could see. Scanning out the window, he saw only the triangular metal spokes of the crane arm.His eyes followed the metal arm out to its end and then down a few feet of wire cables. There he saw a pallet swinging; it was loaded with a clutch of barrels and pipes and was close to where Janice stood.

He looked down at the mass of black rubber-topped levers and tried to make sense of their purpose. Which one would do what he needed?

He looked back at the creature; it seemed to have caught Janice's scent and was moving purposely toward where she was its motions slow and stalking. Janice also seemed to realize the creature was coming for her, and she had begun slowly backing away. He begged the monster to continue its slow process, and he prayed that he could carry out his plan undetected.

"C'mon, come closer. C'mon, you bastard, closer, closer, come closer, please," he desperately whispered.

He tried unsuccessfully to lick his dry lips; the rest of his body was drenched. He was no longer a child, frozen in fear, waiting for his bedroom door to open, for the father-monster on the other side to wreak havoc; this time a part of him kept moving, no longer held rigid by dread. He seized the first lever his fingers reached and used all his energy to yank it down.

Nothing happened.

Dan's hands shook as he tried to fit the cartridge in his hands into the flare gun which seemed to squirm in his grip. His attention kept returning to the screams of men and metal below him. He could see that a man was trapped beneath the thing; he could see red haze above the man's punctured torso, highlighted against his white coat, the man's hands and feet banging against the deck as his head jerked from side to side.

"SHITE, and double fuckin' shit!" Jonnie shouted. "I've fuckin' got something."

As if to emphasize his declaration, the radio crackled static in an aggressive, non-intelligible burst.

Dan looked back to see Jonnie still working under the equipment, with his heels bouncing to their own inner rhythm, which reminded Dan sickly of the scene below. Jonnie had begun crooning to the truculent equipment as if he might coax a tune from its white noise.

"Thank you, Lord," Dan breathed in recognition of the life breathed into the radio. Then, new screams, distant but piercing, drew him stumbling back to the walkway beyond the radio shack. The flare gun and cartridge finally fitted together in a smooth motion, ending in a satisfying click. He looked at his suddenly steady hands as if they were strangers.

A group of men came out onto the deck toting spears, like a savage horde, he thought, and began making an arc around the creature, closing in on it and pushing it back into the sea with their armed cordon. He felt like cheering.

Hoping to aid in scaring off the monstrosity, he sighted the flare gun on the creature. Holding his breath a moment, he then squeezed the trigger till it clicked, and then … nothing.

"Bollocks!" he shouted.

"It's a dud. Try a nuder one!" Jonnie yelled.

Dan clicked out the faulty charge, fumbling for a new one, and looked back outside, where everything had changed in a few seconds. Men were down, and the thing was advancing. He flipped the next cartridge in the stocky breach, snapped it shut, and aimed.

He prayed aloud, "Please, God, help us" … then, as if waiting a moment for God's mercy to commence, he fired. The shockingly bright flare blinded him on its exit, and its heat warmed his face.

As he followed the burning line of the flare, he saw objects were hitting the back of the thing. A large pallet of pipes and barrels rained down, battering the creature. Liquid sprayed from a container as it hit the edge of the canteen block. The monster heaved itself away from the falling debris, straight into the flight path of the flare. The burning spear of light connected with a shower of sparks, and with an inaudible whoosh, the creature's back was suddenly engulfed in flames. Initially, only its arms seemed to register the conflagration, as they went from snakelike weaving to frantic thrashing.

Dan's senses were assaulted by a sonic screeching that made him clap his hands to his ears to block out the sound. The sound seemed to be trying to force the bones of his skull apart. Through his watering eyes, he saw the thing below had gone into an insane dance in the flames, its more external arms flailing around, sending black drill pipes and oil drums sailing through the air. He saw a man go down, sideswiped into the dark by a thrashing limb.

As the pain in Dan's head made him fall to the floor, he looked up into the night toward where the debris had fallen from, and in the crane above he saw Steve, his face lit by the dancing flames below, like some kind of demon ghost part hidden in the blackness.

The pain eased from his eardrums, and Dan once again felt like cheering.

"You see that, Jonnie? Up there! Steve. He got it," Dan said, pointing excitedly.

"'e smashed it up good like, look at dat fucker dance," said Jonnie panting.

Dan looked back at the creature lurching about. Jonnie started laughing.

"We got ya! Ya fuckin' piece of shite!"

The creature abruptly stopped, as if suddenly oblivious to the flames, and started to glow with blue light from within its core, shining out through openings in its carapace. Familiar vibrations came up through the rig floor, Dan could feel them through his teeth, and they seemed to be eddying in the air.

"Oh. My. God," Dan breathed. "It's not dying. We just made it mad … What's it doing now?"

With a sudden massive blue/white blast, every man was knocked to the ground, and every light on board the rig was extinguished.

Dan managed to raise his head from the deck and, through blurred vision, see the burning creature spin in a sideways scuttle, gouging and tearing the deck as it went to the edge of the rig and heaved its bulk into the sea. It fell into the black abyss beyond the rig, like a burning torch into a dark well; the ocean lit up with a flash of blue, like an underwater lightning strike disappearing into a sudden and complete night.

CHAPTER 10 — A TIME TO CONSIDER

The wind whined through the cracked metal of the canteen ceiling above Steve's head with a melancholy lament. The ceiling's symmetrical lines were now dented inward and lined with jagged splits where the assorted falling metal pipes, oil heavy barrels, and the creature had slammed against it. The thrumming moan through the half-lit sweat-filled room dismayed Steve; it sounded as if it were the monster calling out for him from the deep. It only helped increase the chill of dawn and the sense of cold loss that permeated the room. Faces with dark sunken eyes and raw emotion carved on their ill-lit features gaped in silent dismay at the bruised medic in front of them, who was laying out the cost of lives from the night's violence. The canteen was filled with blues of fear, charcoal of loss, and the red shoots of anger.

Of the thirty-two crew of the original oil rig crew, four were missing, and eight were confirmed dead. Two were so seriously injured that it was unlikely they would survive the day, and of the remaining eighteen, not a man was untouched by a small wound, contusion, or abrasion, apart from himself, thought Steve bitterly, the savior of the day.

They had cheered him and called out his name as they celebrated their victory over the nightmare, leaving him astonished and off balance. The real story and his cowardice were locked in his throat, and he dreaded that his panic would signal his deceit to the others. Hands had patted his back, while men with smiling faces had surrounded him with outstretched hands to be shaken, and behind them all, she was there smiling at him.

'Le fat chef' had shaken his hand, with a big smile on his

pockmarked greasy fat face and had recently delivered hot coffee to him, on a tray. Even Lee Jones had clapped him a blow on the shoulder and raised his hand like a champion boxer. But Lee's eyes had shown no fellowship or happiness in the celebration, had not given off any warmth of color or camaraderie in the overtight grip of his hand. Even now, he caught Jones staring, a small smile at the corner of his mouth and his surrounding corona of a light green loathing. His customary red cheeks were pale against the bruising Steve had put there, next to the cuts and abrasions the creature had inflicted. He sensed only brooding animosity in the man's glare.

The ship's medic, Francis Cooper, had finished with his summary of the crew's condition. He seemed to sag with the weight of the sorrowful news he had delivered, and when he raised his head on completion of his report, his eyes were watery and the right side of his darkly swollen face shone with dark blue distress. Steve watched him shuffle back to one side of the canteen and slump against a table as if he hoped it would bear the weight of last night's blood-soaked memories.

Then Steve looked back at the assembled management at the front of the slanting room, shuffling their feet as if they were caught like startled cattle in the bright light cast upon them by the gas lamps. They looked tense under the weight of the eyes watching their every movement.

Chief Johnson and Angus Neil, the platform's OTL (Operations Team Leader, and, in Steve's opinion, a general arse), were in deep conversation with 'Company Man' Hank Storrel. His face had been bleak as he rounded on the two men, who had dropped their heads in deference to his authority.

Off to one side of the management group was the Scouse Control Room Operator, Jonnie, who was in whispered conversation with Dan. Both of whom ignored the pale figure of the head geologist, Lawson, who looked lost and ostracized by the group. He looked as if he might throw up at any second.

Dan caught Steve's look and gave him a smile. He felt that same warm feeling and lump in his throat that he'd felt earlier, after Dan had hailed him as the oil platform's savior. Dan had dismissed his own small role in firing the flare that had set the creature alight as icing on the cake to Steve's triumph. It was 'Steve' who had had quick thinking in climbing the rig crane (in the strong wind and rain) to dump the crane's contents and crush the monster, Dan had proclaimed, and Steve's actions had saved all their lives.

Steve had stood with his heart beating painfully fast in his chest, as if it might explode, as Dan described his heroism. He flashed looks to the faces around him, expecting disbelief at his obvious fraud. Surely they could see his actions were born of cowardice; surely they would see the lie and the guilt that writhed inside him? But when Dan had finished, the battered survivors had cheered his name, shook his hand, and spoke to him like long-lost friends.

His world had stopped when she came up to him and kissed him softly on his cheek.

"I thought you had left me. Instead, you had gone to save me, all of us. Thank you, Steve," she breathed with gratitude, and a touch of something he didn't recognize but which made him a little happily unsteady.

She had given him a frail smile, despite being red-eyed from crying. She had been distraught when they had told her that Barge Engineer Jenkins had been killed. Steve had also felt a strike of sadness that the larger-than-life, friendly man had been taken. He realized that he had always liked him and had never let it reach his lips.

But now he struggled enough with finding himself welcomed by his work colleagues, by the warmth of Janice's lips on his cheek and with the ache of feeling that her blue eyes made him feel.

The guilt from his spineless attempt to hide, which had led to their victory, still lay like a sickness in his stomach, waiting to be vomited up. But worse, as the load from the crane arm had landed on the creature, he had felt its pain and rage as if it had been his own. In that moment he had been the monster being tormented by the flames and had shared the wild unforgiving desire for revenge against the same humans who now surrounded him.

He waited with his newly pronounced comrades to hear the next course of action, now that the creature had been dispatched, the stories and wounds shared, and the desperate terror hidden away.

But all he could think about was the small woman that leaned against him wrapped in a blanket. Despite the lie in his heart, he didn't want her anywhere but near him, so his shame remained locked inside, like so much of his past.

After more hushed talk and further orders from Storrel at the front of the room, Johnson stepped tentatively forward, squinting against the bright gas light into the gloom of the darkened room of men before him.

"Right, men, let's have your attention! Come on, pipe down!" He waited till the hubbub died down, and then continued.

"We have been through a downright bad experience. We have lost some good men, and we have all had quite a scare. We should thank Mr. Staples and r. Giles for their quick thinking in killing the ... erm, thing. But the fact remains that this platform is in a bad state, and we have responsibilities. There is work that needs doing in securing this vastly expensive installation. It's time for us to get back on the job, so to speak and, erm, do the jobs we are paid to do, like professionals. "

There was an exhalation of complaint and rising outrage from the men, outrage to which now-fully-red-faced Lee Jones gave voice.

"Our mates are fresh dead. And you want us back to work? We don't even know what the fuck that thing was."

"No, no, of course not straight back to work," Johnson's tone was now placating. "We have to remember everyone who has died here, and we will have a small service, till we can get back on land and give them a proper farewell. But now this rig is in danger, and we have to get it shipshape while we wait for rescue."

"Sod that, I don't give a shit about this rig!" Brainy shouted. "When is the rescue coming? I don't want anything to do with this fucking place. I want off it."

"Bloody right, man," Jones spat.

"Alright, gentlemen ... calm down, erm, thank you, erm ..." Johnson spluttered.

"What do ya reckon, Staples?" Jones shot a question at Steve, who jumped in surprise and stuttered an answer.

"I, I, think, we should get out of here as quick as possible … what if there is more than one of those things?"

The question hung in the air, gathering body in the sudden silence, like the change in pressure before an oncoming storm. They looked to each other with shared dread, and he felt Janice wrap her hands around his arm, her eyes large with fear.

"Could there be more, Steve?" she whispered.

The plaintive way she asked made him suddenly regret speaking his thoughts out loud; her sad, fearful eyes pricked at his emotions, making him desperately want to take his words back and wipe away her distress.

"Ridiculous," Storrel laughed, too loudly, in the large space.

"Just one of those things was impossible, something never even seen before, and now you think they travel in herds?!" the American said contemptuously.

He swaggered out in front of Johnson, looking them all in the eye as he walked past them.

"This is the time to secure our position, make sensible decisions based on facts," he drawled.

"Fact one is we have no radio contact. Fact two is we have three days to wait for the next ship. Fact three is we don't know how badly damaged this platform is or if it might actually stay afloat," he counted off the points on his fingers. "We all have plenty to do before we can get ourselves safely off this oil rig, gentlemen; it's a matter of survival."

He had everyone's attention; the laying out of this new threat sharpened their focus and silenced any complaints. Storrel's confidence grew despite sweat patches under the arms of his blue shirt; he was in his element, and he was in control.

"We will get ourselves sorted and secure this oil platform, ready to fulfil the duties we are paid for, while making sure we do not lose another good man."

"You can get fucked!" Lee Jones said. "Work fuckin' stopped the minute that fuckin' thing crawled aboard and my mates started dying. I am not working on this bloody rig a moment longer," he spat in menacing tones. "I want off, and I want off now." He bit off each word as he spat them out.

Dan broke the tension by putting his large frame between Jones and Storrel. Palms up in a calming gesture, he said softly, "We need to have a service for our dead, and thank God for our survival. We can't do anything till we get communications back up and running. And Jonnie thinks that could take a while. If we leave this rig, we have only two life rafts with the dive boat gone. We have nowhere to go and no help coming at present. I suggest we make sure we are safe on this rig, and then remember those that died fighting that creature so we could live."

Dan paused, and Steve took in the faces of the men around him; they seemed unimpressed with the idea of taking to the water in rafts. They looked in desperate need of a few months on a beach or hours of therapy, he thought, the crackling blues and shuddering reds that bathed them underlining their state.

"I think we should listen to Dan," Steve found himself saying with sudden confidence. "We need to make sure we are safe."

He shot a look at Dan, who gave him a quick smile in return.

"Alright," said Lee Jones. "At least that makes some sense."

The big man sat down, his face impassive despite his sudden change of opinion, leaving the other standing men looking around with the wind taken from their sails and then finally sitting down in resignation.

Steve looked at Jones and felt apprehension. The man's fleshy face could barely contain his self-satisfaction or the hint of venom in his piggish eyes. Amongst the whirl of emotions from before and after the attack, somewhere in Steve's mind a black shade of fear remained, mixed with the anxiety of this moment and the grief of what had passed. He still felt hunted, or maybe haunted, by the thing that had come from the ocean.

Dan was in conversation with Harry Shore, 'Big C,' the rig's DPO (Dynamic Positioning Operator), who maintained the engines that kept the rig above the pipeline.

"Okay, I guess first thing we need to know is how secure is this platform?" Dan asked the disheveled man, who looked like he would rather hide behind the mug of coffee in his hand.

Harry 'Big C' Shore, as the men called him because of the pun on his second name, shook his bearded face as he spoke, his saggy jowls wobbling as if he couldn't hold the weight of his large head still.

"The engines seem to still be running, and we are still holding water over the drill. I think even with the angle the platform is at that we should be secure, as should the drill pipeline itself. As long as the weather holds."

"That's good news. Thanks, Harry," Dan said. "I think if we spend a few hours securing as much as we can and assessing what we can fix, we will be in better shape."

He turned to the men in ties for confirmation, and after receiving nods, he continued. "Then we can meet back here in five hours, and we can have our service for our friends, to send them into God's mercy."

"I think we would be better praising Staples. He saved our arses, not Jesus bollocks him Christ!" Brainy said in a loud mutter.

Steve felt uncomfortable at being hailed a savior and at how sour Dan's face had gone at the comments; he decided to say nothing though, because frankly he agreed with Brainy that God hadn't done much to help and hadn't shown much mercy, either.

"I think we should all bow our heads, and remember the lost all the same," Dan said.

Some voices were raised in agreement and some heads were nodding.

"Alright," said Johnson, seizing back the initiative. "We have a plan. Let's get on with it, lads. Come on, let's get going. Mr. Neil will assign work tasks."

He clapped his hands like he was encouraging reluctant schoolchildren, and his encouragement was met with dark scowls.

Angus Neil began to marshal out chores in his reedy nasal voice for the jobs that needed immediate doing. Steve was to check the Calor gas supplies for the kitchen and check the gas lines for damage. It seemed, as he listened to the other jobs being handed out, that he had been given light duty. The usually superior Neil had even shaken his hand as he had given it to him, like some cheap quizmaster on a game show announcing a prize. Actually, he was relieved to be on his own for a while; the unusual attention and friendship had unsettled him, and he needed time to gather his thoughts. But all his thoughts scattered when a small warm hand gripped his arm and he turned to look into blue eyes.

Janice had only managed to half concentrate on the meeting of bedraggled and battered oil rig men. She wanted to be involved, to speak her mind, but too much had happened too quickly, and she couldn't seem to stop remembering the faces of her Captain and Jenkins, and oddly she kept remembering her father's funeral. It seemed to leave her weak and unable to be a part of what was happening around her, and even when she began to feel more solid, the creature came out of the darkest corner of her mind to scare her from herself.

She had never depended on anyone before, had always been independent, but now she found that she couldn't be away from Steve without trembling. His almost black-brown eyes and thin face seemed to offer her protection, a place to hide from her fractured feelings and fear. He spoke gently to her, and she felt comfort in his gentle voice and his simple concern.

He had introduced her to a big-framed blond man called Dan, whose friendly smile and kind eyes had also helped her feel more secure. But still the images ran behind her eyes and the memories sapped the life from her heart.

Beyond her grief and the panic that seemed to drain her strength, there was also the fact that whenever she looked up, she felt the piggy eyes of the big Geordie man with the red face on her. He seemed to always be staring at her, and when she met his eyes, she saw no compassion, only lewd obvious desire and the aggressive regard of his lust. She was afraid of him, and the trembling began again in her stomach.

She barely listened to the plans that would affect her, where once she would have leapt to be heard. She could only try to shelter within herself to guard against the crushing horror and loss.

When Steve had said there could be more of the creatures, terror had gripped her anew; it leapt into her chest as if it might compress the air from her lungs and snatch control from her limbs. But the arrogant American laughed the fear off, and his reasoning made sense, calming her emotional storm.

It wasn't until the red-faced man began yelling, the scarlet of his cheeks running down into his swollen neck as his rage surfaced, that she quailed at the violence of him. Then she yearned again for the security Steve brought to her.

Finally the meeting was breaking up and the crew began shambling by. Dan passed and gave her a nod and a grin, and his older skinny companion gave her a shy smile. Till lastly, the big Geordie man passed, giving her a coarse grin and the cold-eyed appraisal of a lizard, making her squirm away from him.

Steve turned toward her, shielding her with his body and long hair, his dark eyes filled with worry as he held her, asking if she was okay.

She held his gaze, hoping to lose herself in it, to escape the bitter world around her and the numbing loss in her mind.

"Can we go somewhere, Steve, alone? Somewhere where it can be just us, and we can lock the door?"

Steve looked deeply into her eyes and nodded.

CHAPTER 11 — CONNECTED DREAMS

Dan watched Steve and Janice as they slipped from the canteen together and felt a smile come to his face; he had never seen Steve look happy before. The reticent and moody roughneck had a look of incredulous amazement on his usually frowning face. Dan's smile disappeared, though, when he caught a glimpse at Janice; she looked desperate, with dark hollows surrounding wild eyes. She reminded him of the Japanese tsunami survivors whom he had seen on the news, forlornly searching the mud for any artifacts of their former lives. It had inspired him to raise charity money running a half marathon to help their plight. His heart seemed to expand in his chest as he thought of how much Janice had been through and lost in the last few hours.

"You can be too generous with your heart," his wife used to say with a smile as she pushed her small frame against him. He recalled her little upturned nose and sparkling green eyes as she hung her arms about his neck—"Just remember you gave it to me."

He could hear the children laughing together at some stupid cartoon in the front room, as he reached his mouth down to kiss her, could smell the wild flowers from her perfume mixed with bacon on the grill. Abruptly, he felt very much alone; he clung desperately to the memory, struggling to keep out the sudden fear that he would never see his family again, which was followed by a rush of determination that he would make it back to land no matter what.

Finally, a nasal voice calling his name dragged him from his memories; Angus Neil was waspishly demanding his attention, and he began the walk up the slope toward the clipboard-carrying man. When he glanced back to see if Steve and Janice were still in sight, he caught a fleeting glimpse of them entering the maintenance block and dismissed the pair from his mind so he could concentrate on Neil's requests. But as he turned away, he saw Lee Jones and two of his lackeys also watching the couple depart, and he felt a moment of unsettling anxiety at the aggressive posture of the big Geordie man, whose sneering face and jutting chin were visible as he talked to the two men who had their backs to Dan. After a brief discussion, the group of the three men moved on, dragging reels of electrical wire and a small generator along with them. But it still left a small spike of worry in Dan, which he tried to put out of mind as a clipboard was once more rattled in his direction.

Brainy was less than surprised when Lee Jones brought them to a stop to watch the couple pass. He also wasn't surprised by Jones's whispered litany of hate that followed as Staples and the elfin ginger girl walked away.

"Why's that little bitch with him?" Jones part-whispered. "Who's that streak of piss think he is? What a piece a shit. It's about time somebody put that cowardly little tosser in his place."

Brainy watched the man's face get redder as he worked up his rhetoric of anger, a familiar sight to Brainy; he had seen similar performances before and knew that behind the show of anger was a preplanned idea that fitted the man's own particular and probably bloody purpose.

He'd seen it before on shore leave with the crew that Jones had a propensity for violence and he carried a knife. But more unpleasant to Brainy was Jones's desire for small and fragile-looking young women. He took pleasure in bringing them pain and humiliation; it seemed to sate his lust and whatever else fueled the man's malicious hunger. Brainy found this behavior more and more unacceptable. He had always had a soft spot for girls. They always seemed the more generous of the species when you were alone with them. Being with a girl ... well, those were some of the only times he had ever really shared himself with anyone, and he remembered again that one dark-haired girl with deep dark eyes. But years growing up with the gangs on the

London housing estate where he was born had taught him it was better to be behind the person with the blade than facing its edge. Jones came across as a mean bastard who was just one of the lads, but underneath he didn't give a shit about anybody else alive, Brainy thought, so in front of the point of Jones's blade was not a place he wanted to be.

"He saved our asses, didn't he, Lee?" Arthur Whitehead asked. He was a roughneck unit from down south who liked too much lager and being on the right side of an uneven fight. Brainy reckoned the weasel would throw babies at a charging bull to save his own arse.

"No way, Art. I reckon that little coward hid up in that crane, probably knocked a lever by mistake. Now everybody is making out he's a fucking hero." Jones's voice was thick with scorn.

"Now he's tricked the knickers of that little lass, and we're the ones did all the fighting. Doesn't seem proper now, does it?"

"No, I suppose not, mate. What should we do about it, mate? I am behind you all the way, you know?" Whitehead asked doubtfully.

Brainy felt contempt for Whitehead's 'dog waiting for a stick' routine and disturbed by where Jones was going with this. Brainy's world had been turned over in the last few hours by the creature. He had never felt such utter desperate fear or gone so far in his response to it; he had changed somewhere inside. The planes and angles of his thoughts had been altered as much as the those of the rig. He could see the malice behind the bruises on Jones's face and the lust behind his hatred. He felt different now, the coverings of his life had been ripped away, and he had looked at himself without all the bullshit ideas of himself he had created; the rules of his life had changed. He believed that Steve and Dan had saved their lives and that maybe they offered the best chance of getting off this rig if things got any worse.

"What do you think, Brainy? Want to have yourself a little party? I'll bring the women and liquor, if you all bring a beating," Jones grinned.

"I don't know, Jones. Would we get away with it?" Whitehead asked, suddenly looking nervous. This gave Brainy time to think; he was being drawn in two directions, toward the new arrangement of his thoughts or toward the loyalty he must display as part of this group.

"Of course, we'll fucking get away with it. Nobody here gives a crap about anything but getting home, mate. They have an 'accident' and it will all get lumped into this same disaster ... and we can have ourselves some proper fun before we get sent back to the same old shit. Might even let you go second on the lass, man," Jones laughed, his eyes gleaming with happy cruelty.

Whitehead matched Jones's hunger-filled laugh. "Bet she couldn't take all of a real man."

"You know what, mate, there's only one way to find out ... after me, of course."

The pair of grinning heads turned to him. He felt coldly distant from the growing lust on their faces, though he had felt the same before in his life. For some reason, looking at their spite, he now felt oddly disgusted and apart, in a way he couldn't explain. But his mouth knew the familiar patter.

"Sounds like it might be a night out to remember," he said, and Jones and Whitehead laughed again as they began moving the equipment.

Steve led Janice to a long white corridor that was interspersed with metal doors down the length of the stores block and stopped at a door marked 'Gas Equipment,' letting her into a room of floor-to-ceiling shelves, chock full of large cable reels, coiled blue and red tubes, crates, boxes, and all manner of equipment, then locked the door behind them.

The metal room was suddenly quiet; the sound of the wind, ocean, and the rig activity was suddenly shut out, leaving only the gentle thrum of the ocean through the submersed structure of the platform. They stood in the three-foot passage between the overfilled steel racking in the thin rectangular room, and he shuddered as the cold settled over him. It was chilly in the locker, like a fridge. He jumped when she put her hand on his arm, as it felt hot on his skin, and he slowly turned to face her. He was afraid he would see revulsion in her eyes at where he had brought her, or the rejection of being locked in this fridge with him.

But her eyes were full of tears, and those negative thoughts dissolved as concern for her overtook him.

"Janice, are you okay? Do you want me to take you back?" He couldn't imagine what he had done, but his happiness seemed to have turned to lead in his chest.

"No, Steve, I want to be here with you … but …" she stammered to a stop. "Tell me, why is someone so sensitive working with a bunch of Cro-Magnon roughnecks?"

He could see distress in her eyes: she was coloured dark yellow with shoots of red, but he could think of no way of making it better, so without even thinking about it, he began telling her about living near the sea, about never seeming to fit in as a kid (not about 'freaky weirdo,' though), and about always finding himself looking out to sea.

"So you wanted to escape where you lived? Was it a horrible place to live?" she asked, but her questions seemed directed inward, almost as if she were questioning herself.

"When it was just me and mum, it was great," he said; he could feel a smile on his face. "She always seemed to make things better, but …" His smile slipped away.

"But?" she said, seeming to come out of her own dark thoughts.

"When my dad came home from the rigs, he was a roughneck. He would drink and become angry and violent; they would be miserable weeks until he went out to sea again."

"So your father was a … roughneck? Then how did you end up working on an oil rig?" She was all sunflower-yellow now, with stirrings of amber.

"After my parents died when I was twelve, I lived with an aunt. She helped me go to the local college, and I just wanted to be good enough. I suppose I wanted to prove my father wrong. He thought I would never achieve much or be able to work like he did, and so I guess I drifted into it that way."

He paused, feeling his own thoughts darken with memories of his father.

She was now her rich orange-gold, but it was flecked with blues.

"He doesn't sound like a very nice man to me?" she asked with a voice full of sympathy.

He could think of nothing to say and just nodded, his throat constricted and tears stinging his eyes.

"Steve," she seemed suddenly intent. "Can I ask you about your dad? Did he hit your mum?" She paused. "Did he hit you?" she asked softly.

Suddenly, he went numb and his emotions seemed far away, as if he was just rediscovering a line of thought. "Yes. When he'd come home drunk and angry, Mum used to make me hide in the bathroom. I could hear her struggle, hear the blows, hear him yell at her."

She looked at him for a long moment, focusing attentively on his face as if she were trying to gather her thoughts and judge what to say next.

"Steve, how did your parents die?" she asked gently, never dropping her gaze.

He felt oddly weak and more detached, and his voice came out as if a stranger were speaking through him.

"Dad came home very drunk one night. He hit Mum as soon as he came in, while she was washing up. Then he rushed at me, slapped me across the face, and I fell on the floor. He stood over me, yelling at me. I remember his eyes; they were wild and white around the edges. He looked like a madman.

"He was shouting that I was worthless and that I would be better off dead. Later in life, I wondered if he really meant himself.

"Mum had gotten up, and she grabbed him away, screaming for me to go and lock myself in the bathroom. He had fallen but was getting back on his feet. Mum grabbed a pan from the draining board and swung it at him, still yelling at me to hide.

"So I ran and locked myself in bathroom. There was screaming and crashes of furniture and plates breaking. I remember crying and jumping with each bang, shout, or shriek. All the while my father kept up this litany of loud accusations and threats that echoed through my door until there was a strangled scream and another loud crash. Then it was silent for a long while, till I heard him outside the door telling me to come out, but his voice was quiet and strange, and I was too afraid. After a while I heard his footsteps go away, and it was silent again, just the sound of the water boiler in the kitchen.

"When I went out Mum was dead on the kitchen floor where he'd strangled her, and he was in his armchair in the lounge with his wrists cut.

"He was still alive and looked at me. His eyes were dull and watery now, and he said, 'It won't be long until you end up this way.' And then he went silent until his eyes went dull."

Steve trailed off, unable to bear the constriction that seemed to bind his chest.

"You don't have to feel like this anymore, Steve. I don't want to feel like this. We're not alone anymore," she said, looking into his eyes, which seemed to have become very dark.

"Make me feel something else, please." Her voice was a husky ache.

She threw her arms around his neck and kissed him with a fiery desperation that slowed into molten urgency. After kissing her deeply, till he felt he might lose all self-control and tear off her clothes, he gently separated himself from her and laid their coats on the metal-grated floor. There was a pause while they looked deeply at one another, and Steve reached out a hand to gently stroke her cheek. Then, with no identifiable ignition point, the fire returned. They fought off their clothes, and hot skin met hot skin, till the heat became a roaring blaze, and their bodies became slick with the rhythmic motion of their flesh. They called out each other's names, tasted, bit, and gripped each other till, in one final conflagration, they collapsed, spent.

Afterward, they lay wrapped around each other, and Steve's mind seemed to be lost in the burnt-out pleasure of the moment as he lay supported by his arms upon her. He was floating upon the luxurious afterglow of their passion, letting every nerve tingle and panted breath drift around him as he closed his eyes, enjoying the warm gratification that ran through his body. He let his mind slide into a pleasant chaos of empty thoughts, and, in that moment, his awareness was grabbed—a blue flash within a white one and his mind was elsewhere; he was now vertiginously below the ocean surface.

He was surging speedily through dark water, lit by fragile

ghost beams of light, while ahead prey maneuvered, glowing brightly with golden workings and leaving a multicolored spectral wake. Other prey scattered in the distant water as he surged toward them, like a box of firework rockets being launched in different directions. Then, with another bright flash of blue-streaked white, Steve was in the coldest blackness he could imagine, but somehow he could see a mountainous sea cliff spectrally highlighted in the blackness. The surfaces around him were lit with lightened edges and vibrant color-rich echoes of light. Blue/white flashed again, and he swam with others toward monolithic structures, lit by the same lightened and iridescent colors, where sound had become sight and light had become revelation.

Another flash took him inside a cavernous water-filled chamber, where impossibly huge beings floated, attended by nightmare creatures like the one that had attacked them last night. They were sending images made of sound through the water, like a shower of iridescent sparks. He understood nothing of the message they sent: his mind staggered under the sensory overload, but he felt importance and the power of purpose, and he knew that these commands had bound him. The flashes came quicker and quicker, too alien for his mind to cope with, too fast, too bright, and he knew he had begun to scream.

Janice felt the chill air like a cool caress on her overheated skin; she breathed deeply, tasting him and the sensual musk of their coupling. She smiled against his neck and felt the muscular strength of his back and the sweat-adhered union of their skin as she tried to hold him a little tighter. The cold miasma of fear that had shrouded her spirit seemed to have been blown away in the storm of passion; now she lay drifting in their shared heat with the comfortable weight of him on her. She had caught up with her feelings and seemed to recognize the inside of herself again.

Maybe in a way that's what sex was, she thought: a magical way of stripping ourselves to the core for brief moments, of being reduced to the base animals that we are, to remember the basic needs of life, especially the need for emotional connection with another member of our species. In this bonding, didn't she want animal passion and to feel protection? Thinking of the compassion and sensitive touch of the man she held, her emotion was suddenly very strong again.

She wanted to kiss him once more and look into his eyes, but then she saw that Steve had his eyes closed, brow furrowed, and eyes moving beneath his eyelids.

"Steve?" she asked, but he made no sign that he was aware that she had spoken, so she decided to pinch him, hoping he would take it as mischief. "Steve?"

The previously caressing coolness of the room now felt like a chill, and Janice began to shake Steve's arm, saying his name repeatedly.

He began to tremble as if he were in a nightmare from which he couldn't wake.

"STEVE!" she yelled his name in his face, and he began to scream, a rending howl filled with terror.

Scared, she pushed herself away from him, as if he had become abruptly dangerous or infectious. His eyes snapped open, and he stared through her with dread, until his eyes focused on her.

"What the fuck?" he said, shaking his head and wiping his hands over his face repeatedly.

"Jesus, Steve, what happened?" Anxiety made her voice high and strident as she struggled to come down from her suddenly heightened unease.

"Are you all right?" she asked.

"Yeah, I think so ... I didn't hurt you, did I?" His face was a caricature of worry, and with a sudden release of tension and despite her best attempts to not, she began to laugh.

"You scared me silly!" she laughed, and though for a brief moment his face darkened, he very quickly began to grin.

"What was going on?" she asked lightly.

His expression clouded, and he shook his head as if it were full of confusion and he could shake it free; he started to speak, and then paused, frowning. She had the impression that he had changed his mind about what to say.

"I guess not enough sleep and too much going on. I guess we have all been pretty stressed ... and I don't think I was ready for the effect you would have on me, Janice," he said with a slightly forced smile.

The unexpectedly gentle words made her serious again, and she thought of their passion. She reached out and caressed his arm, moving into the warmth of his side.

"You've made quite an impression on me." Her voice seemed to have become huskier, and she reached for his face; her lips met his. After several pleasurable seconds, the fire was rekindled, and she felt his response pushing against her side. "Perhaps we should try again," she whispered. "Let's leave the bad memories behind and make new ones."

He hungrily put his mouth to hers and rolled onto her, and she gasped as the red-hot length of him entered her. This time there were no bad moments.

Sometime later, after they had laughed and spoken soft words, they kissed and tried to forget who and where they were. They talked about where they came from, and Janice told him about her dad and the strained relationship with her mother. Steve talked about life with his aunt, minus the parts of his childhood isolation that were related to his unusual gift, a lie detector, his aunt had called it, but it was more of an emotional thermometer. He felt the familiar guilt at his omissions as she expressed her emotions about her father. He did manage to say that he had always had long hair as a kid, but not that it was to hide from seeing other people when their emotional colors became too fierce.

'Freaky weirdo, with a strange hairdo' rang in his ears.

A little later they sneaked furtively from the stores with Steve carrying a roll of gas line and a pack of various fittings, while she carried a plastic toolbox and a gas lamp. They looked at each other and shared a final smile before they went outdoors.

Nobody seemed to be close by. They could hear only the distant metallic banging's and shouted conversations of the crew, so they made for the canteen and crew block.

They managed to arrive unnoticed and set about checking the gas lines. They had started to replace the damaged or stretched gas lines when 'le fat chef' brought them a tray with rough-cut bacon sandwiches, cooked on a camping gas stove, and coffee.

They changed burnt-out fittings and replaced damaged pipes

while finding small reasons to be close, poke fun at the other, or just share a look while they worked.

Steve realized he couldn't ever remember a happier moment in his life. He had been with a few other girls, but the relationships seemed to have been based on shared alcohol and his ability to pay for it. Where he lived in his mother's old flat in a tower block amongst an estate of uniformly shaped concrete flats, people seemed interested only in what they could get from the people, only what they could cheat from another's happiness to make their own life more worth living, or even just bearable. The girls he met from the estate were cold and self-interested, with splintered yellow and grey auras. They were after quick highs and vied with each other for a greater share of social limelight or possession of the better-looking or stronger blokes.

Despite having a decent income, he was a small draw on the social scene due to his long job-related absences, his aloofness, and his constant scowl. All his relationships ended quickly, each one putting the blame of its failure on him; no girl on land ever waited for him, and it had left him a little bitterer each time.

With Janice, though, everything felt different. The dark corners within him seemed to disappear, and he began to feel that he could actually be the person he felt like he was inside. Anger and loneliness had been his constant companions throughout his life, but they seemed to be disappearing when he was in Janice's presence, like a dark emotional compulsion being withdrawn from his mind.

He still felt the memories from before, when they had made love the first time, of being somewhere else, something else, reverberating in the back of his mind, and he was glad he had not shared the experience with Janice; he didn't want to ruin the moment any more than he already had or frighten her with the random craziness blowing through the cave of his mind. He wanted to keep the 'freaky weirdo' for another time. He wondered with a strange new courage about what his self might become, and when he looked at Janice, he was filled with a wild new hope and managed for the moment to put the haunting and unearthly images he had experienced to the back of his consciousness.

CHAPTER 12 — FAREWELL TO THE DEAD

Dan was bone weary when he reached the helipad. He wasn't seeking out the peace and quiet to gather his thoughts but to escape from the demands of those around him. The salt-laced wind was bracing, and as he stared at the ever-changing red length of light cast by the setting sun, he hoped it would blow worry and weariness away in its gusts.

He sought escape from the deeply felt duty of his Christian beliefs that compelled him to provide help and hope for others. His faith was a great boon that gave him support for life's journey and had often been a great comfort in times of his need. But it also demanded he give of himself for all people, even people he could not have cared less about or (despite his great efforts) that he disliked intensely. Chief Johnson was presently top of that list.

Johnson had caught on to Dan's new popularity with the crew after his role in defeating the creature and was dispatching him all across the difficult-to-traverse rig to hand out his instructions—a lot of which were met with disapproval or plain abuse from the tired and frightened men. But Dan fulfilled this duty with patience and acceptance as this was what he believed his God wanted of him. His belief meant that his Christian charity and benevolence could be easily taken advantage of, it was often the reason he hunted for seclusion from his fellow workers, as he'd realized years ago that his kindness could be used as a yoke across his back for those who would use him to his limits without gratitude. He had often felt taken advantage of by those who required his obedient compassion and assistance. He'd taken to having moments of reflection (or just being unfindable) as an escape from the burdens laid on his shoulders. He did not pray to God at these times but sought freedom from the responsibility of his faith, letting his thoughts run until he could find himself again.

He was not disappointed to see Steve on the helipad already, the man's lean figure wrapped in a thick company parker coat against the wind. They had shared this lonely aerie many times, and he knew that Steve would allow him quiet in which to think. Dan thought that the other man was shy and a little repressed, but Steve asked nothing from him and despite his attempts to draw the intense young man out, he remained a mystery. So Dan could talk or share his views without having anything expected of him, no problems to solve or heartache to listen to and no physical or emotional weights to carry.

He stopped alongside Steve, who was leaning on the metal fence. "You okay, Steve?"

Steve seemed to shrink a little away from him as he remained looking out to the darkening white-capped waves below. The silence stretched till Dan thought Steve would say nothing and that his question had been lost between squalls of wind.

"I still see that thing in the water," Steve whispered almost inaudibly.

"Hey, my friend, it's okay. You killed that damn monster. You should be proud of yourself; I know I'm proud of you." He reached out and clasped Steve's shoulder.

Steve nodded but seemed to take no pleasure in the achievement and kept looking at the ocean.

"Where did it come from, that thing? Are there more?" The questions seemed to be being forced out of him. He seemed gripped in some kind of inner conflict that Dan couldn't hazard a guess at, so he attempted to answer the questions he was asked, and he hoped it would help Steve with whatever inner demons were afflicting the man.

"No, I don't think there can be. Storrel is right. It's something never seen before, a mutated creature or maybe some government science project gone wrong. If anything like this existed in the oceans, humanity would have come across it before now." He had answered cautiously, trying to keep his voice even despite the spike of fear he felt when he thought of the creature, not wanting to say the wrong thing and cause Steve more upset, but the other man remained steadfastly silent as if he hadn't heard a word, and the set of his features remained unmoved.

"Is Janice okay, Steve?" he asked, hoping to locate the source of Steve's turmoil.

His companion's features seemed to clench, and Dan knew his shot in the dark had missed its mark. Steve just nodded once, shaking his head slightly after, as if denying this truth.

"She's asleep," he said noncommittally, pushing the matter aside as inconsequential.

There was another drawn-out silence, and finally the introverted man turned his face to Dan; it was dominated by dark, sad eyes that disclosed some sort of inner torment, which made Dan's heart go out to him.

"I don't think any of that is right, about that thing. It came from somewhere else," Steve said suddenly, as if unable to stop the words spilling out.

Dan became concerned for the man and also felt a good amount of confusion. Steve's eyes seemed as wild as the lank black hair that kept obscuring his face as it blew in the wind, like it was trying to keep his face a secret.

"Where else could it be from, Steve?" he asked in as encouraging a tone as he could manage, trying to keep his concern from his voice.

"I think it's somewhere from the deep and the darkness. Somewhere that's not here. It was … was from … I don't know. Having seen that thing, do you still really believe there's a God?"

Dan was surprised at the sudden shift in Steve's conversation; one minute he had been quiet, almost fearfully questioning, and the next, confrontational. He was obviously still scared about the creature, and then aggressive, as if wanting to find who to blame for the fear inside him, Dan thought.

"Well, Dan? Can you still believe, having seen that fucking thing?" he asked again, insistently.

"Of course I still believe in God and his mercy. How can you not after he saved your life and gave you the opportunity to see this day?" He snapped at Steve's hostile attitude, too sharply, instantly regretting the harshness of his words.

"I'm sorry, but God has protected us so far, and with his love we shall continue to prevail."

Steve nodded with no real agreement.

"We should go to your service; we may see some more of your God's mercy for those poor dead buggers."

As Steve strode away, Dan was shocked at this new side of Steve. It left him unnerved and angry. He tried to squash his anger as he believed he should, but little seeds of it were left aflame as he felt his kindness had been thrown back in his face, bringing heat to his cheeks; it would seem gratitude was in short supply today. As quickly as the anger came, it went, leaving the sense that he had taken the quiet man for granted, as a willing vessel to receive his wisdom and knowledge, and that perhaps he had just expected him to be grateful for it. He felt suddenly guilty for his presumption. The seeking of quiet reflection seemed only to have caused him more confusion, and he felt ill prepared for the makeshift funeral ceremony to come.

Steve watched Dan throughout the whole service, his fervent face shadowed by the poor lamplight, which made him seem more wild prophet than priest as he spoke words over the dead from his worn black bible and asked them all to join in the Lord's Prayer (Steve did not). Then Dan spoke of the new life they had been given because of the sacrifice of their lost friends, his voice echoing in the metal rectangular box of the canteen, and how he hoped they could take this gift to make better lives for themselves, in memory of those who had died. The high-pitched whining of the wind through the holed roof seemed a nice counterpoint to the futile nature of the words, Steve thought.

He was bemused as to what the sacrifice had been. If dying beneath the blades of that creature or by having your skull crushed by oil barrels meant something, he was at a loss as to what it was. Then he wondered if all death was some kind of sacrifice to a God who was pruning them for a mysterious long-term 'greater plan.' Did human existence mean no more than that of herded cattle that had only a scheduled butchery to look forward to? The thought left him with a burning rage in his stomach and an acrid, acidic taste in his mouth.

He felt angry and suddenly wanted to rant at Dan's stupidity but was held in check by Janice's warm presence and that the majority of remaining crew bowed their heads and copied the prayer as Dan spoke it. He saw a few that did not share the observance, like Brainy and Jones, whose number he was not sure he wanted to be a part of. One look at Jones's bruised face and he felt the rage gathering in him again, while the others parroted away in a monotone and looked somber. Jones met his look with a thin smile.

Steve's eyes were drawn back to Dan. He was flushed and his eyes were bright with the passion he threw into his speech and prayer. He looked for the entire world like a TV evangelist, Steve thought angrily, an ache growing where his spine joined his skull. He wondered maliciously if, at the prayer's conclusion, they would be asked for their credit card details. But he knew from experience that Dan was genuine, a true believer, and he wondered again why it made him so angry.

For the first time, instead of feeling a little uncomfortable with Dan's religion, he began to irritably resent its banality and false promises of peace and love, along with that growing dull ache in his skull. There was little peace and love in his experience, and he had seen the beast; it had not been manufactured by a benevolent god.

So he waited for the pantomime to finish, looking at the covered bodies with hidden faces he would not see and voices he would not hear again. He waited, fuming and sweating at the prosaic pointlessness while Dan finished with a last prayer from his book.

The others began to filter away, heading into the near-darkness outside. They were gathering in the rec room, where a small generator provided light and heat and where there were no bodies or smell of death, only lager and the company of each other to extinguish dark reminders of the previous night.

He waited behind with no real purpose in mind, just feeling that his anger needed some release but not knowing what outlet was available. There was nothing he could share in from the sterile insights of Dan's bible readings. Perhaps, he thought, a funeral pyre was a better method of passage to a next place; getting lost in the flames appealed to him more as a proper method of freeing the soul to join any spirit world.

"Are you alright, Steve?" Janice asked, holding his arm.

Her voice was like pure honeyed calm to his senses, and he smiled, suddenly very grateful to have her close.

"Sure. I'm fine. It's just difficult to come to terms with so many dead. It all seems so pointless." But as he spoke the words, they didn't seem to match the true feelings churning inside him.

"I know, Steve, but we made it, and we will get through this and get home, together." She smiled as she looked up into his face, and he felt the huge volume of his passion surge.

Two burdened men interrupted the moment as they walked past, helping Cooper (the ship's medic) remove the bodies from the canteen to take to the cold store. Chief Johnson was calling the remaining management staff together. He called over Dan, who responded like a horse to the sound of a whip, Steve thought. He was about to head off when Johnson called his name, too, and waved him over. Bemused by the invitation, he paused, unable to reason why he was wanted, but then walked over.

"We are having a meeting, Mr. Staples. I wondered if you might join us."

Steve was even more surprised. "Er, yeah, I guess ... I mean, yes, sir."

"Can Steve be of some technical assistance to us, Chief?" Dan asked, looking less than pleased with Johnson's request. "I think we should let him join his mates in sharing the loss these men have suffered."

Steve was livid again at Dan; he seemed hell-bent on suggesting that Steve's thoughts and opinions must be worthless compared to his own; it made his anger spill over.

"I might be more use than you telling everyone that everything is okay, or perhaps you can save us all again with your flare gun?" Steve snapped irately.

He turned to Janice and whispered to her that she should go to his cabin, that he would not be long. She looked at him a little surprised.

"You'll be okay there. I won't be long," he said trying to reassure her.

After a moment, she nodded, and with a small anxious glance at Dan, she left the room.

After watching Janice depart (and noticing her look at Dan), Steve stomped off, following the rest of the management team who were leaving, heading to the operations room. His face felt hot, and he could hear the blood surging through his head. Suddenly, the ache was gone, making him feel much better than he had during the service. Having an outlet for his fury made him feel alive and potent.

CHAPTER 13 — A PLAN OF ACTION

When Dan arrived with Johnson in the operations room, everyone else was already there, making the overly warm room feel small and enclosed. Steve had put himself at the back of the room, his arms defensively across his chest, his dark eyes glinting with anger, his head lowered, and his body clenched with impatience.

Dan wondered at the sudden enmity toward himself. Steve seemed to have become a completely different person from the reticent man he had gotten to know, and Dan was beginning to worry about his mental state again. His thoughts were interrupted as Johnson called the meeting to order.

Along with Chief Johnson, Dan, and Steve, the management team consisted of Head Geologist Lawson, Operations Team Leader Neil, Control Room Operator (and electrician) Jonnie Smith, DPO (Dynamic Positioning Operator) Harry 'Big C' Shore, ASP (Automation System Specialist) Rick Carver, and lastly the still dark-suited Hank Storrel, the 'Company Man.' Storrel's hair was greased back and his jowls were quivering with agitation and importance. Dan realized that he had not seen one of these faces on the deck when they had been battling the creature.

It was Storrel who began without preamble, swinging his beer gut around to face Johnson. "The Flomax Oil Company has a large monetary investment in this platform, Mr. Johnson, and in the oil presently being stored and that potentially forthcoming from this facility. I want to be reassured that you are continuing to have the interests of this company at the forefront of your thinking." Storrel spoke with authority, pausing only to remove an indulgently silk-edged white handkerchief to dab at the light sweat on his face.

Dan witnessed sweat springing from the top of Johnson's almost bald head and his neck going as red as if he were attempting to lift a heavy weight. "Of course, I have the company's interests as my top priority, Mr. Storrel. Flomax is my employer, and everyone else's here, too, and so I will obviously do my utmost to represent Flomax's best interests, as I am sure everyone here will," he said with a gush, gesturing to the other men in the room looking for some support. None came.

"But these are somewhat exceptional circumstances, which have created many difficulties, for everyone and for me, to, to keep the continued, erm, running of the platform going," Johnson finished nervously.

"Yes, indeed," Storrel replied. "There have been things beyond your control, and I am sure my report would fully endorse your actions positively and would reflect the effective handling of the situation in glowing terms, should your actions and commitment to the company continue to remain positive."

The obvious threat seemed to galvanize his resolve, and Johnson almost stood to attention in his eagerness to demonstrate his positive commitment to the company.

"Well, yes, Mr. Storrel, I think we can turn our little disaster into a story of success," he beamed. Looking again to everyone in the room, Johnson continued, "We have plenty of work to be done. Let's get our situation assessed and dealt with, so we can get on with the jobs we are paid to do." Without thinking, he wiped the sweat from his face. "Right. Let's start with you, Mr. Carver. Are all systems up and running again?"

Put on the spot by the sudden question, the thin-faced and goateed systems specialist was flustered to silence. He was a tall slender man in his early thirties who was used to quiet conversations over coffee and being mostly ignored at work.

"Erm, well, yes … and no," he stammered, trying to arrange his thoughts. "I think that maybe the, er … damage has been quite severe … So I, er …"

"I think we need a concise answer, thank you, Mr. Carver," Johnson cut in, attempting to sound tough and in control. "Can you tell us where we stand on the running systems of this platform? Have we got the positioning engines running? Do we have capability for main power? What have we achieved today, Mr. Carver?" Johnson finished in his most strident and demanding tones, looking to Storrel with raised eyebrows as if they were sharing his incredulity at what he had to work with.

Carver almost bounced upright. His upper lip twitched, and his eyes flicked nervously around the room, trying to evade contact with Johnson.

"We replaced fuses with everything we had left in storage and as much of the wiring to main systems as we have had time to repair. The positioning motors are up and running. We have some power to the control room. The computers are running to some extent, and we have heat to some areas, and power in the canteen, so food and water is not an issue."

"Excellent, Mr. Carver. Some good news at last," Johnson smiled, and nodded at Storrel as if he had delivered great results and expected to be congratulated. But Storrel remained blank-faced and unreadable.

"Mr. Shore, can you continue to cheer us all up?" he asked loudly with growing confidence in his role.

Harry 'Big C' Shore looked suddenly pale, visibly sweating in the small and increasingly warm room, his light blue shirt darkening at the armpits. He raised his bulk from the table, which creaked as he levered himself up. He stood with his sweat-ridden blond fringe plastered to his forehead, shifting his bulk nervously from one foot to the other as if neither leg could bear his weight for long. His face wore an expression of indecision or trepidation, and the silence hung heavy.

"Well, Mr. Shore? What do you have to report?" Johnson's tone had lost its friendliness and was now sounding petulant as annoyance won over and his mask of professionalism came off.

Big C glanced around the room. "I think we may have a larger problem than I first thought, sir." He stopped briefly to swallow and to take a big breath and exhalation, as if he were struggling to keep his stomach's contents down.

"Yes, and?" Johnson snapped. This seemed to be the kick in the pants that 'Big C' needed, and he began to speak rapidly.

"Well, I based my original calculations on the assumption that the damage that was being caused was directly to the ocean tethers that hold us in position. But I now think this is not the case."

He petered out as color rose in Johnson's cheeks and anger flashed in his eyes; Dan noticed that Big C's face paled in proportion to Johnson's reddening.

Before the heat in Johnson's face became hot air, Storrel calmly interrupted. "Alright, alright, let the man take a breath, Johnson. Then we can all hear what he has to say." Looking back to Big C, Storrel asked with a patient drawl, "Well, my friend, what is it that has changed your opinion?"

Johnson looked like he had just had a large bucket of ice water thrown over him. Dan almost laughed, till he caught Steve's expression out of the corner of his eye. He looked like he was watching a new species of slug give birth, and it was making him nauseated.

With Storrel looking at him patiently and the threat of Johnson no longer hanging over him, Big C stood a little straighter, and with more confidence continued, "Well, sir, when I got some power back to the controls and I checked the engine settings, I discovered that the angle of tilt had changed over the last few hours, and it had affected the impellers' performance. If we were struggling against the tide without the proper tethering, then I would expect sideways movement but not an increase in inclination. Which suggests to me that one of the pontoons keeping us upright appears to be, er, well ... sinking."

His statement left the room in silence, even the usually unshakable and composed Hank Storrel appeared stunned, and the others began to mutter expletives and shared anxiety. After the initial shock, fear took over.

"My God, man, are you saying this goddamn platform is going to sink?" Storrel could no longer contain his disbelief. "How in the name of holy hell is that possible?"

Big C answered in a quite relaxed tone now. The bad news had been revealed, and it seemed to lift a burden from his back; the worst was over, and he could just continue on with the facts.

"Well, I think, from the readings, that it's the ocean moorings that are keeping us upright and the floatation from the undamaged pontoon that's holding the balance. The other pontoon must have had its front section damaged by the creature, which caused the original angle we are at. Maybe it got caught up and that made it mad, and during the struggle, I think, it also damaged the center section of the same pontoon, which has been gradually letting water leak in." He almost smiled as he came gratefully to the end of his report.

"Dat's great. So we survive a fuckin' sea monster and get sunk by a fuckin' oil rig, bloody marvelous," Jonnie chirped. "I tink I wanna change of career, ya know."

His droll humour seemed to drive out the fear in the room. Dan could have hugged the man for his spirit.

"I think we need to know the extent of the danger, Harry. Will the rig sink?" Dan asked patiently.

"Hmm, well, no, Dan, I don't think the pontoon will sink us, but the deeper we go into the water, the more stress it puts on the ocean tethers and the mooring line. If the swell gets up, then that might cause lines to break, and we could be in the shit," Big C pronounced with a cheerful conclusion and a hopeful smile.

Johnson was gaping at Big C as if he were an alien, frowning Storrel had retreated into concentration, and the others all looked as if they were waiting for an axe to fall on their necks—apart from Steve, who looked around the room puzzled, and then asked simply, "Well, can we fix it, 'C'?"

Big C lifted his large bearded face and, pushing his damp mop of hair from his face, looked at Steve, his face split into a big smile. "Yep, I think so, mate."

There were some explosive exhalations as relief sprung from the assembled men. "Why didn't you say so, you daft arse?" said Jonnie, and Dan and mostly everyone else laughed. Not Storrel, though. He looked full of new resolve, as if some essential problem had been settled, and he was released into self-assured motion.

"Well, Big C, that is some fine news. Thank you, and how long do you reckon on those repairs taking?" he asked in a relaxed conversational tone.

"Well, I think if Jonnie can get the electric bailing pump working in the flooded pontoon section, and we have someone who can weld, I think about an hour to pump out the leaking pontoon and potentially one hour of welding, there or there abouts, I think."

"Then would the rig be secure? Could we continue running this platform till the next pick-up ship arrives?" Storrel asked in a faux-casual tone to the now almost chirpy Big C.

"Yes, sir, I am sure we would be okay," he agreed happily.

Dan was watching Storrel's face and saw the satisfaction that registered there, realizing this man had no interest in the crew of this rig, only its cargo and its ability to produce oil.

"I think we need to have the men confident of surviving this experience. They have been through a lot, and maybe setting them back to work might not go down that well, Mr. Storrel," Dan said, trying to remind the men present of the terrifying events that they had all been through.

Not annoyed by his interruption, Storrel looked instead as if he had reached a triumphant point.

"I am sure that with a man they can trust, like Mr. Staples, and the promise of some more-than-healthy bonus payments, we can see this disaster through to a successful conclusion for everyone … Wouldn't you agree, Mr. Staples?" He gave Steve a wide toothy smile.

Suddenly Dan understood why Steve was at this meeting. Storrel wanted to use his new status as hero of the attack as leverage to get the men to play along with Storrel's agenda, which probably included increasing the value of his own shares of the business. He clamped his teeth together at this man's insensitivity to the loss of the crew and to what the survivors had experienced. He was about to rail against the injustice, when Steve answered.

"I expect that the others will work for the money, when they appreciate they have no choice about leaving," Steve spoke dispassionately, and Dan got the feeling Steve wasn't numbering himself amongst the others.

Johnson butted in, obviously trying to seize back control in light of the happier and less perilous circumstances.

"Excellent, Mr. Staples. I am sure you can convince your workmates of the sensible course, while we gentlemen arrange to get this rig back on an even keel, if you will apologize for the pun," Johnson said, attempting to give an all-embracing smile, which ended up coming off as a farcical grin. Dan could see how forced the smile was and how lacking in force Johnson's words were; everyone in the room was waiting for the real voice of command.

"Yeah, the chief is correct. Let's set about getting this rig and the men back to work. It will keep them from worrying or reliving the recent, terrible events," Storrel drawled in his most reasonable voice, with a nod toward Dan.

Then, abruptly changing his tone to a snap of command, Storrel ordered, "Harry, get together the materials and men you require to expedite the repairs you have outlined to secure this rig's integrity. I am sure the chief will give you his full support." Unlike Johnson, Storrel sounded calm and decisive, and the men in the room responded to his tone and authority.

"Mr. Carver, if you could assist in directing essential repairs to the rig's systems while utilizing Mr. Neil's skills in use of manpower and Jonnie's electrical expertise." Carver jumped to his feet, while nodding vigorously.

"I am also sure our esteemed geology department will be able to assist, as they are intelligent individuals." Storrel's drawl seemed to indicate an undercurrent of uncertainty at the last fact.

Dan felt his face go red; he considered it unfair that a mantle of guilt had been thrown over him and the dejected head geologist, Lawson. He wanted to protest the allegation, but Storrel had turned away and gone straight to Steve, whom he was talking to with his over toothed smile, while touching his arm and nodding sagely to whatever Steve was saying. Dan was discomforted again, and, he recognized, maybe a little jealous; neither his advice nor assistance seemed to be required or of any use.

When Steve had finished his conversation and was passing by, Dan's new and unexpected ire at the dark eyed and belligerent man found a voice.

"You seem to have made a new best friend there," Dan said, gesturing to Storrel. "Will you be joining him for drinks later?"

Steve stopped and scowled at Dan, shaking his head, his hair brushing his shoulders and his forehead furrowed.

"He wouldn't listen to me, either. I said we should be getting prepared in case that thing came back. He only wants me to talk to the roughnecks. You're all as stupid as each other," he finished in a caustic and defeated tone.

As he left, Dan remembered the young man whose insecurities and isolation he had felt sorry for and thought maybe that this man was still the same. He suddenly felt ashamed of himself. He had treated Steve as some worthy case he could use his own wisdom and insight to cure, as if he had no fundamental strengths of his own, and he wondered if Steve might be much more of a man than he had ever given him credit for.

But surely the creature had been crushed and burnt? It must be dead or too badly hurt to survive in the ocean, and even if it lived, it would be far too frightened by the fire of its defeat to ever bother humans again, surely, he thought.

CHAPTER 14 — MANMADE REVENGE

As soon as the discussions had finished, Steve's first decision was to go back to his cabin. He told himself that it was to let Janice know what was going on, but it was really mostly because he wanted to see her so badly, he admitted to himself, as he struggled to traverse the rig's slanted stairwells.

Like the tricky journey on the uneven deck, he found himself lurching from one emotion to another, while the ache in the back of his head had returned and grown to such dimensions that it felt as if it might have begun stretching the plates of his skull. His stomach churned with a constant and underlying rage that was almost impossible for him to subdue. But being around Janice was like a cooling cloth on his fevered brow, like the cold flannel his mum used when he had a fever or lumps from his father's fists, and all of his inner consternation and confusion went away and all he felt was the strong emotion to hold and protect her.

He quickened his pace in his urgency, fuming silently about the tilted dark pathways and difficult stairs that confused his steps and slowed him down. He spat angrily at the gusts of oil-tainted wind and cursed its pressure against him, which was delaying his progress to her side. Again a surge of anger filled him, and his eyes swam as the bones of his skull seemed to grind against each other. He started to mumble 'Janice' over and over again as if the litany of just her name would stop the growing splinters of pain in his mind.

As he negotiated the tricky damp and angled walkways, the pressure in his head seemed to render his vision an almost useless blur, and he depended on his memory for direction. His footsteps clanged on the metal and echoed off the steel structure around him, increasing the throbbing in the tortured cave of his mind and the growing rage-filled nausea that swam in his mouth.

In an attempt to quiet his inner turmoil, he thought back to the meeting he had just left, the idiot faces ready to jump through hoops for their shitty careers rather than face the possibility that they weren't safe at all. He tried to recapture the feeling of purpose and determination that he had felt when he had been called to the meeting. But it escaped his mind's reach and left him in the wounded grasp of himself.

He climbed the angled steps and opened the leaning door to his cabin and was met by darkness and an empty room.

Janice was gone.

His stomach dropped, and he became blank; the shock stole away all thought. His mind had become as vacant as the unoccupied room. He waited for his eyes to adjust to the dark and gradually saw shapes become visible out of the murky fog of darkness. It seemed obvious by the bedcovers spilled on the floor and a shelf of books thrown down upon them that there had been some sort of struggle, and panic rose in him, along with a spike of desperation to find Janice.

He turned resolutely to sprint out of the room and down the stairs, only to slide to a halt. Just off to one side, at the bottom of the steps, stood Arthur Whitehead blowing out cigarette smoke with a stupid grin hanging inanely across his face. Steve saw him in a haze of blue-tinged yellow and red.

"Where is she?" he said, enraged.

"Who's that, mate?" Whitehead replied, grinning even more stupidly, with an amateur theatre voice of innocence.

Steve grabbed the front of Whitehead's jacket and forced him up against the railings. "Where is she, you fucker?" he yelled while pushing him back with all his strength, desperately trying to stop himself from pounding the man's head against the metal steps.

"Alright, alright," Whitehead complained. "I'll tell you," he said, sounding injured, the grin gone from his face and his halo of colors lurching into popping sapphire blues.

"She went for a little walk with Jones, you know, to get acquainted and everything," and a dirty smirk replaced his idiot grin, but Steve could see Whitehead's blue fear.

He pushed his forearm into Whitehead's throat, forcing the man to arch his back over the railing while he yelped.

He asked again, "WHERE?"

He felt a rush of pleasure as the other man writhed against his grip and also the urge to unleash his barely contained fury.

"The geology lab, the fucking lab!" Whitehead screeched as his back was further bent. He let out as gasp when Steve released him.

"Fucking hell, I'm just passing on the fucking message, dickhead," Whitehead spat, but there was fear in his eyes, and when his colors fizzed into navy blue, it made Steve feel good. He felt his own mirthless grin appear on his face.

He looked at the man as if from far away, as if he was some worthless organism that had wormed into his view, and he wanted to stomp on it, to squash the weak and pathetic entity before him. Distantly, he wondered if this was how his father had felt as he beat him and his mother, if they shared the same lust for violence, the same need to be potent and to use their power; the thought matched his rage perfectly.

"Show me where, or I'll start breaking bits of you till you can't remember which one I broke first," he breathed uncompromisingly.

He sounded ludicrously mild, compared to the desire to inflict pain that was writhing in him, desperately seeking an outlet for release.

He pushed the man ahead of him and began to follow. Whitehead constantly flicked fearful looks behind, as if he thought he might be attacked at any moment.

Steve felt pleasure again, and the grin was back, like his face had become a rigid grinning mask that hid his mounting need to break and destroy. There was an escalating feeling in him of supremacy; his limbs felt energized, and he felt invulnerable in his growing strength. He would bring his wrath down on Jones and leave him burnt away by the blaze of his anger. His grin grew wider making his cheeks ache.

Dan felt petty and small after the first flush of resentment at Steve's harsh words had passed. Nevertheless, as soon as he considered what Steve had said, an uncomfortable realization sank in. He'd been so interested in the ongoing politics of the situation and his own opinion of what needed to be done for everyone's mental suffering and soul healing that he had failed to even consider that they might be in any further danger.

Feelings rushed through his mind like flitting bats at dusk, moving too quickly to catch hold of. Dark thoughts, memories of the hell-born creature and its striking spear like limbs in the black night, flashed through his mind. He could hear the piercing screech of metal and the screams of dying men. He understood in that moment that they had no reason to think the creature was alone or that there might not be a shoal of the ocean demons for all they knew. They had no reason to feel safe at all.

With a sudden jolt of fear, he knew that those who had been in the control room with him—the people in charge, for goodness sake—were not going to be any help, as usual. They would continue to dismiss the point of view that there was a reasonable chance of danger. With growing sourness in his stomach, he was swiftly out of the warm room and into the cold wind, onto the tilted metal stairwell and out searching in the moonlit darkness for the long-haired lean figure of his … friend?

He caught movement below and set off in the same direction, but in the gloom and maze of steel work, the dark shadows and confused lines, he lost sight of what he hoped was Steve. Guessing by the direction he had seen the man moving in, he headed for the crew quarters.

He made as quickly as he could against the wind, dealing with the wet metal and uneasy footing. The new knowledge of the sinking pontoon below his feet made the deck seem even more treacherous, and as he neared his destination, he came stumbling against an incline to a halt. He caught sight of two moonlit-edged figures moving away from the crew quarters: the person following had long hair; the other, he was pretty sure, was one of the three roughnecks he had seen talking with Jones earlier.

After a moment's hesitation as to how he could follow them from where he stood, looking across the confusingly off-set metal maze of the rig, he made a decision to head to the crew block and try and follow the men from there. He raced down precariously angled and damp steps, gripping cold metal rails to maintain his balance. For some reason, he felt that he couldn't follow fast enough, that Steve was walking into some kind of danger and that if he didn't get there, Steve would face it alone, and that would be bad.

Janice sat huddled against one of the seamless protrusions of the lab's work consoles. She pressed herself as far away as possible from the red-faced man who gawked and leered at her from where he leaned idly against the wall.

Her tongue kept returning to her swollen cheek and the ragged edge where her teeth had torn the inside of her mouth after the big fat bastard had punched her.

He and another man had burst into the room and started dragging her out of the bunk. She came awake with a spurt of fear and adrenaline, kicking and fighting as fiercely as she could while screaming at the top of her lungs.

The sweating and cursing men had soon become irritated with her struggles, and the pig-faced Geordie had hit her with his club like fist, making her head ring with static sparks that left her sprawled on the floor with no strength left in her limbs to stop them. They had part-carried; part-dragged her along the walkways to this room, thrown her on the floor, and the other man had left. But a third man was also in the room, a big and rangy man with cool grey eyes and a constant frown; he looked like he was somehow aggravated by her presence.

But the focus of her distress was the big bloke who menaced her with his cocksure smile and porcine eyes. His stares burnt with lust so tangible it made her flesh crawl and her stomach squirm from across the room; she could see he wanted only her pain and degradation. Each dissolute look at her body screamed his disinterest in her as a person and that she was here only as an object to serve his purposes.

"What do you want?" she asked, hating the fragile break in her voice and its fearful tone.

She couldn't seem to rouse her ire to fight against the terror she felt when he looked her over with his lustful, greedy eyes.

"Don't worry, lass, we'll get to you. You won't miss out on all the fun. Right after we have a nice little chat with your fella, it'll be your time."

He grinned without humour, but his wet-rimmed eyes glinted with pleasure.

She realized then that it was Steve whom the heavy ape was really after and that she was only secondary to his desires. Abruptly, her fear turned to desperation. Steve would stand no chance on his own against the two men. She looked at the man with grey eyes, and his look was impassive, his frown unchanged. She noticed belatedly that he was holding a metal bar down by his leg.

Urgently she looked around for a weapon or a way to warn someone or call attention to where they were. But the wreckage in the room was down by where the tall thick-set man stood by the door; nothing else was in reach.

Both men were watching her; the pig seemed to enjoy her anxiety and dread, and the frown on grey eye's brow just deepened.

She had never paid attention to the foul comments of her shipmates, never paid attention to any dark undertones in their comments or looks and never been afraid, because she had been so confident in who she was. She had seen herself through her father's eyes and through her own accomplishments, which she'd wrapped around herself like armor; now, abruptly, that all felt like so many layers of self-deceit. Now she felt the fear of what had lain hidden behind her happy indifference, the fear of what she had ignored, that lust and violence were linked. She was noticing for the first time the feral nature of men that she had heard about but ignored. She was suddenly face-to-face with the reality, and it left her innards cold, and she felt that the beliefs of her life had been violated. It was as if they were blowing away like the ash from burning newspapers.

"That's right, little lady, no need to worry. We'll all show you a proper good time." He laughed, obviously taking his own perverse pleasure in the consternation on her face.

She felt so suddenly lost and that she might begin to weep as her carefully built image of life was brutally swept away. She felt the pain in her face from the earlier blow and understood terror. She wanted to curl up and feel protected, to escape the sickening heat that came in waves, with sweat and sour breath, from the animal that loomed above her.

But just as she felt she might collapse beneath the weight of her vulnerability and beg them not to hurt her, she found the inner belligerence that had been the keystone of her life. From that moment as a child when she had cut her hand on a boat cleat and refused to go back to shore with her dad despite his concern, till when her mother had forbidden her to sail after her father's death, and still later when she had had to fight to become accepted on the ships she crewed on, she was strong and determined. She knew her own mind.

She would not back down; she couldn't. It was what made her believe in herself, her capacity to always be able to do the thing that she wanted, no matter the obstacles. She would not be forced to do anything she didn't want; her mother had never learned that lesson and had not grasped that by being the barrier she enforced the behavior. Buttressed by the strength of her memories, she forced open her eyes and returned Jones's look with her own hate. His face changed from gloating to annoyance and then a sneer, but he looked away first.

She slowly worked her feet back beneath her, so she could launch herself if need be. Steve was coming, and he would need her help, and these bastards were not going to break her or make her less of herself.

As she gathered herself, a third roughneck entered the room, bringing with him a gust of chill wind and clean salt air. The new man was White, or some name like that; he had a grin on his face as he gave a mocking looking behind him, and she saw that he had led Steve to this trap using her as bait. Her heart quailed as she realized they had no hope against three men.

She saw Steve's face as he came up the steps, and for a moment she felt a surge of hope. He looked unafraid and powerfully confident, as if he had found resources beyond himself and become somehow unassailable. He entered the room and seemed to almost smile around his snarl at Jones.

"Shut that door, Brainy; don't let that fucker out no matter what," Jones yelled, "Right, you bastard, let's be having you."

Without thinking she flung herself at Jones's legs and held on. The big man struggled with his balance against the deck and her grip; then, like a slow-motion tree felling, he began to fall.

The third roughneck paused in confusion, and Steve struck, two fast blows to the man's face, and then swung his right elbow into the man's nose so hard that it cracked with a sound similar to a crab being stomped on.

Before she could cheer him on, Jones yanked his leg out of her grasp and kicked her straight-legged in the head with a nauseating impact and a blinding flash of pain that left her on her back, unfocused and sickeningly woozy. She watched in blurred motion as Jones jumped up and attacked Steve's exposed back.

Dan carried on up the walkway to the stairs and stopped to listen for sounds. He had lost view of the men he had been following. But he could still hear the clangs of their footsteps from above and made quickly up the canted steps, stopping at the top to listen again.

The gangway ahead was empty, only steps up to some of the rooms were visible in the thin light from above him, and he suddenly understood the light was coming from the room above. He made toward the stairs, when he heard a shout and a large thud that resounded through the metal beneath his feet, and like a starter gun had gone off, he flew up the stairs.

As he swung open the heavy metal door, he stepped into the room and saw Steve struggling with two men. Janice was crawling across the floor toward him, and in the same moment he became aware of a shape beside him, and he turned with a spike of adrenaline, ready to fight, to find the roughneck Brainy with his palms up facing him in surrender.

"I want no part of that pair. If you want my help, you can have it, mate," he said with a flat statement. "And if I can have the bloke on the right, I would appreciate it," he said with a happy hunger in his voice.

In a snap decision Dan decided to take the man at his word.

"Alright, c'mon."

He saw one of the men stand up and look around at the voices behind him, with confusion on his face.

"What the fuck are you doing, Brainy, you dickhead?" he panted, wiping blood from his nose and looking down to shake Jones's shoulder and make him aware of the shift in circumstances, but he was ignored as the other man was busy trying to strike Steve cleanly in the face. By the time Whitehead looked back up, he had one moment of horrible realization before Brainy came upon him like a rock fall.

Dan made to grab the big round head of Jones, as the man was busy holding onto the thrashing Steve beneath him. The torment of Steve's struggle drew Dan's attention to the bloodied man, who was screaming and had his eyes rolled back in his head. Even more troubling, Dan noticed, Steve seemed oblivious to the blows raining down on his and to his wounds.

Dan's shock at his friend's condition gave Jones the pause he needed to get his feet under his knees and launch himself. His shoulder hit Dan from below, knocking him off his feet. For a second Dan was back on a rugby pitch somewhere wet and muddy, but his landing shocked him quickly back to reality. His elbow was jarred on impact with the solid floor, sending a sharp stabbing pain up his arm. He kicked out with his feet, catching some part of Jones, and rolled away quickly. Wincing at the pain in his arm, Dan stood as the red-faced Jones also regained his feet.

Dan was looking directly into the man's eyes and saw they were near the same height; the man's piggy eyes regarded him with vehement malice. He took in that the man was a similar size and guessed he would be violent and not likely to have a laugh and joke about a scrap in the rugby club bar later.

They sized each other up, with hands raised defensively like boxers. Jones snapped a surprisingly quick punch with his left hand, which Dan managed to evade by snapping his head back; that punch was almost instantly followed by a prodigious haymaker of a right, which, if it had connected, would have probably removed his head. But thanks to some martial arts he had learnt as a lad, against his clamoring instincts Dan stepped inside of the arc of the swing. Suddenly, to his and his opponent's surprise, they found themselves momentarily face to face, till the momentum of the swing threw them together and Dan found himself grappling with the sweaty man in a loveless embrace.

He was struggling frantically to keep his feet while urgently trying to find a way of striking the other man or using his strength to throw Jones down, but physically they were too evenly matched. They reeled around, thumping into the walls until there was a final thump, and suddenly the man Dan was holding onto dropped like a dead weight in front of him, almost dragging him to the floor.

There Brainy stood, holding an iron bar and wearing a satisfied smile. Dan felt the air explode out of his lungs with relief, and suddenly the consequences of the adrenaline-fueled scuffle hit him, making him feel both sick and exhausted.

"Thanks, mate," he struggled to catch his breath, feeling his hands shaking as he put them on his hips in a bent-over recovery position.

Brainy nodded and gripped Dan's hand, looking down at the groaning heap at their feet with another tightly vicious smile. Brainy's hands were steady and his grip was firm.

"A pleasure to be honest, I've been dying to do that for quite a while. Think this is the time for people with some brains to stick together," he smiled, admiring his own humor.

Dan gave a thin laugh. He seemed to be having a day of misjudging people. Somewhat taken aback, he realized that he had always considered the roughnecks as being a group free of 'sharp tools.' But this man seemed to have a full grasp of their situation and what was needed to deal with it.

He saw Janice struggling to her feet and leapt to help her, getting her steady. He took in the bruise on her face with a glance and felt a rush of anger toward the men who had abused her. It was only then that he saw her gaze and focus were fixed in another direction.

Looking around and expecting to see Steve still stretched out on the floor, he was astonished to see him on his feet, standing above the stretched-out body of the other roughneck, as if in no pain or discomfort from his attack. Despite the bloody, leaking wounds on his face and livid inflammation on his cheek and brow, his eyes were not pain-filled but intense as they bulged wildly in his head with some inner vision or compulsion. The white around his black pupils flashed with his heated stare, looking through them with an otherness of sight that teetered between crazed and prophetic.

Janice reached out her hand and croaked his name, "Steve? Are you alright?" Pain and worry crowded her eyes.

He turned to her, and with a voice that seemed too full of force, too close to almost inhuman, he spat out through swollen lips, "Agony—rend—defilers."

He seemed like he contained some inner, 'other' presence, like a medium channeling a voice of the dead. The tableau held till Steve began to cough in a hacking choke as if he were trying to expel the phantom from his throat. He collapsed to his knees, retching.

He shook his head as if to chase out the source of the words and looked as if the blows had finally come to have effect as he half-stumbled to the terminal table to his side.

As Dan and Janice moved toward him to keep him from falling, he raised his palm to stop them and, looking up from his position, half-folded on the console.

"The beast is coming," he croaked from his ravaged throat. "It's close. I can, can … feel it. We have to get up high. We can't stop it. We must keep away from the water, and we must move. We must move NOW!"

Agrushell had never in his long existence experienced such excruciating pain; he could feel it radiating down from the burns across his carapace. Blazes of white agony flowed down from the rigid wounds in consuming red-hot currents that scrambled his body's neurology, inducing part-formed limbs to propagate in spasmodic aborted growths from his liquid interior.

He lay beneath a rock shelf and attempted to endure the searing pain produced by the wounds that had left him with a permanently hardened crust, as though his enemies' fire still burnt him.

His bodily structure shook with the effort of withstanding the effects of the damage he had suffered and the painful humiliation of his defeat by the pitiful beings above. In the throes of his agony he cursed the light-water creatures' cowardly nature and tried to rein in the blue fire within him as it flared uncontrollably in syncopation with each nerve-rending lance of pain, blasting into the ocean around him, boiling the seawater and sending up plumes of sand. Each thrust of energy and detonation was like a discharge of his torment and hatred.

He lay overwhelmed by the pain, till eventually his tortured mind fled the agony into the flashed images of his memory.

He remembered the moment of his beginning and the multitudes of his tiny birth brothers. He relived again the fearful moments of the endless journey back to the abyss of the ancients, trailing behind the vast shadow presence of the father and guardian, whom he would have the honour of succeeding.

Countless of his brothers perished of exhaustion during the journey, unable to keep pace with the old guardian; more had succumbed to the ocean hunters: shark, squid, and tuna. Only the fast, strong, and clever survived in the guardian's wake.

But lessons truly began in the deep; the simple crushing weight of the depth took a massive toll on his siblings as did hunting lessons with a prey who could easily strike back, dragging the slow and hesitant into adhesive tentacles and hungry beaks. Till eventually only he remained to travel through the gateway of illuminations, back to the old ones and the expansion of his mind.

As his memory traveled light shafts of blue-edged clarity, he remembered the gift of his potency and the burden of his purpose. But his thoughts were disturbingly fractured with glimpses of the light-water construction and of his enemy. They seemed to haunt his memories and taint the sacred recollections of his journey to ascension amongst his kind.

Compressed beneath the weight of his agony, a rage began to grow in equal measure, a growing thunder of furious denial. It built wave upon wave in challenge to his wounds, in answer to his antipathy. The puissance within began to build to a burgeoning pressure inside, till it seemed every particle in his body shook with force, every cell was alight with the vicious desire to immolate himself and the source of his enmity.

He considered from the cold analytical compartment of his

mind, far distant from the conflagrations within him, that perhaps his wounds were fatal; he knew that he would never again glide in the depths or hunt the black cliff faces in elevated ocean harmony. He would never be perfection again; he was crippled.

His purpose was all but at an end; only one constraint to expending himself in vengeance remained. He must relinquish his role and unfetter himself from millennia-old constraints by summoning the change.

As he drifted abstracted from his pain, he focused on the ghosts of his destructive fantasies, fantasies made rich by his desire to strike back, to bring pain and death to the creatures that had cowardly brought extermination to his kind and inflicted his own craven wounding.

The weak creatures were devious and callously destructive, using lifeless shells, mineral fluids, and foul elements to contaminate and destroy. To meet the requirements of the pressure inside, he would bring their metal architecture down into the sea, so they could be torn asunder as the pitiful prey they were. He would not attack full with hubris at his own superiority again. This time he would destroy and kill from a position of strength and drag them down below the waves, where he could eradicate the construction of their flesh and they could meet the black expanse of his vitriolic retribution.

He let his icy fury build, letting it wash the fiery torment from his consciousness, till all he could feel was the expanding blue fire yearning for release within him. And when all thought was obliterated and he felt that the incandescent potentiality inside must consume him, he released with a violent spasm the pent-up energy, creating a massive sonic boom of puissant blue potency, whose frequency would reach around the waters of the globe.

He surged from beneath the coral up toward the faint silvery light from the celestial body above, toward the shadow structure overhead.

Moving his damaged anatomy from side to side, he closed the gap made in his perceptions by the hardened wounds as his multiple senses read the structure above. He began to understand how it functioned in the light water; he read its motion, saw the lines stretched out to the seafloor around him. He began to understand how to bring about the structure's downfall.

He knew the darkness beneath the rig would hide him from his prey above. He drifted underneath the massive length and metal lines and severed four of the six thick bound metal wires in controlled bursts; they were like super dense ocean weed but came apart simply with a narrowly focused flow of his energy, which caused the metal to heat and break.

He came in from beneath, darkened and invisible from sight above, wraithlike and armed with multiple hardened spike projections, with every sense pitched to catch vibration or activity in the water, in case of attack or defense.

He landed silently beneath one of the large air-filled metal chambers, the mirror to the one he'd damaged previously. This time the damage would be more extensive, till the whole construction was submerged to join him.

He was attracted by loud vibrations thrumming through the water from the opposite chamber, and silently he glided with shadow stealth to its surface.

He sensed the electrical makeup of several light-water creatures within and also flows of energy, one of which sent out a sharp static noise. The crackle of its emanations was like blades plunging into his senses, increasing his anger and confusing his sense of direction. One of the creatures was directly above him, holding one of the weakling's devices, which gave off a white energy of wrongness, and he felt an irresistible urge to attack.

He began to bleed his own blue power into the metal, sensing when its composition began to soften. Meanwhile, he grew a thick blade-ended limb, whose tip he hardened and serrated into a cutting edge.

CHAPTER 15 — REPAIRING THE DAMAGE

Harry 'Big C' Shore had two men helping him hump the heavy welding equipment needed for the repairs on the leaking pontoon. Ahead of him was the double-chinned and ever-grumbling maintenance specialist Brian Locke, followed by young Billy, the quiet junior welder, his head held high and long blond hair ruffling in the breeze. He looked unbowed and filled with vitality, despite carrying a fifteen-kilo reel of MIG wire and the hefty load of cable he had wrapped over his shoulder.

They arrived at the lower deck hatch that opened into the massive rig leg and led down into the rig pontoon that hung in the sea below them. At the hatchway they met a grinning Jonnie, who was shaking his head exaggeratedly and pointing at his watch while 'tutting' at their tardy arrival, which made everyone, minus Locke, smile.

After a brief discussion filled with Locke-related whining and Jonnie's acerbic put-downs, they came to an agreement on how best to shift the equipment down the metal wall ladders that ran the inside length of the hollow steel of the rig leg.

Billy was first and leapt down the metal ladder like a junior Spiderman. Gripping a torch in his teeth, he almost flew down the rungs with his lightweight wiry frame and youthful energy.

Brian Locke heaved his pot-bellied figure down next, with a tirade of complaint from the mustached man until his bald pate finally disappeared from view down the black opening.

Harry followed next, leaving Jonnie to start tying on equipment to be lowered down. Harry sweated heavily with the effort of heaving his own large weight downward; the added weight of a thick coil of sturdy rope over his shoulder and torso did not help.

The oppressive space and humid air, mixed with the strong ocean smell, seemed to make each breath a labour as he went down repetitive rung after rung. Muffled waves accompanied his efforts, echoing through the long metallic cavity. He also noted the occasional clangs and shouts from his colleagues.

The slight rocking motion on the already-angled ladder was making the sweat run down his back as he concentrated on keeping a firm grip. He arrived at the first leg joint and stood back onto a small platform with a sigh of relief and decided he really wasn't made for assault courses.

Shining his torch upward into the dark tube, looking for the first piece of gear to appear, he watched as moisture ran in droplets down the interior surface, like the metal was sweating and the ocean sounds were the subdued breaths of a living entity. He was snapped out of his peculiar train of thought by Jonnie's resonating shout from above: "'Ere it comes."

Each piece of equipment was to be passed down on a line to a man at each section opening, reattached to a new line, and then lowered on to the next man below, and then to the next, till it reached the pontoon's outer hull.

After what seemed an interminably long period of back-breaking time and after the last gas bottle had been passed on down, Harry gathered himself with some deep breaths and a final woeful groan and then began the final climb down into the black depths of the massive rig leg below.

On reaching the next joint space, he stopped for a rest, a drink of water, and a badly-needed Snickers bar. When he heard the echoing sounds of Jonnie coming down from above, he decided to move on, but he took every opportunity to rest along the way.

After a long, breathless, and sweaty eternity, he splashed down on the damp outer hull and sucked in some deep breaths of relief.

He turned around to look at the dark, dank chamber that he, Billy, and Locke stood in. More ominous-sounding echoes rolled through the clammy moisture-laden air, and he felt cold and sticky.

Impossibly, when Jonnie arrived sweaty and splashing through the thin water, he seemed in great spirits, much to Locke's chagrin and Billy's amusement.

"Welcome to the Midnight Grotto, ladies. I'm afraid we are out of punch, but we 'ave plenty of water, and we'll be 'avin a disco later." His Scouse accent seemed to catch the giggles in Big C, and he laughed wholeheartedly along with Billy, and even Locke, despite his generally stodgy nature, joined in.

Harry mopped his brow and wondered about Jonnie's sanity but was very glad the man was here as they began unpacking the equipment they had humped down.

When they had wired up the welding cable to Jonnie's jury-rigged generator at the section opening above, then attached the CO_2 bottle to the MIG welder, they lowered it through the final hatch to hover above the water-logged base from where they would have to carry it. Jonnie would stay above to monitor the generator.

"So, Big C, da pumps are runnin' and dat last readin' of our angle of dangle shows us more upright. I tink we're good to see what da damage under dere is like." As Jonnie reported, his face was a mask of seriousness which was betrayed only by his twinkling eyes in the torchlight.

Still smiling at the lively Liverpudlian, Big C went to the last top-locked door and looked down into the pontoon's inner hull.

"All right, then, fellas, shall we see what is going on in the basement?" he said, trying to sound as hopeful and confident as Jonnie.

"Not unless we have to. It's bloody cold down here," Locke griped, his face looking pasty in the meager gas-lamp illumination.

With the aid of the lamp Jonnie had fashioned and their own hand-held torches, they climbed down a last metal ladder into the cavernous central space of the pontoon. The bottom of the hull was about two feet deep in chemical-filmed seawater and smelt unpleasantly of sea-corroded metal and oil. The thrum of the water pump reverberated through the massive space, as though the dark itself resounded in the vaulted space around them. Big C shivered involuntarily and, with a conscious effort, tried to shake the chill out of his thoughts.

"So, first things first, lads. Let's find out where the water is coming in, and then we can get it stopped and go home to applause and hopefully an ice cold beer," his voice echoed unnervingly in the large space.

"Let's get a move on, too. My feet are bloody freezing in these wellies." His attempted humour seemed hollow and lost in the echoes. The other men's faces remained unnerved and disheartened by the cold damp vault they found themselves in.

The location of the seepage was relatively easy to find by shining a torch over the surface; the small disturbances and eddies in the water could be easily seen.

Brian Locke, the rig's experienced maintenance technician, retrieved the tubes of black water-tight sealant from his rucksack and set about forcing the material into the strained-opened seam, whining all the time about the chill water, cold air, and the sticky bastard nature of the sealant. After a further half an hour of pumping, the water level had dropped to about half a foot.

Trembling a little in the cold dark and wanting to get out of the oppressive space, Big C signaled Billy to get the welder ready. The twenty-two-year-old splashed enthusiastically over to prepare his welder. Since his boss had been speared through the chest during the creature's attack, he was taking his new responsibility as senior welder very seriously.

The yellow rectangular metal box of a welder was wheeled over, and Billy plugged in the extension cabling, plugged in a welding torch, and tinkered with the black controls on the front of the box. When Billy was finally satisfied and Harry felt his nerves were starting to shred, Billy put the light reactive welding mask on top of his head, pulled on thick brown welder's gloves, and looked to Locke for a go-ahead.

With a sour face, Locke nodded. "Go ahead, knock yourself out, kid."

With only the residual water gathered in the concave bottom of the hull, the position of the damaged join was now above the water level. Some luck at last, thought Big C.

Next he and Locke brought over the first of two steel plates to weld over the split in the pontoon seam. The plates were heavy and ice cold, and he was delighted when they dropped down the last of the two plates, with a resounding clang that rang into the blackness beyond the light.

"Right. Then, Billy lad, show me where you want these plates," Big C asked as they bent to grab the ends of each piece of steel.

"Put the first one just by the seam for the minute, sir, and we can use the grinder to prime the metal. Then I'll clean with the pre-clean spray. Then we can get these plates welded on fast as you like," Billy smiled keenly.

Big C couldn't get over how Billy could be excited at the prospect of working in the freezing-cold, pitch-black hole. But the young lad seemed to take it all as a new great adventure. He had to smile at his boyish energy, wondering if he had ever been so full of life, even before he had reached thirty-eight years old and three stone overweight. He shook his head, his damp fringe falling across his face and wondered where the time had gone. He'd achieved so few of his own life's ambitions, realized so few of the dreams of his own youth. He pondered as Billy sprayed the metal and he thought how little he had to draw him back home to land, beyond a smart house and nice car, neither seemed to be of any real value to him after seeing the monster on the deck above. He was glad to be in Billy's company, though. He was able to put aside his age and feel a little younger and full of the potential of life, if only for a little while.

Billy finished meticulously cleaning and drying the area for the first plate, and they lifted the metal into the place Billy indicated.

"If you can just hold her still there, till I get some weld into it, Mr. Shore."

Billy looked odd in the harsh lamplight with his welding helmet up; it made his head look far too big and his features far too small.

Big C smiled at the boy's seriousness. "Just call me Big C, or Harry, if you like, Billy. You call me 'sir,' and I'm looking around for a headmaster."

He almost laughed aloud at Billy's reaction. He looked bewildered, reluctant, and finally he was left with a shy smile on his face. "Erm, sure thing, Mr. Sh ... er, Harry. Sorry."

He did laugh this time. "Not to worry, me lad, close enough." They smiled at each other, both realizing that this might be a friendship in the making.

"Okay, then, Harry, if you get hold, I will start. Just remember to not look directly at the light from the welder. The UV it produces can blind, if you look directly at it," he said with more confidence and a growing edge of pride in the knowing of his trade. "Don't want you getting 'red eye' on account of me," he said with a grin.

"Thanks, Billy, that's a useful tip. I want to be able to see my beer when we finish here." He winked at Billy, who smiled back again

"Too right," he said, and flipped down the black glass-fronted helmet, positioning the silver tip of the black plastic-gripped torch alongside the metal plate.

"I can taste that beer already," Billy mumbled from behind his mask.

As Billy struck an incandescent weld and Harry hurriedly remembered to face away from the glaring light of the welder, seeing flashes of the arcing bright blue light behind him, the welding sputtered and crackled like noisy bacon, without the appetizing aroma. The smoke was harsh and acrid, and Harry was glad not to be working directly over it like Billy. As he waited he watched the bright light flicker and chase shadows across the revealed ceiling of the pontoon above.

After the first plate had been finished and he and Locke had got up to stretch their legs, he asked Billy if it was safe to work with such noxious vapors. Billy said it was dangerous in high concentrations, but in a large area like this and only a reasonably small amount to weld, it shouldn't be a problem. It very much smelt like a problem to Harry, and Locke suggested he'd rather not learn to breathe smoke for a living.

Harry's role involved little more than sitting on one quarter of the plate to hold it still, so his mind began to wander again, and he started to search the darkness with his two-cell torch.

He could see the closest walls and part of the inner ceiling of the pontoon, both of which held little interest. So he shone the beam down in front of him, locating the edge of the water caught in the base of the pontoon. It seemed with the motion of the rig to be lapping on the edge of the seam they were on, as if he were sitting at the edge of some wind-driven lake. He cast the beam out on the surface, imagining himself on its waters in his small CJR fishing boat. He was just mentally casting out across the water, when he noticed the surface of the water had vibration circles rolling across it. He thought, 'Are there fish?' Then he felt a light vibration through the metal, which just as suddenly stopped. He scanned the now-still surface, and suddenly a chill ran over him.

Billy interrupted his frozen shock. "Okay, Harry, just one more and it's lagers all round," he chirped happily.

He mumbled, "Yep, sure. No problem, lad." Then he continued looking over the water with the torch. Billy caught his distraction.

"You okay there, Harry? Your mind not on the job, mate? That lager will be getting warm," he admonished, smiling.

With a last look into the blackness, Big C shook his head clear. "Nothing, lad, seeing ghosts, I think." He laughed. "Right, let's get that plate down, followed by that beer. Then we can thaw out, and forget this hole ever existed."

"Any time today would be good. My butt is frozen solid," Locke grumped from behind him.

"I am on the job, lads. Have this done in no time," Billy affirmed and flipped his mask down again.

They returned to their positions and the welding torch resumed its electric light show, crackling and spitting. Big C laughed to himself, as he shone the light across the water, which had resumed its regular lapping motion. Shining the light across the surface, he looked for ripples, and after a while of seeing nothing, he began to relax back into reverie.

A massive twang of metal giving way under stress and a sharp grinding of steel made him almost levitate off the metal plate he sat on. The sound of the tormented steel echoed around the cavernous space, making locating the direction of the sound impossible.

He grabbed the lamp and used it to stare out into the dark.

"What the hell was that, Billy?" The spattering noise of the welder had stopped as had the light show behind him. Billy must be searching for the source of the sound himself.

He got to his knees, holding the lamp out in front of him. It was then he saw the abrupt torrent of water flowing from beneath the plate he sat on.

"What's happened, Billy? Billy? Did the plate crack or

something?" No reply. He turned with the lamp to shine it on Billy, whose back was to him and half-hidden by the yellow welding equipment. But the top half of his body seemed to be shaking, and Billy let out a low muffled animal moan.

Locke was shining his torch around, looking pale and wide-eyed. "What the fuck? What the fuck was that?"

"What did you do, Billy? Did you hurt yourself, lad?" Harry stumbled around the welder to shine the light fully on the boy's bent-over form.

Water was bubbling through past the three-inch round black rod that had punctured the steel floor and penetrated the middle of Billy's body. When he shone the light to see Billy's face, he found scared, pained eyes looking back at him; Billy was moaning and breathing the word "please" over and over. He was crying bloody, red tears.

Billy reached out his hand to Big C, who started to reach for him, when the vibrations began again. Billy dropped his hands to the black spear through his middle and went rigid.

Big C knew it was back, that thing. It was back and was right outside the metal of the pontoon. He started to back away, but his hand was still reaching out to Billy, and he stopped, transfixed by Billy's agony-filled face.

"Please," Billy breathed the word again. "Please."

The boy's white face contrasted with the tears he was bleeding, while blood slowly dripped from his mouth. "Pleeease, Haarrye."

Big C felt sick with fear and torn with the irresistible request of Billy's words and face. He could hear Locke screaming behind him, but the sound seemed distant and irrelevant; the only thing in the frozen moment was the suffering boy's face. In that moment of indecision, his mind closed down in the face of what was happening, and his instincts took over; he moved to help the young boy.

"Aaah, Hharee, Pleease ... Ruunn!" Billy looked at him with agonized entreaty etched on his face. "Ruunn!!"

Harry stopped, and with confused desperation whirling in his mind he looked, nodded, and then turned and ran. He was following the distant rolling light beam and splashing echoes of Locke ahead of him. His pulse was thumping in his head, and desperation gathered in his chest, as they both pelted toward the ladder and the distant disc of light above. It hung overhead like a faraway chance of escape, a way out of the darkness and the terror that was made real within it.

He clambered as quickly as he could drag his substantial frame up the ladder to the hatch opening above, till he flopped over the edge of the door entrance with Jonnie's assistance. Breathless and drained of energy, he collapsed on the deck and ignored Jonnie's shocked questions while he gasped for air.

"Shhut … the … hhhatch!" he heavily panted out, too exhausted to do anything but exhale out words after each sucked-in breath. "Shhut hhit!"

"Where the fuckin' 'ell is Billy?" Jonnie said, shining his torch into the blackness below.

"Dead." He exhaled each word in between despairingly gasped breaths: "Shhho … shho … whill … whee bhee … hhif, hhyou … hhdon't, shhhut, thhhe, hhhatch!"

Jonnie looked hard at him; multiple emotions seemed to be fighting for domination of his face. Harry looked back at him, thinking 'What do you want me to do?' He felt like he had weights on his chest, and his limbs had disowned his body.

Jonnie struggled alone to lift the heavy pontoon hatch, but finally swung it over till it slammed down, ringing like a pealing bell for souls to enter an afterworld, and Harry was sure that hell was right below them. He was grabbed by the arm and shaken out of his inner vision.

"'arry, what d'fuck 'appened down dere?" Jonnie shouted wildly at him.

Having gained some of his breath back, he levered himself up with some assistance from Jonnie. Leaning on his shoulder, he looked directly into the man's panicked eyes and wondered what the man saw in his, because the only thing in Harry's mind was dread.

"We have to get up, up and out of here," he said, pulling Jonnie weakly toward the ladder. "That fucking thing is back, and it's coming through the hulls. Where's Locke?" He abruptly remembered the other man.

"Pushed past me like a mad man, and den went straight up

d'ladder, as fast das 'is beer belly wud let'im," Jonnie muttered in an oddly subdued tone, and they both looked at the opening up into the rig leg and the wall-mounted ladder lit by Jonnie's torch.

As they watched, a faint blue light seem to glow in the dark circle above them, and water began showering down, spattering loudly on the steel floor below.

They both stepped back involuntarily as a loud crack sounded like a detonation in the small space above and rang down through the metal with a heart-stopping intensity, quickly followed by another gush of liquid and more resounding thumps, until a body thumped wetly onto the deck in front of them, spraying red water.

They stood frozen, looking at the near-decapitated and contorted body before them; it looked as if the bones beneath the skin had conspired to reshape the flesh in its final throes.

With a jerk of realization as the cold water began to form around his feet, and despite the dread that seemed to numb his mind, Harry knew they, too, would have to climb the ladder in front of them.

"Jonnie, we have to go up. This room will be full of water in minutes. That thing lives in water; we have to go up, we have to."

He gripped Jonnie's shoulder. His voice sounded hollow and shock-suffused, and his hands were shaking as if he were chilled to the bone.

"Fuck dat! Dat fuckin' ting's waitin' for us!" Jonnie shouted. He was wide-eyed and kept staring back at Locke's remains, as if they signaled a point he could not pass.

"Jonnie, if we don't climb out, we'll drown," he said, dragging the man's eyes down with his to look at the water level, which was already at the ankles of their boots.

"We haven't got a choice. Follow me, and we'll go quietly, really fucking quietly, alright, Jonnie?"

Before Jonnie could answer or Harry gave himself time to think about what he was doing, he went to the ladder, edging around Locke's broken corpse that was heaped in the water below the opening. One of the crookedly bent arms was floating on the surface, waving him on with one last gesture from the beyond, and his heart seemed to freeze in his chest.

Looking up into the blackness, he found he was contained

within a shower curtain of falling seawater, and the black tunnel above, beyond his torchlight, seemed to be looking back at him, making his flesh crawl and tension cramp his chest. He quickly shot a glance behind him to see that Jonnie was following. With a rapid twitch of resolution and with a wince against the insanity of his actions, he started to climb the ladder.

Inside the dark tube all of his senses were focused on sound, the harshness of his breaths, the squeaking of his rubber boots on the wet rungs, and the distant muffled sea sounds outside. In those distant sounds he strained to pick up any noise, any movement of life, which might indicate the creature's presence, till his concentration almost, stopped him moving.

He forced himself on, begging in his mind that the cobalt radiance would not return and that the metal would not rupture out in front of him in a spray of ice-cold water and death.

Each rung became a focus for his inner pleading, 'One more, just one more.' And 'Come on. Come on,' endlessly repeating as he reached cautiously from one rung to the next.

He heard Jonnie start up from below; the sound of him climbing seemed unbelievably loud and echoing in the confined blackness, and for an insane moment he felt like screaming down at the man below him to be quiet. But his mouth was stopped dry with fear, and he just kept climbing, a small part of him hoping that Jonnie's noise would lead the predator away from him.

His arms were becoming leaden with the slow, quiet pace, and finally he had to stop and suck in oxygen and rest from the agonizing pressure building in his shoulders. It was then he noticed that he was hanging much more to the right, and he could reach out his leg to touch the side wall. The tunnel up which they were climbing had become more like the downslope of a waterslide, and putting his feet down, he could almost walk up the slope, using the ladder to keep his balance and help pull him upward.

He passed a place where water was spraying like a fire hose. After passing it, he turned on his torch and saw the punctured metal and guessed he had reached as far in his climb as Locke had.

After a moment of frozen horror, he struggled on a little

quicker with the adrenaline that the shot of fear gave him, but soon had to stop again to rest, hoping the noise of the water would mask his desperate gulps for air. The spray of water had soaked his clothes, cooling off the heat he had generated with the effort of the climb.

He was nearly shocked off his feet when the ladder vibrated in his hands and grunting sounds approached. He was close to laughing out loud when he realized that what he'd noticed was Jonnie coming up right behind him. The laughter bubbled maniacally in his chest, but he didn't have the breath to spare.

The angle of the tube had declined even more, to a gentle slope, and he began to walk as fast as he dared, as quietly as he could, and after a few minutes the dark ahead lightened, and he added to his pace in a rush of excitement.

"C'mon, Jonnie, we're there. It's just up ahead. One last push, mate," he whispered behind him hoarsely and stood up out through the hatch, looking up the oil rig that now towered above him like a near vertical cliff face and up the walkway they had crossed that looked more like a coal chute leading to an insane climbing frame of stairs. Incongruously, the stars twinkled overhead.

He looked down in shock, and he saw the platform side they were on was becoming submerged below the dark moonlit waterline. From the hatchway he looked over the side and could see dark foam-crested waves crashing into the metal curve of the access tunnel they stood in. He looked around urgently for a way to get up the rig, but he could only see areas above that they couldn't reach. As Jonnie joined him at the hatch entrance, their heads poking out into the wind and sea spray, Big C grasped that the platform was sinking and that they were trapped between a near-impossible climb and the rapidly approaching ocean waves that might contain the creature beneath.

With a small itch of regret, Agrushell dragged himself forcibly away from hunting the individual creatures that slowly crawled beneath him like flaccid worms on the seabed. His design was of a larger nature, and he felt potent and purposefully close to its completion.

Jetting away from the metal wall and the helplessly weak beings inside the steel cylinder, he moved back down its tubular length, to the top surface of the chamber at its base and landed with ethereal elegance upon it. Anchoring himself with sprouting multiple sucker-lined limbs, he placed the core of his power above the shell of the hollow space beneath.

Constricting his central form he began to build his internal puissance, tightening his inner chambers to create a swirling force, constricting and building its power within him. Blue light began to show through the gaps in his outer shell, making the water around Agrushell dance in beams of light blue force. The water that surrounded him became agitated and finally began to boil away from his skin with small bubble streamers.

The power built and built as he squeezed, straining his structure and endurance, until finally with a throb of pleasure he released, driving the force directly into the metal plates below him. If he had not anchored himself, he would have been blown away from the rig by the potency of the release. But holding himself against the blast, he directed his power in a four-foot circular pillar of blue energy that blew a hole the same size through the pontoon's hull.

Drifting emptily down the pontoon's length, he anchored himself again, resting for a brief while as he regained his strength in the expended cells of his core and then slowly began to rebuild the energy inside himself. As force was fed into his central chamber within and funneled and clenched, it began to build inside anew, water began to seethe around him, vibrations grew as waves of force within built their pitch up to a thunderous vibration, and he blew another hole at the opposite end of the chamber.

Already he sensed the angle of the structure changing and beginning to sink into the deeper water. He wearily glided beneath the sinking edge of the compartment, hidden from attack, and accepted that his rage had taken him beyond his limits; he must rest to be ready to strike again with all his strength.

CHAPTER 16 — SURVIVAL

Steve could feel shadows move in the cavern of his mind, like ghost memories. Alien concepts invaded his thoughts, and he felt flushes of a cold desire, deeper and more disturbing than any he could imagine. He knew where they had to go, and it was as far from that strange subzero desire that pervaded his own emotions as he could possibly get.

So, using the urgent imperative to move away from the black rolling sea below, he urged and cajoled Janice, Dan and Brainy to to climb to where he knew the rig's highest point would be when the rig capsized, pushing the group to move as quickly as possible.

As the rig turned sideways in the sea, the rest of them began to realize the danger, which provoked a headlong dash to reach the top of the overturning rig, before the walkways became near-vertical surfaces.

They arrived at the uppermost edge of the oil platform; the once side walls of the platform had now become flat surfaces. They stood upon the large white corrugated blocks that made up the equipment and oil stores, with the canteen running adjacent down to their left. Below them was the now-sheer cliff face of the helipad, and the crane and derrick protruded out below. Staring down the now vertical face of the sinking rig, to where the living quarters and operations block from which they had climbed had been, all they could see was now below the rising ocean surface

They all stood silently looking down on the tortured and sunken oil platform that had been their home and had now become a broken shell, fighting to survive the rocking motions of the sea.

Finally Janice suggested that they would be safer inside, and the general consensus was that they should head for the canteen. After their mad climb up the stricken rig, the fear of falling, and the last of their adrenaline being exhausted, they were tired, thirsty, and in need of the security that came from being around their fellow human kind. It didn't meet the design in Steve's mind, and he refused.

Janice tried to persuade him that he was hurt, that he needed to get looked at, and that they needed to tell the others of how he had been attacked. They hadn't seen any sign of his assailants since they had started the harrowing ascent.

The urgency of her requests and the painful need in her eyes had no effect on him. His emotions seemed distant, like they were contained in an assembly of distinct chambers that he could sense as a whole but only access through instinctive need or with a strong impetus of thought. The pains in his body and the wounds on his face were dull aches, compartmentalized and shut away by the necessity of what he needed to accomplish.

He recognized that Janice, Dan and Brainy were going to do was going to push him in a direction he didn't want to go, so he searched, found, and prepared a means to keep them away from the rest of the crew. He knew with cold reason that gathering with the others would only speed their fate.

A sudden intuition made Steve look down to near the surf line of the stricken rig, near where waves broke against the semi-submerged platform, and he could see two tiny faces below. He knew it was Jonnie and Big C, knew that the others would attempt their rescue.

Dan would certainly side with him, Brainy had become a follower, and kindhearted Janice would be compelled to want to save them. A simple distraction keeping them, as per his design, separate from the rest of the human herd as they attempted the rescue. All of these thoughts were simultaneous and far beyond any way that he had reasoned before.

"Down there," Steve shouted. "Near the water, two people are trapped."

He looked to the others while pointing urgently toward the distant white faces highlighted in the moonlight below.

"How the fuck are we going to help them?" Brainy asked. "They are too fucking far down to climb after; everything is wet and slippery as fuck. We won't get any grip, and it's a hundred-

and-fifty-foot drop easy. I'm not risking it, not with this pissin' rig being rocked about all over the place by the bloody sea."

"We don't have any ropes, or any way down," Dan agreed, looking thoughtfully down the rig's face, his hair being ruffled by the wind.

Steve's mind had already run through the options.

"We are standing on the stores; if someone can lower me down to the door," he leaned over the edge, "I can get inside and get ropes and equipment."

He turned back and awaited the obvious result.

Dan came and looked over the edge, accessing the distance down to the door into the stores. He pursed his lips and nodded.

"That looks possible, but I think if Janice is up to it, she is the lightest, and Brainy and I can lower her. You're too knocked about to be risking yourself, mate."

His design was being unexpected altered by Dan's concern for his well-being.

Dan turned with a serious face to look directly at Janice.

"Do you think you could do it? We'll lower you by your legs so you can reach the handle, then bring you up and lower you by your hands, so your feet reach the opening. Could you do that?"

As different emotions flitted across Janice's face, they all waited for her reply.

Hearing the concern and appeal in Dan's tone, Steve felt his strategy being blown apart. Would Janice accept? He saw hesitation, then resolution gather in Janice's face and the blue lightning in her aura fade.

"I'm fine. I should go. There's no need to take a risk with Janice. I can do this!" Steve could hear that his voice sounded desperate, and his sudden lack of mental control led to the pain in his ribs returning, sparking a coughing fit that left him hugging himself as if his rib cage might come apart.

Janice came to him and held his cheeks in her hands; he could feel tears in his eyes as she kissed him deeply. He felt his heart ache painfully in his chest with the fear of losing her and the stinging resignation that he could not stop her.

"I'll be okay. Don't worry, my dear. I won't lose you now that I've found you." She looked deeply into his eyes, and the words seemed to be rebuilding the very nature of his heart inside him.

"Be careful, Janice. I don't think I could bear it … bear it, if you got hurt." He kissed her firmly again. "Go on, you can do this."

He smiled for her but felt a loss and sadness suddenly grip his stomach.

She nodded and went over to the two men solemnly waiting for her. She lay next to the corrugated edge while they each took an ankle and slowly lowered her down, while he watched with his passion mixing with his anxiety.

He looked down only once; the sight of her floating above the drop below made him vertiginous and sick to his stomach with trepidation. He retreated back five feet and sat with his knees cramped below his chin, watching the edge and sky beyond, until after an eternity she returned slickly red-faced and wreathed in golden orange from triumphantly opening the storeroom door.

He embraced her as if he hadn't seen her in months.

All too soon she was rested and ready to attempt getting into the stores through the open door below, which was banging against the wall with the structure's yawing motion, creating tension and urgency from Dan and Brainy that it might slam close.

So they lowered her again, this time by her wrists, and with their grunts of effort, he saw her pale, determined face pass below the white-painted metal edge. This time he had to watch over the side, as she requested that the straining men gently swing her toward the open door and on her shout of 'now' for Dan to release her hand. With hands clenched painfully by his sides in nervous tension, Steve watched in vivid clarity and almost slow motion as she screamed 'NOW!' and let go of Dan's hand, grabbing for the door frame.

She flung out her hand and grabbed the door, hanging on precariously for a few seconds before pulling herself along the door to the entrance, and then both the men gently lowered her through its frame.

With a struggle she finally managed to pull herself in and vanished into the black rectangle of the doorway beneath them.

He let loose the breath he hadn't realized he'd been holding, and it seemed to leave his stomach empty and shaking.

Moments seemed to move in normal time again as relief flooded through him, leaving him a trembling mess, until a rope arced up from below which Dan caught in his large hands with casual ease.

Steve thought in a separate part of his mind, 'With his easy nature and friendly demeanor, you sometimes forget that Dan is a large and physically adept man, a potentially dangerous man'—the consideration surprised him.

Tying ropes off on the mounted walkway posts and using several carabiner and a small pulley block, they fashioned a rope line they could attach themselves to and a way of hauling up the men from below.

Janice also attached a large tool bag to a rope for them to lift up, filled with torches, water bottles, and sealed food packs. When she was hoisted back up, they slaked their thirsts and ate a quick meal to prepare them for the effort ahead.

They used the torches to flash at the men below, until they received answering flashes of light from them. This time Janice volunteered to be lowered down to the men, and there were no arguments. But Steve felt relaxed; he was oddly unconcerned about Janice encountering any danger, and he listened calmly as Dan outlined to her how many flashes for 'up' and how many for 'wait' and 'go.'

He helped the others as much as he could to gently release the line she was on. He stood in a painfully long, braced stance that made his shoulders, arms, and bruised ribs ache, as he passed taut rope through his hands.

When the line went suddenly slack, he nearly fell because of the tense strain he had been exerting in the opposite direction, and his heart jumped and he shouted out her name.

But Dan, at the front of their line, shouted, "Don't worry! She made it. She'll signal us when they're ready to start coming up."

They took the opportunity to shake out their arms and take in some welcome deep breaths of sea air.

Dan and Steve silently took in their impossible view, while Brainy sat with his eyes down on the store wall, like the view below was an insult to the balance of his mind. The wind gently pushed against them in liquid-flecked gusts, seagulls screeched above them, and they struggled to accept the normality of a world turned insane as they waited for the signal.

When the distant torchlight flashed three times, they began hauling on the rope. This time the effort was different, and they could get a rhythm going to heave the burden up more quickly, until to his delight Janice's glorious and success-filled face appeared with a corona of glittering golden orange.

After a few minutes of mutual congratulations and a fierce hug between Janice and himself, they signaled for the first man below to come up.

With Janice helping lift the next one up, it was easier still, and the pale and oddly lackluster face of Jonnie appeared. He immediately collapsed on the deck as if his legs couldn't support the burden of his endeavors and lay there panting severely.

After a few shared puzzled looks, they waited until Jonnie climbed to his feet to question him. "Are you alright to help, Jonnie?" Dan asked, looking at the man with concern.

Jonnie nodded, though he seemed dazed or in shock.

"Yeah, yeah. I'll be alright," he mumbled.

So they flashed the torch again and started lifting the man below, whose weight seemed twice that of Jonnie. But with five of them drawing up the line, the large bulk and stricken white face of Big C soon appeared.

As they began dragging him onto the relatively flat surface of the stores, they heard noises from behind and saw two men crawling on their hands and knees across the top of the steel walkway meshing that linked them to the canteen block. The approaching men were shouting, but between the wind and distance Steve could not pick out the words. In unspoken agreement they put down their ropes and waited for the men to arrive.

"What the fuck is he saying?" said Brainy, his face screwed up in concentration trying to hear. That probably added no assistance to his hearing, Steve thought.

They saw Chief Johnson and Operations Team Leader Angus Neil crawling toward them, fear on both their faces, which, Steve thought, with the now semi-submerged rig being buffeted like a floundering ship in the waves, even in these reasonably calm waters, it didn't surprise him they looked ashen-faced.

They arrived, and he understood immediately that the blue of the chief's fear was about to turn to indignant red iridescent anger. He felt separate from emotions in a way he'd never felt in his life. Usually his inner memories and accompanying dread would have backed away from the confrontation and thrown up a wall of defensive anger. Now he was sublimely relaxed and was ready to watch the ensuing confrontation with a critically appraising eye.

The man's face screwed up and reddened as he came to the boil.

"Mr. Shore, how have you managed to compromise this platform? What in the name of all that is holy, what have you done, you bloody incompetent idiot?!"

Big C lay on the floor unmoving, his face dull and his eyes watery, but his beard bristled at the injustice.

"Well, man, have you nothing to say? You have sunk this rig and will be liable for charges of criminal negligence. Have you nothing to say, Mr. Shore?"

Harry lay still, with a look of fiery disbelief on his face; he looked as if he might begin screaming, when with a sudden frown and a softening of his features, he began to laugh. It was harsh and contained a hint of hysteria in the gale force of its release.

"Very well, Shore, your attitude will become part of the evidence of your blatant disregard for the safety of this vessel and the crew members whose lives you have jeopardized." But the chief's rhetoric had become a bemused litany as his anger was drained away by the other man's indifference.

"Ha ha ha! You stupid bastard, Johnson, what makes you think any of us will survive the next hour?" There was no humour left on Big C's face; it had become bleak with an absence of hope or care. "You can blame my corpse when we're all floating face down in the ocean."

The chief began to sputter with returning indignation but seemed unable to formulate a response. Angus Neil came to his defense.

"Rescue will be coming shortly. This rig has been out of contact for two days, and I would expect an investigating vessel or chopper as soon as it becomes light, so you will not escape the justice that your actions deserve."

Big C started laughing again, then very abruptly stopped. "Shut up, you prick! No, I don't think rescue will be coming in time, do you know why not?"

Steve instantly knew why; perhaps he'd known from the minute the creature had fallen from the rig. He watched the scene play out in front of him, part of him chilled with fear, part calculating consequences, and the cold reason of his consciousness awaited the moment for action.

Chief Johnson continued to look baffled, while Neil's dander was up after Big C's insult.

"Why don't you enlighten us before you go to jail, arsehole?" he spat contemptuously.

Big C nodded to himself, sat up and looked directly at Neil.

"Because Billy's dead, Brian Locke is dead, and this fucking rig is sinking because that fucking creature punched holes through three inches of steel to kill them and seems pretty fucking intent on dragging this platform and us down to the bottom of the ocean with it. So, fuck you both, sir."

Silence followed his statement, a silence that seemed to drag at their collective courage and introduce a slow freeze into their veins.

"It can't be?" Johnson persisted. "We saw that thing die … We saw it." He seemed to run out of words and looked forlornly at Neil for support.

Neil was shaking his head and looking down the rig to the oil-black ocean below; he seemed to be conjuring up images of terror from his memory.

Johnson turned to the rest of them. "What do we do? What do we do now? I must report back to Mr. Storrel … This is his responsibility. He'll know the best way forward. Yes, Storrel will know."

He turned and began scrambling back across the walkway mesh as fast as he could on his hands and knees.

This seemed to click Neil out of his inner horror show, and with a haunted look at the small group, he scrambled quickly off to follow Chief Johnson's frantically wobbling rear.

Each of them seemed to be reacting to Big C's revelation in

their own way, Steve thought, as he took in Janice's dread, Dan's fierce concentration, and Brainy's look of miserable loss.

His mind shifted into the moment of action.

"We need to make defensive weapons, be prepared to send a distress signal, and find a way to harm this creature or drive it off the rig," he said with complete confidence, the assembled parts of his mind falling into place.

Dan looked at him with surprise, and then quickly looked determined and ready to hear a way forward.

"What fucking weapons?" Big C asked despondently. "We don't have any military hardware, and we are short on submarines."

Steve smiled inwardly; each reaction was becoming obvious, and each could be turned around to directly benefit his intentions.

"The scaffold poles will give us distance. I would think a bunch as resourceful as we are can fashion some basic spears," he said with resolve.

He turned to Jonnie. "But the hard work falls to you, mate. We need to be able to send a radio distress signal. We'll need help as quickly as possible. I think this thing uses some form of electrical clout, from how it knocked out our power before, so it can only be a short-blast signal, or the creature will attack that same way again … and …" he paused, weighing up the man.

"Christ, wat more do ya want me to do in ten minutes?" Jonnie groaned.

"If this thing is using some kind of electrical power, maybe we can short its systems, too. I was thinking … some kind of trap? Perhaps we can bring this organism a bit of electrical hell," Steve said, his tone gaining determination.

He gave Jonnie a tight grin and saw the man's startled face, which was followed by a look of deadly commitment and a malicious grin in return.

"Maybe we can, at dat like," Jonnie said.

"Do you really think we can stop it, that thing? It's so massive." Janice's voice sounded lost and full of fear.

"We don't need to stop it, just to keep it away from us and us out of the water. After that, with a distress call sent, help should be with us quickly." He tried to sound as reassuring as possible, holding the trembling girl in his arms and feeling the same tremble in his stomach.

"Don't we need the others to help? Aren't we stronger fighting together?" Dan asked with urgent emphasis on the word *together*.

"They will refuse to believe at first. They will argue that Big C is lying, trying to save his skin. They will argue and shout each other down. But that help must be here early tomorrow, and that creature must be hurt and unable to climb the remaining height to reach us here. By the time the rest of them are ready to act, things will be beyond their control." He reeled off the facts of the situation as he saw them as if he were reading them their share of the bill at a restaurant.

He awaited the crucial question, the answer to which might mean they wouldn't trust him.

In the end, Dan asked, which didn't surprise Steve; Dan was intelligent and would be the first to wonder at Steve's absolute confidence. "How can you know, Steve?"

"Because," he paused, perceiving that he was leaping into the unknown, "I've been feeling that thing for at least a day, and I can still feel it now. We have hurt it, but it isn't incapacitated. It won't risk itself too far from the water again; it wants us where it's strongest, where we're weakest, in the sea."

"You sound very sure. You may be risking our lives on a feeling you've got," Dan stated with worry and suspicion.

"Fuck me, are you saying you know what that fucker is thinking? That sounds bat-shit insane to me." Brainy almost choked on his anger, disbelief, and fear, which were making his aura waver in blue sparks.

They had come to the crux of whether they would trust him or not, and as he had predicted, their untenable circumstances and fear would be the driving motivation behind their decision.

"You don't have to believe me, or vote me as leader, or any of that shit. Just trust the logic of what I've said against the alternative, which is if we don't get off this oil platform that monster will drag every one of us down into the ocean."

His voice was calm, and he raised his eyebrows, willing Brainy to see the reasonableness of his words. He felt no fright, just purpose and the necessity of getting off this rig. He was shocked to find he was no longer a prisoner of his childhood home, consumed by terror, but free and alive. He almost smiled.

Brainy looked wild-eyed at Steve for a couple of seconds, as if amazed at the person he was talking to. "Yeah, alright, mate. Let's do it."

"We have to keep up high, away from where it's strongest, and use where we are strongest to keep it away, or we will have no chance against it. We do not have any more time to talk about it; we have to get the radio working and get prepared for when it comes, so we can stay alive and get OFF this bloody rig."

Momentarily dumbfounded by the new Steve they were hearing from, the group stood in momentary shock, and there were several open mouths. Only Janice's eyes gleamed with support.

"I think the sooner we move, the greater chance we have of surviving," Steve suggested dryly as they gaped at him, and he smiled at Janice.

His words seemed to galvanize them; Jonnie recovered the quickest, whilst Dan was still looking at Steve as if he was a stranger.

"I tink we need watever weapons we can get to 'old dis ting off, ya know. I 'ave an idea for sometin special. Come on, Brainy, let's go and grab one of tose large mobile generators from the stores and get it up 'ere. Dan and youse can work on it like, while I scavenge for radio parts."

As the light of the astral plasma sphere at the center of the system rose past the arced edge of the world, multitudes of radiating light rays hit the vast surface of the sea and rang through the upper levels of the ocean. The light minutely vibrated in different tones across the immense marine surface like music.

The symphony of light and music stirred Agrushell, and he began to reengage his primary senses with the conscious parts of his mind.

He focused the following collaboration of logic and thought input into a hunting mode. He began ranging his full breadth of sensory capabilities around him, giving him a more complete image of his immediate environment.

As he built a full mental representation of the structure's position in and out of the water, he assessed the floating capability of the construction, its remaining air-filled chambers, and the viability of its remaining seabed-moored lines. Then, with infinite care, he started to locate individual creatures on and within its metal assembly, one by one, till he found every remaining lifeform.

He located one creature dead within one of the metal cave structures and broke through the clear panels to drag the flaccid corpse out; with abstract fury he tore the corpse in two and let the split body parts sink down to the waiting crabs below.

Agrushell discovered that the majority of the creatures in their boned jellyfish flesh had gathered near the peak of the structure as far from his grasp as possible, while others had collected in a large iron cavern that ran partway down its side. Perhaps, he considered, they felt secure in their metal-bound cave, hoping its solid walls would keep them safe.

They would soon feel their lack of safety, feel the dread of his arrival, and with his frigid rage unleashed, they would understand without hope that they were doomed.

Yet the strange resonance of thoughts and sights still flickered in his mind from the one above, like a warm eddy of images in his awareness.

Ignoring this strangeness, part of his mind instigated the factoring of distances, conditions, and the possibilities of sinking the rig further, till he was unbearably distracted by the close electrical signals of a lifeform.

The nearby lure of one of the abhorrent prey became an overwhelming urge, far too sweet a call to resist.

The feeble enemy being was only a small distance above the surface, hiding in a thin steel shell. Agrushell examined the protective capability of the thin metal sheath, and he glided until he was directly beneath the lifeform.

He sensed light vibrations emanating from the thick upper part of the being's torso, rhythmic noises that tasted like distress, and he felt a hunter's calm again.

With slow care and a surety of his opponent's weakness, he moved almost silently from the water on great suckered limbs, drawing himself with infinite patience up the metal surface to attack.

CHAPTER 17 — FISHING

Head Geologist John Lawson sat in the crane cabin about twenty five feet above the water. He was cold and had his arms wrapped around his torso. When the platform had begun listing dramatically, he had climbed up the rig as fast as he could but had soon become tired. He seemed drained of energy and purpose, so he looked for the closest place to rest, and the crane cab had been his nearest shelter, secure under the shadow of the rig's derrick.

Now he looked down through the plexi-glass to the white scuffed tops of the waves below and felt no desire to move. His fear had been replaced with a growing separation from the events around him, ever since he had suffered the ignominy and displacement of being removed from his important role as one of the key management staff.

He had become a pariah amongst the crew, being shunned and ignored by the very people who had once respected him, who had once deferred to his opinion. He couldn't have known or even begun to guess that something like that abnormal monster could be alive, a thing that had no right existing, but still they made him the villain. Meanwhile, Mr. Perfect, good-looking sportsman and font-of-all-wisdom Dan, his bloody junior, was hailed as a hero. Listened to at meetings and called upon for his 'expert' opinion.

He laughed to himself—Dan was an 'expert' in self-important arrogance, nothing more, and the youngster was barely out of his school trousers. He began again with the litany of curses at the conceited, bloated image of Dan that his mind kept conjuring.

His inner misery returned him to memories of his own boarding school life, when he had felt as devalued and as alone as he did now, where he'd been despised by everyone. His parents had not been wealthy or connected enough; this had rendered him socially poor because of their financial impotence, leaving him worthless in the eyes of the school's social glitterati. He had spent years living in misery as the dorm's whipping boy.

But on leaving that hellhole and taking up his new profession, he had found respect and significance. All of which had been swept away so easily by that monstrosity's appearance and by Dan's puffed up self-superiority.

He began his inner monologue of cursing again, till it became a mental noise that blocked out the frightening reality outside.

He looked emptily out of his glass and metal chamber, perched on the vinyl seat's edge, as the crane cab peaked and yawned gently with the motion of the waves below. The dawn had begun to rise in front of him; red-tinged grey clouds were pierced by light shafts that spotlighted parts of the ocean as the sun rose over the hazed edge of the horizon. But he watched the changes that came across the world of water without hope or curiosity.

Looking at the lead-shaded clouds that had become defined and edged by dawn, he saw lighter, sun struck grey clouds chasing below, and the growing brightness caught diamond-tipped undulations on the surface of the ocean beneath him. He felt tears dropping from his cheeks, and a tight band of sorrow form across his chest; he dropped his face into his hands and began to sob at the futility of himself.

He was unaware of the darkness that had appeared at the base of the crane window; he was unaware of the light rasping of friction between two hard surfaces. He finally became aware only as pain slammed into his leg. He barely had a moment to glance down and take in the black encrusted lance, as hard as iron, which had pierced the cab wall and stabbed through his right leg. His mind became a red torrent of frozen pinpricks, and a scream gurgled, trapped behind the panic in his throat.

As forcefully as the spear had entered his flesh, it was withdrawn with a screech of abused steel, leaving stomach-sickening agony and a spray of blood. He clasped one hand to the bloodied exit wound and heaved himself away from the pierced metal wall to the cab door, flinging it open with a metallic creak. A blast of cold sea air seemed to clear his mental anguish, and he looked down to the sea below, transfixed for a moment by the impossible perspective.

He turned in pain to look behind him to see wrapped around the crane cab was the nightmare of two days ago gradually curling its hooked limbs toward him as its bulk threatened from below the crane cab's steel shell. Then, in a sudden thrust of motion, several of the limbs undulated, smashing their ends against the deck with a cacophonous ringing of metal that vibrated through the deck below his feet.

As the metal rang out deafening him, he looked frantically for an escape route, even as the monster's edged and spiked limbs crept sinuously closer.

In desperation, he looked up and around, but there was nowhere to climb and his uninjured leg shook with the effort of supporting him, as waves of sickening hurt shot up from his injury. His head seemed to bulge with the pain and the impossible fear.

He had nowhere to go.

A black-flaked and anaconda-like limb grated across the metal below where he leaned out from the cab with a painfully high-pitched screech. From the corner of his eye, he saw the mass of the nightmare's body very slowly drawing up toward him. It seemed to be in no great hurry, as if it was anticipating the moment.

The creature's black bulk was angled up, as if it was looking above him, and his eyes followed that elevation. He could see distant faces high above, too far away to help and too high to hear him beg for it. The scraping of a spiked limb above him caused a flush of icy desperation through his limbs; he looked down at the only place left to escape to, and with a stomach-sinking desolation of will and an excruciating stab of pain from his leg that seemed to blacken the edges of his sight, he pushed himself off into space.

Chief Johnson fumed; he wanted to kick and punch that bloody idiot Big C in his imbecilic fat face.

He passed the sullen figure of Jones at the top of the ladder, his battered visage and bruised aggressive squint promising violent impending reactions.

He started down the ladder to deliver his impossibly bad news and felt a sudden strong urge for the toilet. He was totally sure his news would not fall on kind ears.

"It's ... back ... the bloody thing is back," he called apprehensively down into the hollow dark.

He was panting, and sweat dripped from his nose after his efforts crawling on the overturned rig walkway and clambering down the makeshift steps, but most of all in anticipation of his approaching conversation with the Company Man.

The canteen room was dark as he climbed the rest of the way down the hastily erected scaffold ladder. It had been used previously as a stretcher; its occupant had not survived the rig's latest reconfiguration.

Pale faces, lit by the light above and the weak orange glow of propane lamps, looked up at him, sat on the edges of table and chair units that were welded to the deck of the canteen block. The crew's wan and battered faces made him abruptly think he was looking at lost souls in one of the rings of hell. The echoing room was filled with ill-contained anger, fright, and the need to blame.

He looked down from the ladder and, in ghostly lit precision, saw the deep frown on the large face of the barrel-chested, black-shirted Storrel. There was not a bead of sweat on his unforgiving features, and Johnson felt his stomach squirm. This man was his every chance of progressing in the company, and his good opinion could make or break Johnson's future in the industry.

"Harry Shore says that the creature is back. It broke in through the pontoon hull, killing Billy and Locke. He says that that thing is back and trying to sink us, sir."

Johnson then lapsed into silence, unnerved by the echo made by his voice as he waited for Storrel's response.

The big American's eyes seemed to pulse with fury, and his frown grew deeper.

"What a ridiculous pile of crap, Johnson. Don't tell me you believe this fantasy story?" he snapped.

"Well, no, sir. I assume he's trying to save his own neck ... but I thought it important to apprise you of all the, erm, facts, sir ... so, I came straight to you and erm ..." Johnson tried desperately to pitch his tone as competent but respectful, but it only sounded tremulous and desperate.

"Enough," Storrel interrupted Johnson's nervous reply with firm control. "Did you say the pontoon hull has been breached? That bloody idiot has managed to sink a facility worth hundreds of millions of dollars; I'm going to have his ass handed to him on a silver fucking platter," Storrel spat out the final word.

"What do we do next, Mr. Storrel, sir?" Johnson was relieved to be out of the firing line but was desperate for reassurance, as the solidity of his world had shockingly become as choppy and uncertain as the motion of the waves.

"We need to launch the nearest available life raft, get in, and wait for its automatic beacon to signal for help. Then we sit tight and play some cards until we're rescued." His tone was solid with confidence.

"But, I want everyone's reassurance that during any proceeding enquiry that everyone will confirm that Mr. Shore's actions were responsible for this oil platform's demise," Storrel announced. He scowled at the ill-lit insipid faces around him, waiting to be contradicted.

As he asked his unspoken question, vibrations ran through the metal under their feet, and above them they could hear disbelief and frightened swearing.

The battered face of Lee Jones appeared in the brightly lit doorway above.

"You'd better wait on that fucking life raft, and come and see this shit." Jones was wild-eyed around his bruises, and panic strained his voice.

At once Storrel started up the ladder past Johnson as if he'd ceased to exist, and the others started to clamber up from the tables and chairs toward him. Desperate to be close to the toughness and protection of Storrel, Johnson also grabbed the rungs and started upward.

He climbed into the growing light above into the cold wind of a pale dawn and joined Storrel and Jones on their knees at the edge of the canteen wall, looking down to the ocean below. What he saw made him want to back away from the edge in shock.

Through the triangle-shaped metalwork of the crane arm and derrick below he could see the creature's arms wrapped around the crane cab almost directly below them, as if it meant to crush it. The bulk of its body was under cover behind the metal cabin, as if peeking up at them from below. He could also see the tiny horror-stricken face of his head geologist, Lawson, staring up at them, his mouth open in a soundless scream. Johnson didn't want to look at the man's face; it was bone pale and filled with hopelessness, but he could not look away.

Lawson stopped looking up, and his head snapped around to look back at the approaching creature, which had crept nearer to him, its tentacle-like limbs coiling out to clutch him with their hooked ends. Then with a sudden lurch and without a final look back at the men above (to Johnson's relief), Lawson threw himself out away from the rig, falling briefly, then hitting the water in a badly executed dive. As he fell, the creature retracted its arms and also dove away from the rig into the sea, like an alien multi-limbed whale smashing into the water.

Other men from inside the canteen block had gathered around them. No one spoke until Lawson came to the surface, spinning in the water and searching the waves around him.

"We've got to help him. Can't we do something?" the overweight canteen manager said in a plaintive tone. His pudgy white face was patchy and red-stained like his white apron, as if he had come from a brutal murder scene. But Johnson thought he looked more like a victim than a perpetrator.

The man's voice seemed to snap them out of the mesmeric lure of the events unfolding below them.

Storrel took immediate control.

"Someone grab the life ring from under that walkway wall and get it down to him. Mr. Neil, go across to that group of miscreants over there and get us line we can attach to haul that man back up with."

"Yes, sir, but do we have time for that?" Neil sounded doubtful, and he was eyeing the reverberating metal wall-cum-walkway nervously.

"Move, mister, and now! You still work for this company and directly for me." Storrel's face had gone an explosive red, and his eyes bulged threateningly.

As Angus Neil stumbled to comply under the impetus of

Storrel's savage stare, the tableau was interrupted by a shout of "Catch this, mate" from behind them.

Johnson looked down in time to see the bright orange ring gliding toward the man's small dark head that bobbed in the waves below.

The ring splashed down close to the man, who, with painful slowness, swam to it and dragged it over his head, till it was beneath his armpits. Lawson then started scooping at the water with his hands, spinning the orange preserver as he began searching the waves around him again.

Everyone looked across to see Neil jogging away from the group to the stores block to collect a coil of rope, which he slung over his shoulder as he began heading back at a light jog to the walkway. Then, dropping to his knees, he started to crawl urgently, but the movement of the rig between swells hampered his frantic momentum.

Johnson looked back to the sea surface and felt the air freeze in his lungs; below the orange circle holding the man above the waves a large shadow was growing. He wanted to scream out a warning, to attract the attention of the others, but the ice in his chest seemed to have sealed the words in his dry gullet.

As he watched, parts of the shadow broke the surface; black-hooked limbs with a membrane of flesh curved between them all rose around the helpless man encircling him. Like windbreaks on the beach, Johnson thought absently, but hung with black tissue. The man in the ring began wheeling his small craft around in ever more desperate circles, searching for a hole of escape in the membrane curtain around him.

"Holy fucking shite. Look, look at fucking that … Fuck me, look …" the large roughneck Jones gasped out in shock, till his words seemed to run out.

In the water just above the shadow, a whiter circular construction could be seen. It had a central aperture that contained a white-beaked mouth that was an open maw of anticipation. The arms began to close in and over their victim like the petals of an alien lily drawing the frantic figure into its embrace. The grey-black umbrella of flesh closed like a flower in reverse. There was a seemingly endless pause; then, in the blink of an eye, the whole creation vanished beneath the waves with a white plume that rained down on the boiling surface.

The rig's men stood in silence, watching the white splash of foaming water disappear into the waves. Across the gap, the other group also stood watching, and there was no doubt that the thing that had stalked all their nightmares had returned.

"What the fuck are we going to do now? What the fuck can we do against that?" Jones's face was pale and his eyes wild; his sentiments and expression were mirrored on every face Johnson looked at.

As they all stood transfixed by the sea surface, the orange ring reappeared, bobbing up from below the surface like the spat-out remains of a meal.

Only Storrel looked different, as if he was trying to come to terms with the fear. His face looked like he was trying to force himself past it.

"That thing changed. It was different. That motherfucker can change its shape. There's nothing we can do to stop it. We're all getting pulled down there with it," Neil said panting, his eyes dilated. No one made to disagree or reassure him, Johnson realized. They could only agree with him. He could only agree with him. There was nothing they could do.

"It's not fuckin' possible! Nothing like that can exist," Neil continued. "What can we do? Where is the fucking rescue helicopter, for fuck's sake? What do we do?" Neil sounded as if he was about to collapse in on himself, his voice becoming shrill and despairing.

Out of the blue, the canteen manager spoke up. Johnson didn't know his name; everyone just called him Chef.

"We have propane bottles in the galley?!" he spoke directly to Storrel in an uncertain and diffident tone.

"What?" Storrel said in tense surprise. "Propane bottles? So what!?"

"We have some propane bottles for the kitchen, sir. They could do some damage if we could blow them up near the, that thing, if we had some way of setting them off," the overweight canteen manager suggested timidly.

His pudgy white face was flushed red around his greasy skin.

He probably ate too much of his own greasy food, Johnson thought absently, his mind trying to forget the sight of Lawson vanishing, wrapped in the creature's membranous embrace.

"We could blow those bottles up, near the creature, if we could get close enough," Storrel said wonderingly. His tone was still as tense as a whiplash, but some of the drawl was leaking back in. He stopped, lost in thought, as he stared at the ocean below; then, he looked up directly at Johnson, and his eyes were filled with a deadly purpose.

Storrel had a lifetime of maintaining his mental resolve in the face of intimidation—many years of boardroom negotiations, on-site problem-solving, and in-office political astuteness that had made him the ideal company man. He was expert in dealing with people and stress; he had been able to manage people and situations since he was a kid on the streets of Phoenix. He'd developed an ability to convince others into courses of action, with logic, persuasion, but mostly with leverage. He also had become expert at being able to use the skills of others to benefit himself. It had protected him from the violent local gangs of his home streets, propelled him quickly up the business ladder and into the consideration of boardroom empire builders who needed tough-minded men like him to protect their investments.

But he could never have imagined stress like this.

Using his hard-earned experience and innate self-belief enabled him to hold on to his calm in the face of a terror that seemed insurmountable. Despite the fear clamoring inside, he knew he would survive—no matter what or who he had to use to make it happen. And he would hold on to his resolve to do it.

In his experience, problems were never intractable if you used the correct measure of persuasion, force, or influence. To fail here would be a threat to his carefully crafted image and would be viewed badly by his employers. More importantly, he smelt opportunity: if he executed things correctly, it could make him a serious player in the company's infrastructure, a hero pitbull who would be able to choose his own course in the company.

He had been here only to overview a company initiative to reduce its investments in North Sea oil as reserves dwindled, but now he was prepared to sacrifice every life on this rig to survive and take this golden opportunity for his advancement.

"Okay! Alright. Very well, gentlemen, the question is very simple: How can we make those propane bottles blow remotely, and how do we go about getting them near that goddamn piece-of-shit creature down there?" He looked from one numb face to another and waited, then looked at the slack end of line, still held tightly gripped in Neil's hands, and the inkling of an idea came to him.

"C'mon, how do we blow these bottles up from a distance? C'mon, if we do nothing, that thing gets us all. Nobody goes home. I need ideas!"

"Does Dan Giles still have that flare gun? The one he set light to it with before?" Johnson asked him questioningly, as if expecting a slap for his gall. His needy desperation made Storrel feel nauseated, as usual.

"Neil, get your-self over there again and find out if that flare gun is still around. That gun could set the gas canisters off, if they were already pumping out gas."

He felt a dark confidence building up inside him, and he flashed Johnson a smile of congratulations, as Johnson had solved his plan's first problem.

"But how do we get anywhere near that thing, and open those bottles of gas, without someone getting ripped to bits?" Jones asked in a woebegone tone.

The big roughneck Jones stared at Storrel questioningly. His piggy eyes were wet with desperation and surrounded by an angry, bruised swelling, Storrel noticed unsympathetically.

"I'll be honest, lads; it's going to be tricky and dangerous. But I reckon with a bit of teamwork and a brave man to volunteer to help all of his shipmates, we might be able to pull it off and save every man here." He spoke with growing self-assurance, the plan falling together perfectly in his mind.

"With all due respect, Mr. Storrel, what did you have in mind?" Johnson asked with renewed confidence after his suggestion of using the flare gun had been so successfully received.

"Well, Mr. Johnson, I think with the right bait, that creature will come where we want it. So we'll strap cylinders to a life preserver and put a man on top to lure the thing in."

He looked around the group, who were nodding and joining with him."And when it comes up for the kill, then our man opens up the bottles releasing the gas, and we haul him up on a line. While we lift him to safety, he fires a flare at his leisure into the bottles, which explode right in that motherfucker's face, without him getting blown up or ripped up." Storrel poured as much honey as possible into his tone to radiate his assurance.

Most of the faces around him were looking more animated as they bought into his idea, Johnson was positively hanging on his every word, and he smiled to himself. Only the chef was looking dubious.

"Who on earth is going to volunteer to do that?" the chef asked incredulously.

"I think we need a man whose first interest is to the rig and its crew, a man of leadership, a man who takes his responsibility for this installation seriously and is ready to stand up and be counted." He ended his sentence with another smile, his gaze fixed on Chief Johnson.

The pathetic little man went white and began to splutter.

"Surely, there must be someone … er, must be, erm, a safer way? Maybe there is a way of remotely, um, exploding the bottles, sir. Perhaps a younger man might be more capable, for such a difficult, erm, such a physically difficult task," Johnson appealed. His voice was becoming whiny and annoyingly desperate, Storrel thought.

Despite Johnson's writhing on the hook, he would give in. Storrel knew how desperate the little man was for advancement, to get past the post and earn his retirement package. It made him a malleable and easily managed tool.

"Nonsense, Johnson, we'll need the strength of every younger man available to lower you and to haul you back up safely out of harm's way. All you need to do is open the valves, and when you're on your way up, fire the flare down. Simple. As a man who has the company's and the crew's interests at heart, as a man responsible for all the lives on this vessel, you can do it."

He let the point hang, watching Johnson squirm while his fear battled against his ambition, till finally in a strained tone of resignation, he agreed.

"Excellent, Chief Johnson. I'm sure every man here appreciates your courage, as will the company that employs them," he said, clapping Johnson briefly on the back and then as quickly dismissing him from mind.

"Now, lads, let's get things prepared, before that creature gets a chance to try anything else. I think it's time for us to do us a little fishing," he wisecracked, looking around at the expectant faces with self-congratulation and the applause of the boardroom ringing in his ears.

CHAPTER 18 — AN END OF GAMES

Agrushell was inquisitive by nature, and the heavy deep was a place of limited change and of very little new stimuli for his minds to explore. So, though he sought the destruction of the enemy above, they were also incongruously fascinating. Their aggressive actions and constructions spoke to a deadly intelligence, yet the weakness and pitiful defense of their form, along with the ill-positioning of the ocean reef they inhabited, suggested they were little more than clever animals.

And yet they used tools, technology, and had a primitive knowledge of the blue potency to communicate and run their machinery. But their limited knowledge was just a primitive reflection of the Old Ones and their wisdom of power—they were the galaxy minds who had transcended flesh—and still, there was something about the creatures above.

He remained fascinated by the contradictory nature of his enemy, the signs of intelligence and of their callous savagery. And more, there were the flash visions and the sharing's with the one above, the glimpses of a world through another's senses, basic perceptions, combined with perplexing clarity. He saw the world he knew, but from a new perspective, and a new world. He shared the confusing emotional contexts and baffling desire-based thinking in one section of his mind, analyzing each flash of sensation. But the cold rage and icy purpose continued down the channel of his planning without pause or indecision.

He approached with every sense stretched and sharpened, ready for his assault, and at once the design of his hunt was changed by the prey. Another body had entered through the light-water barrier, and the thrashing signals of prey carried through the aquatic volume, overlaid with electro-acoustic positioning information. He moved to an attack posture, but then the chemical and metal taste reached his senses. He tasted the deception of the simple creatures he stalked and changed the course of his own impending incursion to accommodate their bait.

Dan had always found his direction in life simple. He knew what he desired from his life and lived by the tenets of his heart and faith. But the radical changes in his circumstances and the debilitating fear of the dark monster that now seemed to gnaw icily at his bones had shaken his impervious faith, and now he knew doubt. He doubted himself, his beliefs, and even his past actions ... Should he have ever left his family so far behind, so undefended?

But the worst blow to his certainties was the new, unnaturally and superhumanly confident figure that Steve Staples had become.

The unbelievable change in the man's behaviour, his new force of will, left Dan feeling oddly humbled and weak. He had always believed that his strength of belief would carry him through any storm or past any danger, but he felt unmanned and adrift in the wake of Steve's cold assurance; Dan was in control of nothing.

He looked over at Steve and Janice, feeling a lurch in his heart and a yearning to be holding his wife the way the other man was holding his woman. If it wasn't for the emotions and reactions that Steve showed to Janice, he would question whether Steve was human at all.

But Steve's feelings for Janice were written all over his face, and this left him with the same dilemma. He didn't feel strong enough to deal with what was happening to him; he didn't feel he might survive to see his children again, and because of this, a black terror seemed to be eroding his hope. Steve had become the linchpin holding him and the others together; Steve had become his only hope.

He was afraid of Steve, too.

Keeping in motion helped them forget their fear; working on the tasks Steve had given them so they could fight had given them courage. He could see the sense in the planning and the beginning of results, but it all seemed to make him more dependent on the man, on Steve's plans for survival that left no room for any other thoughts. Steve had become the sum of his faith and will, leaving him too afraid to think beyond each moment and the tasks that Steve had given him.

Their work was intermittently suspended by what was going on with the rest of the crew on the canteen block, eventually bringing them to a standstill as they stopped to watch the other group's peculiar actions. They watched as they lowered the chief down on a life ring strapped with propane cylinders toward the waves, in what seemed like an act of wanton human sacrifice. Yet inside, despite his shock and discomfort with what they were doing, Dan wanted it to work desperately.

Johnson's pasty white face looked back up as he was lowered down by the men by rope; he sat uncomfortably astride the propane bottles. He looked like he was riding his doom down into the ocean below.

More of the cylinders sat on top of the canteen block, like leftover rounds of super-sized ammunition for non-existent giant cannons, he thought.

They all watched in fascinated horror as the chief reached the water and sank in up to his waist, with the orange life preserver and cylinders sinking below him. He sat anxiously looking down into the green depths of the water with a black rubber scuba mask they had scavenged from the stores.

Everything seemed to have come to a halt. Every eye watched the scene below; every nerve seemed stretched taut, and patience strained more as the seconds passed.

They waited for the demon to come, hoping their staked-out offering would be an enticement to the beast. They waited like millennium-old hunters of their kind had, poised with spears around a baited trap.

Dan knew he should protest, that he should be screaming against what was happening that he should fight against such a lack of humanity and feeling. But the dread was in his bones, and in that secret place in his mind, he prayed for the plan to work, no matter if Johnson survived or not.

Time passed. The man below bobbed on the waves. The sun broke through the clouds, spotlighting sections of the ocean. The wind picked up and began to blow the tops off the waves. The strong breeze buffeted the observers in gusts as they leaned out to look down, gripping onto the wire they'd strung across the edge of the maintenance block for support.

The freshening salt breeze blew the long black hair off Steve's face, making him look like some kind of holy mystic looking out to sea. Dan looked down again to see Johnson suddenly sit up and start waving his mask frantically.

Glancing across, he saw Storrel with his arm across the men gathered on the rope attached to Johnson, delaying any action until he was ready. Looking back, he saw Johnson was waving and screaming at them from below, but the distance and the wind took the words away, and then he noticed a shadow edged with a faint unearthly blue glow was appearing from below.

Without warning Chief Johnson was hauled up into the air, and the propane tanks and a flash of the orange preserver he'd sat on bobbed up in the waves as his weight was removed. Meanwhile, in the sea beneath, the pall of blue light grew stronger and larger beneath the surface. A refracted silhouette of the creature became visible within the glow as it rose inexorably slowly toward the surface.

Swinging and spiralling like a drunken trapeze artist, Johnson attempted to get himself into position to fire the flare gun he held. He swung once precariously close to the rig, then with much shifting of his body weight against the direction of swing managed to get his body to face toward the rising nightmare.

He aimed and fired the flare, shooting a bright burning rocket vaguely in the direction of his target.

But with the cylinders pumping propane gas into the air, the flare caught the fumes, sending an instantaneous wave of flame down into the cylinders. They exploded with a 'Whoomph' and sent up a billow of flame-filled black smoke, metal fragments, and tiny orange flecks into the air. After concussion-filled moments, while the fragments rained down and the column of smoke dissipated, everyone's attention snapped back to the foamy and splash-ringed surface. Where was the evidence of the creature's demise? Where was evidence of its destroyed body raining down?

He wondered fancifully, as hopeful relief warmed his mind, if they might see a pool of oil arise, as if they had depth-charged a submarine. But he wiped this image from his mind as the turmoil dissipated, and the sea surface began to settle.

Storrel joined in with the shouts of enthusiasm and retribution that had come from the men at the edge of the canteen as the propane bottles exploded in the water. They had temporarily drawn back to avoid the heat and glare, but now they returned to see the rewards of their efforts.

The blue glow had gone, and the shadow had decreased massively in size. Surely, he thought, the creature had been damaged or killed by the blast.

"Quickly, another one," Storrel shouted. "Let's finish this bastard thing off. We hurt it bad. Now let's make sure it knows we're boss."

They grabbed another orange ring and began urgently lashing propane bottles to it, gently cracking the seals to let the flow of gas out.

The stout chef and the medic Cooper positioned themselves at the rail, preparing to throw the ring and bottles down, looking back to Storrel as they awaited his command.

Storrel was watching the ocean below like a hawk, waiting for the massive shadow to return. If they could finish this thing now, then they could still come out of this with the rig and the men on board intact.

His mind wandered slightly into the boardroom, imagining the back slapping and the kudos he would gain from pulling this one out of the fire, single-handedly saving the rig and the image of the company. His confidence soared as it always did when he wrapped himself in his own self-image, basking in his own inner glory. So lost was he in the congratulations that he missed the return of the blue hue in the water and the shadow within it, as it hurtled toward the surface.

"There it is," shouted Cooper, pointing at the rapidly growing light below.

But the creature didn't breach the surface; instead an intense ball of blue rippling force ripped explosively out of the sea and sped like a rocket toward them and into the top edge of the canteen block, the blue blaze igniting the cylinders and the men holding them in a conflagration of energy and fire.

Dan watched as the explosion tore out the top of the metalwork, blowing men into the air like so many of Dan's sons' action figures, their bodies flung out into free-fall while other flying objects were body parts, metal and unidentifiable burning debris. The canteen block was left with a ragged hole from which flames and black smoke poured like a chimney, mixed with the screams of the men echoing inside.

Dan watched as his mind stumbled to grasp what was happening; the terror in him seemed to block out all rational thought. He just watched in numbed horror as men and wreckage fell to the ocean below as one.

Johnson wrenched his neck watching the ball of puissant blue might flash past him, crackling the air around it as it passed and leaving a smell of burnt ozone in its wake. He saw as it struck with a bright flash and red explosion above, and then Johnson found himself plummeting down toward the water below.

He let out a disbelieving scream as he plunged with a stomach-churning slap into the sea, sinking deep below the surface, scrabbling desperately to turn himself back the right way up as he clawed at the water breathlessly for the light above.

He surfaced sputtering and gulping air thick with fire, smoke, and burnt meat. He gasped as he felt a sickening pain in his side and leg and turned to escape from the pain in his side.

As he came to terms with breathing again, he found bizarrely that the scorched bodies of several men were floating around him. There seemed to be too many bits and a mist of red in the sea.

Reality hit him with a slap as the cold of the water snapped him back into himself. Then fear replaced his confusion; he was in the water, with the creature.

It felt like a clawed fist had gripped his innards, and he looked desperately at the distance to the rig. He attempted to turn silently in the water, to find something floating to which he could hold on.

His leg and side hurt, but his instincts were to just keep quietly stroking for the rig, to keep the saltwater from his mouth, and pray the creature didn't hear or taste him in amongst all the other meat in the water. Struggling to paddle as his side hurt more and more, he briefly reached down toward the pain, and his hand contacted something metal that caused a sharp pain to lance up through the left side of his ribcage.

Gasping involuntarily against the pain, he clamped his mouth shut, glancing desperately around in fear of being exposed. As he swam he recognized the body he was swimming past. It was wearing Storrel's distinctive black shirt; though the man's face was in the water and coated by slick wet hair, Johnson knew it was him.

He made to turn Storrel over, wincing at the pain in his side, but the shredded torso flipped over too easily, and he was confronted by ripped and burnt tissue, with the absence of any recognizable face. The whole other side of Storrel's body was missing, and Johnson pushed the cleaved corpse away with a shudder of revulsion and felt vomit choking his throat.

A cloud of dark red hovered in the water around the body like an ethereal shadow. His first thought was to be afraid of it attracting sharks, and then he remembered that a worse danger was already in the water.

He looked around in the waves, moaning slightly as his side sent another bolt of shooting pain through him as he tried to maneuver. He could see someone else attempting to swim, toward the platform's side. As the figure made another stroke, he saw that the arm went only to the elbow, ending in a ragged red stump. A blue haze seemed to be forming around the swimmer, and he recognized Niels ginger hair as he was abruptly yanked below the sea, some hundred feet from where Johnson swam, between him and the nearest part of the rig.

Above him there was another explosion, a bright flash, and a dark angular piece of the canteen substructure crashed into the sea, almost exactly where the man had been snatched down. The blue haze retreated and disappeared.

He had never been much of a religious man, going to the local Christian church with the wife on holidays and the odd Sunday service when he was on shore leave. But now he began to beg God with all his heart.

"Please, Lord, don't let it have me ... Save me, please, God ... oh, God, please!"

He breathed the words out with each exhalation, blowing the words with the saltwater from his mouth after each agonizing stroke, as he aimed toward the rig and the chance of safety. In a corner of his mind he remembered the saying that there were no atheists in a foxhole and that told you everything you needed to know about foxholes.

But here, alone in the water, praying for any chance of surviving was all that mattered to him; he continued his breathless prayers for his life as he brokenly breast stroked, trying desperately not to disturb the water.

The blue was moving now, beneath bodies to the right of him, coming inexorably back toward him; he began trying to increase his speed, causing more discharges of pain and a growing burning feeling in his leg. In one part of his mind, he knew that his movement was attracting the death that was coming for him, but his panic drove him on for a few more yards. His wet clothes seemed to be dragging at him, and he was sinking as he swam, his face going under a little more each time he pushed his arms forward to a breaststroke. He thought he saw a figure climbing out of the water onto the rig, but his chest was too tight and breathless to call out.

He was feeling dizzy now; his arms and legs were weighted with lead and becoming impossible to lift. He saw obscurely, as he sank again, that his hands and arms seemed to have a blue glow around them in the water, and beneath him he saw dark shadow limbs. He lost control of his bladder as the darkness flickered beneath him, moving shapes and lengths all around him; his mouth was too dry to scream despite the water, his throat parched as though all the liquid in his mouth had been burned away.

As suddenly as it came, the blue in the water moved away toward the rig and seemed to disappear from the surface. With a despairing last hope and a last surge of adrenaline, he began to agonizingly stroke his way toward the rig, in a kind of one-armed breaststroke, painfully slowly, trying to protect his damaged side from movement and fiery pain.

He looked up to the top of the rig edge only fifty feet above him and knew he would never make it back up. He could make out faces above and attempted to shout his desperation, but his throat was constricted and his lungs could barely use the meager oxygen available. He tried to wave or reach for the help above, but the pain flared with agony, and he sank momentarily, gulping water.

He surfaced, choking out water, his body racked with pain. He felt the cold dragging at his limbs, numbing his effort, the frantic effort, to keep his head above water.

Recognition of the stark fatality of his position hit him; his fear took him another ten feet, and then he had to stop, urgently attempting to tread water and grasp breaths. He sank quickly, the weight of his clothes finally dragging him down; he could see the blue glow a way off through the water. His body bucked with his first lungful of ocean; he fought briefly against the lack of air as his lungs burned. His last thought was of his wife and their garden, as black lassitude swept as over him.

Dan stared down onto the ocean's surface; it was scattered with dark shapes and slicks of dark liquid and fuel. He could see moving shapes. Miraculously, some of those below had survived the blast that had left the top corner of the canteen block looking as if some fiery giant had taken a bite out of it, leaving the edges jagged and blackened.

"Steve, what can we do? Can we help them?" he asked with a strained voice. He had a frantic desire to try and save them, despite his distress about what that would mean.

Before any answer could come, the shroud of blue and its dread silhouette returned, and one of the moving figures in the sea was yanked beneath the surface.

"There's nothing we can do, Dan. We have to take this opportunity. We have some more time to prepare ourselves, and for Jonnie's signal for help to get an answer. We have time. We have to use it to save ourselves."

Though Steve sounded conciliatory, Dan could feel the uncompromising message and will in his tone. Those below were lost.

Dan felt resentment at Steve's instant dismissal of the lives below, but at the same time he could see no way to save them or to help them. The rest of what Steve had said seemed finally to filter past his hurt at leaving the men to die in the sea.

"How do you know we have time?" he said suddenly looking back at Steve in surprise. "How do you know that bloody monster won't attack at any moment?"

Steve looked at him with an unwavering stare, pausing as if weighing up what information he needed to reveal.

"I think it must be an enormous drain to create that kind of power it just did, to fire a ball of force hundreds of feet. It must cost in energy and strength. Also, it's not moving fast down there, more drifting about like it's exhausted," he said with conviction.

"But that's still guesswork. You can't know that," Dan said, bemused.

Steve nodded and thought for another second.

"Maybe it is guesswork, but here's some more. Jonnie has been sending a distress signal since those idiots tried to blow it up with propane bottles and that thing down there hasn't come for us. What does that tell you?" Steve's voice was filled with certainty.

Steve grabbed one of the ropes attached to their makeshift lifeline and lowered himself down into the stores' doorway, leaving Dan with as many questions as answers. But Dan's mouth seemed closed by his own doubts and Steve's extraordinary change in strength of will and his need for Steve to be right.

What if the thing was too exhausted to attack? What if they had a chance?

He turned away from the sights below to help Brainy wind thin steel wire around individual heavier lengths of cable. Jonnie was joining the overlaid cables together with a solder gun run by a small generator, and already a steel net was beginning to take shape.

CHAPTER 19 — A QUIET TIME

In the hours that followed, Dan and the small remaining group frantically prepared themselves for the creature's next attack. Their nerves were stretched taut, like overburdened crane cables, burnt out with tiredness because of lack of sleep and the ever-present debilitating trepidation of the creature that hunted them.

They created spears from scaffold pipe scavenged from the rig's derrick and built wire up and around their position on more scaffold tubing, driven into the corrugated edges of the stores' block, till they had created a makeshift wire cage. Steve hoped the wires would slow the creature's questing spear limbs and give them time to fight back, but his eyes seem to slide away to the sea as he said it.

They finally finished putting together Jonnie's metal net in one last group effort, working almost silently, each trying to avoid the fear in the others' haunted eyes. As they wound wire and sweated in the high sun, Steve urged them on with a whispered monotone of dogged confidence.

The time passed, the sun stood at its highest in the sky, and they were ready.

After several hours without incident, Dan's mind was troubled by the thought someone might have lived through the fireball attack and that they might need their help. He approached Steve and quietly asked if he could go and make sure there were no survivors in the fractured, torn, and burnt metal shell of the canteen block that their gazes were constantly drawn to.

Steve agreed, though he was distracted and almost lost in his own thoughts. He seemed unconcerned about any danger and indifferent to their discussion and Dan's decision. He dismissed his presence and quickly became closed off to everyone, with the exception of Janice. He stared at the waves with a fixed impenetrable gaze.

So Dan, Jonnie, and Harry voted themselves a makeshift, and probably useless, rescue squad and gathered rope and medical supplies.

"Right den, lads, let's go an see what we can do for dem poor devils," said Jonnie; his face was pale and determined. He held a first aid kit from the stores, which he used to indicate the distance across the long drop to the sea to the light grey smoke wafting in the breeze from the black cavity of the canteen.

They crawled across the cold metal fencing of the corrugated block, moving with apprehensive reluctance as the foul smell of the smoke became stronger. Along with the fuel-laced smell of burning was the interlaced, unpleasant smell of burnt meat.

As they arrived in a slow procession, the extent of the explosion became clear. They came to the torn, blackened metal edge, and they saw the red, cracked skin of a man's severed arm, which had become hooked onto the sharp edges of the blasted steel, left behind as its owner had been blown away.

Wrinkling his nose as he edged around the charred limb, Jonnie leaned over and looked down into the smoking chimney, and nausea contorted his face. Dan crawled up alongside Jonnie and stared down, trying not to gag on the acrid smoke, while letting his eyes adjust to the darkness below.

Gradually, shapes started to emerge out of the darkness, and he could see the angles of the fixed canteen tables, and then the bodies and their remnants draped over the furniture. Some of the furniture and unmoving lumps were still smoldering, fueled by the layers of blackened grease and residue of life that was spattered around the room.

The corrugated walls were bowed outward and broken by the blast near the top, and as he looked farther down into the smoky gloom, past the shadow forms and into the murkier depths, he saw a glimpse of movement near the water-logged bottom of the canteen.

"Look, Jonnie," he said, pointing into the devastated canteen room. "There. You see? There's someone alive. We have to get down there." He was suddenly lifted with the excitement of hope that they might save someone.

"Alright, lad, calm down. We'll need a line like, and youse two will 'ave to lower me down. I'm not tryin' to lift a big lad like youse, and dat 'arry 'as got no 'ope," Jonnie said without Dan's enthusiasm but a familiar, if strained, humour.

Dan turned away, hurrying as quickly as possible back to a white-faced Harry, who was sitting on the edge of the walkway with the line they would need over one of his shoulders, his wet eyes fixed on the severed limb on the breached metal. He looked as if the structure of his face had begun to lose its integrity under the weight of his dismay.

"C'mon, mate, we need that rope, and I need you to help me lower Jonnie down. There's one of our lads in need of our help down there," he said, dragging Big C along with him back to the ruptured-metal mouth.

After some quick discussion, securing the rope, and getting their grip on the heavy nylon cord, they began lowering Jonnie into the darkness. They strained against his weight as his head disappeared below the rim and they were left in the sun staring into the dark pit. Sweat began running down Dan's back as he tried to maintain a taut line, gradually feeding out more, with only brief rests as Jonnie negotiated the tables below.

Jonnie felt unnerved by the choking stench, which seemed to set off a stomach-sinking revulsion as he breathed in the thick air. His descent into the blackness seemed to trigger dread and fear at every sound and touch; it seemed to enfold him within the smoke-filled air, and the cloying stink seemed to invade through his senses and skin as the acrid fumes stung his eyes.

The nylon rope bit uncomfortably around his armpits, feeling as though it were rubbing directly on his skin, with a burn of friction each time he swung in the air.

The blue sky above was being swallowed by the sides of the hole, like it was closing in, trapping him in this sickening well of death.

He distracted himself by shouting downward into the echoing space.

"Don't worry, lad, we're 'ere. We'll get ya out of dere quick like. I'm comin … I'm comin … You'll be alright … I'll be dere in a minute, mate."

Barely listening to the words he was using, he kept calling down, trying to sound reassuring to the man below as much as to keep the darkness from himself, as his senses were repelled by the smells and noxious atmosphere.

He passed the burnt lumps of men. He winced when he made contact with dead flesh and clambered gingerly through the mixed smears of liquids and charcoaled surfaces as he put his hands down on table ends and slid down the greasy blackened vinyl of burnt tabletops.

He could hear movement below him, wet slaps and an agonized moaning, that seemed to aggravate his nerves and stretch his anxiety in the enclosed death-filled chamber. Ice seemed to course through his veins. But he pushed on, wanting to help the poor soul below who was in so much pain.

He stopped when he was close to the water-covered end of the canteen room; he balanced on the top edge of a table and tried to catch his breath despite the stench. The moans below had become nerve-jinglingly loud and unnervingly close. He could hear each splash of movement, which seemed to be accompanied by a moan from the suffering man, right beneath him.

He paused for a second gathering of his courage, then reached into his body-warmer pocket to retrieve his torch and shone it below.

A charcoal-blackened hand reached up toward him, skin hanging in tatters from its fingers whose seared flesh leaked liquid from around exposed white bone.

Shining the torch down the ragged blackened arm, Jonnie's stomach turned as he saw the rest of the man. He'd lost his countenance, as if it had been smeared off by a burning wipe, leaving only a red, raw, scorched reminder of human features.

His stomach in his throat and fighting his own repulsion, he reached down to offer aid, but he couldn't imagine what form his aid might take, or of what use it would be. The thin lipless remains of a mouth dribbled thick drool shot with blood, and after a strangled choking, the hand dropped with a wet thump into the congested water and was still.

Jonnie felt a wave of sadness edged with relief as he shone the torch across the rest of the lumpen shapes in the water to reassure himself no one else had survived.

He was about to put the torch in the side pocket of his overalls, when he heard a clank against the metal wall to his left. He shone the torch back around to the entranceway that led to the back of the kitchen and adjoining buildings. In the passage between rooms, he shone his torch on a large figure wearing torn and blackened and bloodied overalls. Snapping the light up, he shone the beam on Lee Jones's raw, burned, and begrimed face, and he gasped in shock.

The man's eyes looked too wide and white against his charcoal-smeared cheeks. Blood trickled down his face from a cut in his scalp, and one of his ears appeared to have been burnt down to a red and blackened stump. What made him gasp in shock, though, was the man's insane grin.

"Jesus Christ, Jones, are you alright, man?" his voice sounding stunned at the damage the man seemed to bear without discomfort.

Suddenly, Jones moved, and before Jonnie could react, he felt a thump in his chest that was quickly followed by another. It felt as though he was looking down from a distance as Jones jammed a spear of metal into his chest. He looked shocked at the blood running down him. Pain seemed to hit him with a consciousness-vibrating force, making the edge of his vision go dark.

"That's right, fucker. You and all of Staples's little shit buddies are fuckin' dead. That fuckin' creature wants all your blood, and I'm giving it to him," he spat, and the spittle drooled from his bloodied mouth.

The spear stabbed again into Jonnie's chest, sending a burning flame from his chest into his left arm. He fell like a lead statue, face forward, with no ability to move his arms or stop his fall; he hit the thick water, pushing aside the floating body remains, and felt the cold liquid flood his lungs as the pain went quickly away.

"Jonnie! ... Jonnie!" Dan shouted down into the echoing

depths of the shattered canteen's guts and waited for an answer.

"What should we do, Dan?" Harry asked his voice anxious and fearful.

"We get him up. Now!" he said, the decision made up instantly in his mind.

They began hauling on the rope, but Dan felt only a dead weight. His mind was ringing with alarm at the lack of movement on the line.

"C'mon, Harry, let's get him out of there," he yelled at the man behind him.

They came to a sudden stop as the rope became taut and they were unable to pull it up farther.

"We'll give it some slack and try and unsnag him," Dan breathed.

"What the fuck has happened to Jonnie? Is he alright, Dan?" Harry panted breathlessly.

Dan gathered himself, then shot a glance downward. "I don't know. I can only see the shape of him. I can't see him moving. Maybe he hit his head or something … Let's get him up."

They tried again, and again, and suddenly they seemed to drag Jonnie free after some more concerted pulling that had Dan sweating heavily and, by the sounds of his agonized breathing, had Harry close to having a heart attack.

With a sudden last haul, Jonnie's wet and limp body came up over the edge, and they dragged him to the level area.

As soon as his body came to a stop, they could see the blood in the wet smear left behind on the surface they had dragged him over. Dan turned Jonnie over, and murky water spilled from his lips. Looking down Jonnie's body, he could see the blood-soaked front of his overalls and the dark red holes where something had stabbed through into his chest.

"Christ, that thing is down there. It's fucking down there, and we've got to get out of here, Dan, for fuck's sake, come on." Harry ran toward the walkway, his bulk quivering with the sudden activity.

Dan checked Jonnie for a pulse, the hairs on the back of Dan's neck standing up, but he couldn't bring himself to leave Jonnie behind. Jonnie had been a good man, someone he'd cared about, someone he'd called a friend. He felt a lump at the back of his throat, and tears stood in his eyes, blurring out the man's lifeless corpse.

Wiping the tears from his eyes and with a fearful last glance at the menacing black void, he began to creep as silently as he could toward the walkway, leaving Jonnie's corpse behind along with a part of himself.

He arrived shortly after Harry and was met by Steve, Janice, and Brainy. He could hear the discussion as Harry told them how the creature had killed Jonnie, having somehow entered the buildings below the canteen block. Brainy seemed to think something that big would struggle to get through that amount of small spaces.

"It can rip through steel like it's not there. It could climb through this rig like a beetle burrowing through rotten fucking wood," Harry was arguing.

Steve was standing apart from them. He seemed oddly tranquil, even as he objected to the possibility of Harry's statement. He was almost glassy-eyed and was unruffled by Harry's desperate and unequivocal demands that he was wrong.

"Steve, it's true. Jonnie was stabbed through the chest, many times. What else could have done that?" Dan said with concern. Steve looked as if he were on some sort of drug as he slowly swiveled his head around to face Dan.

"No, Dan. It can't have been it." Steve's voice sounded almost indistinct, as if he were calling in his thoughts from a great distance.

"Christ, man, the body's over there. We've seen it. How else, who else, could have done it? That thing is there, man, goddamn it." Dan felt his temper rising with his fear and distress at losing Jonnie.

"No, that's not possible Dan, because it's still down in the water. Look," he said dreamily, pointing down to the surface of the sea.

Dan and Harry both rushed to the wire wrapped around their perch, and they looked down on the ocean below.

Much of the detritus floating on the surface had dispersed; the bodies had floated farther out to sea, apart from one corpse that had washed up on the rig and become ensnared. Looking down into the upper light-shafted sea, Dan spotted a blurry shadow hanging about ominously in the depths.

"That can't be. It can't. What killed Jonnie? What the fuck is happening?" Harry panted his eyes white-edged with shock and fear.

Dan turned back to look at Steve.

"Do you know what killed Jonnie? Do you know what that thing is going to do, Steve?" he said, urgently needing some explanation and reassurance from Steve. He needed to believe Steve could still be counted on to know what was going on and what they should do.

From one second to the next Steve's face seemed to undergo a transformation, from slack-featured and dull-eyed to animated and keen.

"We've got to move," Steve announced. "We've got to get to the canteen and quickly."

"What the fuck for? We've got this place defended," Brainy complained.

"No fucking way," Harry agreed. "I'm not going back over there."

"We have to go. Now!" Steve shouted.

Janice, holding his arm, looked alarmed. "Is the creature coming, Steve?"

"No ... but it will hear that helicopter coming, the same as I can."

They all looked with shocked disbelief in the direction Steve was pointing.

"It can't land near here, with the wires we've put up. We need to move to the canteen, so it can get near us," he said, squinting into the distance.

And they all strained their eyes in the same direction.

"There!" Brainy said, pointing. "There it is. It's a fucking chopper. We're fucking saved!" he said with cheer in his voice.

"Not unless we move, right now," Steve cajoled. "It will hear it, too. We have to get on that 'copter and off this rig before it can get up here. So MOVE!" He ended with a yell, trying to break through the sudden euphoria that had come over them, holding them in a stupor.

Dragging Janice, Steve sprinted for the walkway and got her up on top and crawling. His sudden action broke the ice, and the others all ran to join him at the edge, looking up again for a sight of their flying savior or down in dread that the creature would reappear.

As Steve got Harry on the walkway and crawling, Brainy was looking down at the ocean. "Oh, shit! Oh, fucking shit!" he breathed, full of dread. "It's moving. It's bloody coming. Oh, shit. Shit! Come on, come on. We have to go," he said, pushing himself past Dan to the edge of the stores' block and the outside surface of the walkway.

"Go, go," Steve said, almost pushing him onto the metal chain-link of the walkway.

The sound of the helicopter was becoming a constant thrum in the background, and with a glance up, Steve saw the vehicle angling toward them, the cockpit glass glinting in the sunlight, with the promise of rescue and joyful survival.

"Let's go, Dan," he said, clapping the man on the shoulder. "We're getting out of here."

Agrushell drifted against the current, using just enough motion of his outer limbs to maintain his position in the water in relation to the stricken and sinking metal coral. He floated using only enough energy to let his senses range around him, while he registered the damage within. He assessed the information about his injuries coming from his body and felt the seared and dying cells in the complex chambers at his core. The massive effort of producing a globe of so much power had scoured his interior membrane, leaving only a charred hollow. He could feel the scorched flesh of his interior sending out strands of inner fire that seemed to blaze in electric shorts through the networks of his structure.

He could feel the fire, painful and acute, in his every fiber and limb; he could taste the fiery seeds of his death as they seemed to sparkle and ignite in small lightning shocks of pain. The flashes of pain were like the flash information of his senses that had once communicated pure information, vision and thought. Now the information was broken and fragmented, as if the world around him had become as flickering and dappled as the sunlight through the undulating ocean's skin.

He assessed the incoming signals and motion from the rig, slowly forming it into comprehensible fragmented pictures. He perceived the swimmers agitating the water above and, with fading strength, managed to coat himself in the last reserves of his blue puissance, the effort sending sporadic veins of hot agony through his extremities. But he must protect himself from another light-water trap; his enemy was not without hunting skills, teeth, or cunning.

With slow cautious patience, he snatched each swimming organism down, dispatching them with stabbing limbs, and then drifted on to the next till the sea was quiet of vibrations and electrical signals, and he rested again.

Gliding deeper, to the bottom of the metal coral, he wound limbs around the broken rig and let himself rest without expending effort, let the cold water through his outer carapace to soothe the burns of the blue fire and let his mind recover from its mind-numbing expenditure of force.

He recognized that some of the compartments of his mind had closed, the secondary minds in his body no longer responded; he was left enclosed in his mind's central nucleus. But he was beyond its recall or being turned away from his purpose.

The contact with the metal increased his connection with the creatures above and his sharing with the other. He watched in bemusement but also in jealousy as one creature killed another, stealing away the life of one of his prey. He marked the killer, separate from the group, as his next quarry for vengeance.

He began to build the strength of will to hunt this lone thief, who had stolen his prey, when another rhythmic vibration reached his damaged senses. He was aware of its machine nature and what it meant.

He was uplifted by a surge of urgency and anger as he jetted toward the surface and, breaking into the light water, began to climb the structure from the water's edge. He fueled his might with his desperate need to avenge his kind and bandaged his pain with an icy determined hatred.

There would be no rescue for the life stealers above.

CHAPTER 20 — RESCUE AND RECKONING

The red and white sea rescue Sikorsky helicopter hovered above them, thrumming the air and drowning all other sound out. It blasted air down upon them with a gale force draft that threatened to push them from their roost on the canteen end as it caught in the folds of their clothes. But for Janice, it was like a fanfare that sent her heart racing with the excitement and relief of survival.

As she pushed aside the hair whipping across her face, she saw a man in a bright yellow flotation suit, with a red life preserver at his neck, being hoisted down toward them on a wire line, swinging in the downdraft of the thumping rotor blades above.

As Janice looked up into the force of the wind, its strength hurting her eyes, she wanted to scream for the swaying man overhead to hurry. She could still feel the beast at their backs. She'd heard Brainy shouting behind her as the helicopter hovered toward them that it was down there and it had started to climb up the sinking rig.

Fearfully she glanced behind her, as if the beast might appear there at any moment. Steve held her arm, turning her away from the precipice of her fear, and hurried her to the front of their small group, to be lifted up first. Relief and gratitude seemed to clog her throat as tears welled in her eyes. She wished she could see his face through her windblown hair.

Beneath the noise of the helicopter and with the fear and confusion spinning in her mind, she could barely focus on anything but the wonderful hope that she would be lifted away from this place of nightmare and horror. Soon she would be returned to the so beautiful, normal world, where nightmares didn't hunt and where she could remember what feeling safe was like.

The buoyancy of relief seemed to make her dizzy, and she felt her legs might collapse as the weight of impending death was lifted from her. The promise of liberation seemed to empty the dread that had underpinned her every moment.

She could escape the visions in her mind of the creature stabbing into her body with its black, crusted spears or dragging her beneath the sea surface with its suckered limbs, to be fed upon as she drowned.

Awash in her respite, her thoughts drowned out by the helicopter and the comforting reassurance of Steve's embrace, it seemed to take her forever to realize that the face of the man being lowered from the helicopter had become contorted with emotion and that he was pointing wildly and shouting soundlessly.

She turned to look behind her; her brain took in the scene being played out in detached slow motion. Everyone seemed to be moving at once. Brainy had been clubbed to the floor with an inch-thick grey steel bar from behind. Before Harry had a chance to raise his hands to stave off a similar blow, he was also bludgeoned directly over the head; the metal bar bent slightly with the force of the impact. She heard the sound of it in her head and experienced an empathetic and visceral response to the blow, feeling like she was the one who had been attacked. Harry dropped forward with glazed, unfocused eyes, falling like a lifeless puppet.

As Harry's body toppled out of her line of vision, the fleshy face of the big Geordie man Jones was revealed. His face was bloodily scorched and blackened; his eyes flashed wild and white-edged as he swung his steel cudgel at Dan.

Turning just in time, Dan threw up his hands to stop the blow, but the steel connected with one of his out-thrust arms, smashing it downward. He flung himself away, out of further reach, screaming soundlessly into the roar of the rescue 'copter above, falling to his knees, clasping his damaged arm to his chest.

Shock ran down Janice's spine when Steve caught hold of her from behind, pulling her behind him and putting himself between her and Lee Jones.

Jones grinned at him with blood-smeared teeth, gesturing for Steve to come toward him, and Steve launched himself at the shaking face of Jones. Steve reached up to grab Jones's weapon before he had a chance to swing it down again, but he was fractionally too late to grab at the weapon at the apex of its strike. Instead, he arrived in time to get beneath the swing and grasp Jones's arms, stopping him mid-swing.

For a few moments they swayed back and forth struggling for control, but clasping Jones's upraised arms from underneath put Steve in a weaker position. The big man could bring his height and weight to bear, and it was giving Jones the advantage. Slowly he brought his arms downward, pushing Steve onto his knees. The wild-eyed man was grinning again, showing his blood-rimmed teeth and leaking muddy spittle from one side of his rictus.

With a sudden movement, Jones brought up a knee, smacking Steve in the top of his chest, knocking him to the ground. He was left sprawling and at the mercy of the man standing with weapon raised above him.

Jones gripped the bar fiercely, his eyes wet and glazed with maniac delight, his grin so wide Janice wondered if it wouldn't begin to split the seams of his mouth. She prepared to launch herself at him, though fear made her stomach tremble and limbs feel weak.

Jones looked down on his victim and tensed himself to deliver as massive a blow as he could muster, when his crazed features went suddenly slack with shocked surprise. He looked down at his chest, with a string of drool falling from his mouth.

She followed his look down.

A conical spike was protruding from the centre of his chest, and she instantly recognized the black flake–encrusted surface of one of the creature's deadly spear appendages.

With casual ease, Jones's body was lifted up and thrown out into space in a powerfully dismissive toss, disappearing past the end of the canteen block's edge. She looked up, hoping to reach up for rescue from the helicopter crew but saw the helmeted man screaming into his radio headset and gesturing to be brought up and away from the nightmare below.

Bereft of hope, she turned to see the creature arise onto the flat surface; it was close enough now that she could see details of its black, indented skin. She noticed that a blistered white crown crested the area where a head might be as the colossal creature crept toward her.

Her stomach became churning liquid and her bladder painful till, not even realizing, she voided a hot stream down her leg. The heat of it seemed to flee her body as terror filled her veins with ice water. She couldn't blame the fleeing man at all.

She watched in defeat as the creature seemed to part pour, part clamber its bulk atop the building. She waited despairingly for its limbs to gather around itself and come with spears of death for her. With a snakelike undulation and slow inevitability the spears came searching for her as she stood unmoving in her horror.

The black arms extended over where Steve lay prostrate, looking up with desperation in his eyes, as the sharpened limbs hung and turned above him. But they milled about as if unsure of their prey, and then slowly moved away, changing shape to tentacles more like those of an octopus.

Bypassing Steve, the limbs shifted again, once more sharp, and began reaching up for the man dangling from the helicopter; he continued his screams noiselessly beneath the helicopter's roar, swinging and trying to kick away the approaching limbs with his feet, his face contorted with panic.

But the creature could not be resisted, and it speared the man with the same ease it had Jones. It stabbed him through the centre of his torso and then withdrew with a jerk, tearing out his innards so that they hung down the front of the man's yellow dry suit in red tatters.

Its other suckered black arms thickened and began wrapping and coiling in an ever-tightening grip around the wire cable that led up to the helicopter.

She watched in dread dismay, unable to form a thought as the creature took grip and began to haul on the wire line; the howling down thrust from the helicopter's attempt to pull away sprayed blood from the dead man above into her face.

Steve swung her around by her shoulders and made her jump out of her skin; he was yelling at her as he tried to manoeuvre her away and back toward the walkway.

He was shouting at her, gesturing for her to go back across, and without thought she started crawling across the metal fretwork, as Steve returned to the others. With the thunder of the helicopter behind her, the wind from its rotors seemed to blow her quickly across, and reaching her destination, she fell onto the cold metal looking back up at the mammoth tug-of-war between monster and machinery.

The beast was dragging the craft down painfully slowly into range of its multiple arms, which she saw had now become very large and thickly suckered, ready to clasp onto its target.

The helicopter tried to dip and dive and strain away, its engines pushed to the maximum. But half the creature's bulk was now fully in view, and it had secured itself to the deck, becoming an immovable anchor.

She looked in fascinated dismay at the flexing dolphin-like skin and the apertures of the creature's construction that exposed the inner configuration of its body. She saw mighty limbs that seemed to sprout from the very skin of the mass of the creature. She could see a vivid white coating on its top; it looked like melted plastic had been poured onto the thing to form a hardened shell that was at odds with its flexible surface.

This couldn't be the same creature as before; it was no longer crab-like or hard-shelled to the point of invulnerability. This monster was now constructed more like some alien black squid, she thought.

Her eyes were dragged away from the tableau before her as Dan crawled into view, and she realized, with guilt, that she had let him crawl across using only one arm, as the other was quite obviously broken. With nausea at the sight of his out-of-shape limb, she helped him onto the flat surface, where he collapsed to look back across the chasm between buildings at the raging battle.

With belated concern she looked frantically to see where Steve was, and she saw him half-carrying Brainy onto the walkway side, getting on first, and with small assistance from a bloody-faced Brainy, pulling the man onto the walkway, part-dragging him along behind him across the gap to where she watched helplessly.

She could not fit on the walkway to help them, so she waited with mounting anxiety as she watched the conflict behind them.

The chopper was being reeled in, despite the defiant scream of its engines.

The creature had the helicopter low enough to catch its landing struts with an arm that curled around the metal. In the chopper, she saw a man with a knife being swung about by the struggle, desperately attempting to hack at the metal line which the creature was using to reel them in. But now it was reaching the fuselage with its limbs; it seemed that he was too late, and it was too late for them all.

Steve arrived screaming at her to get Dan and herself into the storerooms beneath them. He pushed her toward Dan, still shouting to be heard over the strained and erratic sounds being made by the stressed engines of the helicopter and the screaming of the angle-strained rotors.

She reached down to Dan's uninjured side and began to attempt to lift him. He raised his head and, white-faced, managed a nod and began getting onto his feet. They quickly went to the edge, and she wrapped a line under his armpits. Using his good arm to hold on, Dan helped Janice get him to their destination as best he could. Janice managed to successfully lower him down using the pulley.

Steve briskly attached the line to her, glancing constantly to the monumentally deafening contest being fought across from them. "Get into a storeroom. Dan can pull you in. When that helicopter hits the rig, it's going to blow shrapnel out like an explosion," he yelled in her ear. "We'll be down to join you in a few seconds."

His face was grim with deep lines of stress, and for a moment he gazed into her eyes and gave her arm a brief squeeze, and she wanted to hold him very badly.

He swung her down, and she passed instructions to Dan to pull the pair through the now-horizontal doorway, then headed for the nearest room, waiting outside the next sideways door for the others to catch up to her.

She saw Dan pull Brainy in with his good arm and in a few seconds reach up for Steve. As they struggled to close the door, the rig was shaken by violent vibrations. The entrance door slammed echoingly shut, and all light ahead of her disappeared.

An explosion hammered through the rig's framework, rocking the floor, knocking her off her feet, and sending her sprawling across the painted metal floor that was once the wall. She lay on the chill metal in the pitch black, listening to what sounded like heavyweight hailstones raining on the outside walls, and then there was a very sudden silence that seemed to stretch on and on.

Finally she gathered her courage, and she crawled back down the passageway to find the others, calling Steve's name and praying that he'd made it inside safely.

"Don't worry. I'm fine, Janice," Steve said with a deep sigh of relief, his voice resounding in the confined space. "I'm over here. Near the entrance," he said, trying to guide her with his voice.

"My fucking head hurts," Brainy said with a moan of complaint, and for no apparent reason she began to laugh out loud.

Everyone joined in as if it were the funniest thing they had ever heard, apart from Brainy, who asked in a thin voice if they could shut up as his skull was ringing.

It set them all off again.

Janice found Steve's side, and they hugged fiercely in the blackness, letting the laughter briefly wash away the stress of fear that had held them in strained anxiety for so long.

Dan groaned loudly in the silence after the laughter subsided. "I think my arm may be broken," Dan complained, wincing.

His injury came back to her memory suddenly, and she flinched inwardly.

"Steve, have you got a torch? I'll go and see if I can find bandages and a splint for Dan's arm in the stores." She wanted to make up for her spinelessness inaction earlier.

A light beam ignited in the dark, and as the torch was passed, she caught flashed glimpses of drawn, desperate faces, looking like miners trapped below ground and entombed by a ceiling collapse.

Not wanting to think beyond the moment, she hurried back down the corridor, shining the light before her, looking for the supplies. She tried not to think about what lay outside the walls she passed or how fragile their protection was from the creature outside. She felt very alone in the reverberating metal corridor, and every echoing sound jangled her nerves and made her jump.

She found a medical kit and a solid wooden measuring ruler that she thought would fit her purpose; clasping the items to her chest, she rushed back as quickly as she could out of the lonely space that seemed filled with the dark danger of the creature.

As she approached the men by the door, she heard Dan ask, "What happened to Harry, Steve?" His voice was trembling and full of distress; it echoed in the resonant corridor.

"He was dead when I got to him. Jones cracked his head open with that metal bar," Steve said with bitter anger.

Janice felt all the laughter of before drain from her, and all at once the nightmare fear of what remained outside the door of the stores came flooding back. She stopped in the dark, fear making her quail from the pain and misery ahead of her.

"Did that explosion kill the thing out there, Steve?" Dan asked without doubt that Steve would be able to answer his question. Nor was there any uncertainty in his voice about the existence of a relationship between the creature and the man in the dark with him.

There was a long pause.

"No, it didn't kill it, hurt it some more, I think … Its, its thoughts seem confused. It is definitely hurt, damaged badly."

His voice was soft in the dark, and Janice abruptly felt a need to see the face of the man she had fallen so quickly in love with. She shone her torch near where she thought he was. His head was down, his face covered by his hair, but as her light beam picked him out, he raised his head and gave a thin smile, just for her. Then he closed his eyes.

"A hurt animal is dangerous, and this one is very, very dangerous. I can't fully sense its thoughts or actions. Its pain and injury are acting like a camouflage … but I can still feel it out there." His voice fell to silence.

"Oh, my dear God," Dan whispered. "May the Lord protect us."

Brainy wondered what it would be like to be able to let go of all his fears and worries, to let his faith in some magical being take away all of the distress and anguish. It sounded great. But he didn't believe it for a second. No god would make life so harsh, a torture, for those creatures it claimed to love.

Where was this super being when his sister was rotting painfully to death of cancer at age twenty? Where was a god when his father drank and beat his mother, then later him, with his old belt and its silver buckle?

No, there was no god to save them and no place to hide from what was down there in the ocean. He shuddered as he remembered the beast sharpening its black limbs into blades, as he remembered the nightmare apparition the first night it had come aboard. His body still trembled as he remembered it hanging above him, preparing to cut him open while he squirmed in terror. To distract himself, he touched his fingertips to the tender wound on his head, which antagonized its ache.

He listened to the other three talking quietly in the torchlight and felt suddenly soothed by the companionship of their voices; he drank in their faces, thought how odd it was that, despite his own self-interest, he had come to know such decent, courageous people.

He felt oddly comfortable in their company, and for once in his life, he was not trying to shield what he thought or felt; he wasn't concerned that they might try and take from him or that they might use him somehow. They had shared horrors and survived together and now shared a bond. For the first time in his life, he realized that he was with people who had become like family, born of the terrors they had endured together. He recognized that this was one of the few times in his life, despite the throb in his skull, that he felt he belonged.

The positive feeling was short-lived as he listened to Steve confide that they were still in danger; the monster was awaiting them. Steve's next words made cold fear clench his guts.

"We have to go back outside. We can't defend ourselves from it in here. It will punch through these walls like they're cardboard, and there is nowhere in here where we can hide from it. We must be able to fight, and we must fight it off, or … kill it, if we want to still be here to be rescued."

Steve's voice was soft and full of sadness, but with a timber of resigned determination.

"We're in no shape for a fight. Dan's only got one working arm," Brainy said, hearing the plaintive sound in his voice and wondering if his fear had always remained just under the skin, hidden beneath false bravado and self-conceit.

"Can we … Can we kill that thing?" he asked, a tremble in his voice.

"If we want to survive, we have to," Steve stated unhappily.

They had all come to trust Steve, so they waited while Janice finished splinting and binding Dan's arm and then turned her ministrations to Brainy. Janice gave him paracetamol with some water. He sat passively as she worked at bandaging his head. When everyone was ready, Steve approached the door and stopped, tensed before it.

They held their breaths collectively while Steve waited, building up courage to pull down the door handle and swing it open. With a sudden spasmodic jerk of action, he opened the door with a push and quickly jumped back as the door shrieked on its hinges, swinging down out of sight to crash into the metal below, ringing like a bell.

Light shone in through the horizontal rectangle of the door opening. They tensed, waiting for black limbs to appear around the edges of the entry, but only the sound of the wind and waves entered their metal cave.

After a long and anxiety-crammed interval, Steve finally leaned out of the door space and looked around outside. They watched his every move with fearful tension. Brainy found the pressure running up his spine stopped like a boulder inside his chest; his mouth was dry, and his vision seemed acutely rimmed with the crystalline sharp pains in his head.

Despite their anxiety, only the distant sounds of seagull shrieks drifted through the hatchway. With a communal, if tentative, release of tension, they prepared to return topside.

Steve led the way, followed by Janice, who slipped out lithely and scrambled quickly up out of view.

Next came an ashen-faced Dan, who struggled, despite Brainy's assistance, as he tried to shield his damaged arm, wincing and occasionally sucking in his breath when his arm was jarred about, but finally he was up and away.

Then Brainy was left alone in the dark passageway, the ocean moving and vibrating the metal beneath him. He could smell the sea air, and for a moment he drank in the blue, almost cloudless, sky beyond the post box–like opening before him.

With a reluctant sigh, he leaned out of the entranceway, feeling the breeze on his face, and saw the metal embedded up the outside of the stores' wall. It had changed into a macabre and dangerous version of a climbing wall. Metal pieces from the rotors' and helicopter's explosion had showered the surrounding area with jagged shrapnel.

He looked below to the sea, but there was no sign of helicopter wreckage or of the creature. The canteen block was pared open down one side like a partially peeled iron banana skin, exposing the blackened interior. In the sky above the damaged canteen, many seagulls were circling in a vague vortex of v-shaped wings.

The sun was lower now, glinting off the ocean, but the sea air was fresh and clean and seemed to reduce the swelling inside his head.

Brainy clambered up onto the block, and with the assistance of Steve, he slid beneath the wires they had erected and stood looking at his new friends, feeling the warmth of the sun on his back as he untied the line around him.

"There's no sign of the thing, Steve. I think this time it's too damaged to come after us. All we have to do is sit tight till more help arrives. They must have radioed out for help before they went down," he said with a heartfelt confidence, enjoying the late-day sun and the strong possibility of life, as the cool breeze ran gently along his side and leg.

He looked at Steve, who was frowning.

"I don't know, Brainy. It's still around, but I can't seem to feel any coherent pattern of thought. I can't feel where it is. We've still got to be prepared for anything," he said with concern and worry evident in his tone.

"I think we're okay, mate. We can make it. We've made it this far, and we will make it home, I know it," he said, trying to cheer up his friend. But Steve's eyes had flicked down to Brainy's feet and widened, and his mouth was forming a shout.

Brainy looked down.

He froze, watching a black squid-like arm curl around his leg; then he yelled out loud as it coiled around his thigh. He couldn't seem to understand what was happening as the suckered surface scraped along his skin. The whole thing was too unreal. Finally, he seemed to realize that voices were screaming warnings at him, and he looked up into the familiar fear-filled faces before him.

With a wrench and a blur of movement, he was dragged into the air and backward into the metal wires behind him, which bent with the strain of his body's contact. He felt pain as the wires cut into his flesh like burning nooses, and he was left hanging below them with his mind shutting down from shock and pain as his friends' hands reached down to help him.

Agrushell had dragged the machine down, hardening his surface as the whirling metal blades of the machine came close. The ill-wrought flying contrivance coughed out noxious chemical gas and battered his acoustic senses with a barrage of vibrations that seemed to shake his fractured mind, till with an explosion of rage, he jerked the machine down into the metal corral.

It detonated into lethal metal fragments and liquid fire that seemed to wash over him. It blasted him from his anchored perch, tearing away limb ends and blinding his senses with an inferno of pain. The blast blew out all thought and sensation, so that he fell insensibly into an ocean of darkness.

Unknown amounts of black time passed until sharp discomfort began to drag him from the well of his oblivion; lightning and confusion rolled through his nerves, shaking his inner core. But no light of vision seemed to find him between the bright lightning strikes of agony, each shock rolling over him in red agonizing explosions in the darkness.

When the confused images began to gradually filter between the aftershocks of pain, they were of the jumbled images of the enemy above, seen through the sight of the one above. He saw the bright light-water sky and the fleshy weak creatures as they moved awkwardly under their own weight.

The sight came back again and again of the female, overlaid with some emotional context that was alien and peculiar. Yet he welcomed the sight of the female foe, even though her visage was revisited in a way he could not begin to comprehend.

As more of him became aware, he felt the damage and deep wounds that seemed to float on a bottomless current of weariness and weakness. But he was drawn to the one above; an internal tide pulled at him with an inexorable draw to the creature whose sight he shared.

With painful slowness and force of will against the pull of the blackness gathering like oceanic depths in his mind, he pulled himself toward the light-water realm and began to climb. He struggled to produce limbs and power to drag his weight upward across the metal coral, till finally he stopped in the shadow below the jutting construction they stood upon above and gathered himself for a final attack.

CHAPTER 21 — LEFT AT THE LAST

With Janice's scream of dismay and animal panic ringing in his ears, Steve ran to follow Brainy's form as it flew into the metal cables which they had stretched around the top corner of the stores block. He watched as Brainy hit the lines and was dragged down by the leg, the wire sagging beneath his weight and the force of the creature's wrenching tug.

Smaller arms began to wrap themselves around Brainy's torso, increasing the creature's grip. Steve feared that the force and weight of the heaving tentacles pulling Brainy against the taut metal strands would begin to cut through Brainy's clothes and into his flesh, like a cheese wire, because of the powerful heaving pressure being exerted by the beast below.

He reached the edge of the block, trying to grab Brainy back from the thing's grasp but finding he was inches beyond his reach. The man lay immobile on the tautly strained wires as he was stretched against them. His eyes were looking up unseeingly, his pupils black dilated pools of shock.

With both Dan (with his one good arm) and Janice trying to anchor him as he stretched out, Steve's fingertips just managed to brush Brainy's stained orange boiler suit. He attempted to extend himself farther, but still couldn't reach him. He saw dark patches of blood seeping around where Brainy's limbs were caught up, under and around his arms and legs; he knew Brainy would have to reach back up to him, and quickly.

"Brainy! For God's sake, Brainy, help us … Brainy, snap out of it!" Steve yelled at the man underneath him, trying to spark some urgency in him. Brainy was shaking as if he was having some sort of fit, his mouth moving as though he were trying to describe the pain on his purpling face. Abruptly his eyes focused on Steve and he let loose a strangled moan, filled with pain-ridden loss, filled with the realization that death had a tight hold and was squeezing out his life.

"Please, Brainy, reach up your hand," Janice begged. "We can still pull you up."

She was crying, her desperation making her voice break as she continued to beg him to reach up to her.

Steve felt as if he could hear Brainy's skin being sliced by the tightly strung, singing metal lines and feel Brainy's flesh beginning to give way before them, like his mum's old egg slicer he used to love using in the kitchen, forcing the steel lines through the helpless white then yellow meat of the egg.

But just when he thought meat would give way to steel, Brainy began to move his hand upward, his eyes fixed on Janice. Some new force of will or wild desperation to fight for his life had grasped him. Despite the agony on his strangled face, the saliva that dribbled from his mouth, and his eyes bulging large with bloodshot dread, he fought to be saved.

Steve caught his hand, and as he did, Brainy's arm became detached with a twang of stressed metal being released; this seemed to signal some final capitulation of Brainy's flesh, as first Brainy's head, and then his other arm, detached with more metallic twangs. Blood sprayed, and the body was snatched away, leaving only the fleshy residue that dripped red off the metal wires as they danced with release.

Steve stared unbelievingly at where Brainy had been, and then down at the creature below and at the hand and arm he still gripped. With a visceral spasm, he released the separated appendage to fall with the rest of its previous owner.

His attention snapped back to Brainy's slaughterer below; its surface seemed ragged and torn. Metal jutted from parts of its carapace; the tentacles, some stunted, seemed to move in spasmodic jerks. The bulk of the creature seemed to shift toward him as if turning to look in his direction. They regarded each other, and for a moment, Steve found himself looking at himself through the creature's vision.

He looked like an active ultrasound, an electrical chart of his makeup and assembly that was lit up in his vision. Every fiber was detailed in glowing color and every vein mapped in fragile pulsing detail.

The image surged to focus on his head, and he looked through a million cross-sections of his eyes into the electrical storm of his brain, watching hue and heat change with the electrical fields that generated tiny multicolored lighting storms.

For just an instant, the tableau held, and then his normal sight returned in a blurry rush, and the creature came back up toward them with a deadly single-mindedness.

Steve threw himself backward, away from the edge, toward the simple spears they had made for their defense.

"Janice, get away, get back," he screamed as he leapt. "Get behind me."

He grabbed one of the scaffold spears and rolled it toward Dan, sending it ringing across the deck, then grabbed another spear and pushed himself onto his feet.

He spun to see that Janice stood only ten feet from the edge, where a dark shape was rising; the late afternoon sun cast an orange line down the side of its ragged contours. Tentacles appeared over the edge, suckered and large, that adhered themselves to the deck, supporting the creature's weight. New thinner limbs joined them; these were the same black encrusted bringers of death they had seen previously; they curved sinuously over the side. The new limbs began to flatten like blades or tip themselves with crude sharpened points, while others had aborted stump-like ends.

They gathered around Janice, seeming to point to their favourite part of her anatomy, while they poised themselves like rattlesnakes around her, ready to strike.

Steve's mind went red with the pressure of desperation and the need for violent release; the winds in the cave of his mind screamed with a hurricane of growing internal compression, till with a feral mindless yell, he launched himself and his spear at the nearest limb. He swung his scaffold pole with fury, and it made heavy contact across the breadth of the nearest pointed limb, leaving the metal tube ringing in his hands.

The limb flinched away a little but no mark was left where his blow landed, and the spearheads still menaced the fragile form of Janice before them.

He jumped in front of Janice's petrified form and swept her behind him with his arm, then began frantically swinging at as many of the spear ends as he could reach, the long metal tube ringing again and again till his hands began to feel numb as he desperately tried to keep the black-flaked lances away.

Dan joined in the battle as best he could, stabbing at the weaving appendages with his own spear gripped in his one good arm and balanced under his other arm, but his blows seem to similarly have little effect. Then one of the creature's many limbs seemed to grow bored with his intrusion and batted him away with a swipe that left him sprawling and screaming as his broken arm made direct contact with the floor.

So Steve faced the dark demon from his mind alone. He looked at its nightmare shape as his arms burned from repeatedly swinging his homemade spear and began to feel as if they were made from lead. He staggered a little backward after a missed blow, and the behemoth slowly followed, dragging more of its bulk up onto the side of the metal stores. The weight made the metal protest in strident shrieks and loud metallic groans as the large suckered arms put tension on the building's construction, and then once again the spear-tipped limbs began to encircle him. Wearily, he raised his spear and snatched a quick look back at Janice, who quivered hollow-eyed behind him. She had squirmed as far back across the floor as she could, to the edge of the rectangle of white-painted metal they stood on.

He turned back with a rage of last defiance, determined to keep the thing away from her as long as possible. The rattlesnake motion of the black spears had begun again and he prepared to himself to fight, when the sound of a motor starting distracted him.

The limbs seemed equally surprised, their motion stopping and turning protectively to face the new unexpected roar.

"Get away from it, Steve," Dan yelled.

Steve jumped back and watched Dan bend down swiftly to attach a large silver crocodile clamp to the generator he had just started. There was an explosion of sparks as intense electric light arced from beneath the creature.

The thing became upright and rigid; liquid spurted from the wounds on its immense flanks, and its menacing spears came down in one abrupt convulsion of motion, punching through the metal of the deck. Its stump-ended limbs began banging in a rhythmic beat on the metal, which echoed like huge drums through the storerooms below.

Steve smelled burnt seaweed and fish, a combination that took him back to his mother burning his father's tea-time mackerel, and he remembered how afraid he had been of his rage as his father had entered the smoke-filled kitchen. So much of his life seemed to come down to the fear of his father and the love of his mother. He wondered, in the shocked detachment of the moment, which one had mattered in his life most.

With a static report, the generator stopped, leaving a detonation of silence, and the creature sagged instantly down onto the deck. Its body had suddenly become flaccid over the more ridged substructure of its being, its limbs becoming soft, formless tubes of skin. Looking like a floppy jellyfish corpse, it sagged over the edge as if it had been spilled onto the deck.

Steve couldn't seem to take his eyes off the alien body before him, as much because he feared it might come to life again at any second as because of the surreality of its outlandish mass spread before him.

A screech of metal on metal made him jump as Dan dragged his spear over to them, eyeing the unmoving mound of flesh fearfully as he approached.

"Is it dead?" he asked querulously and then tentatively approached one of the formless arms and, with a sudden motion, poked it and jumped back. He looked wide-eyed in fearful anticipation of its retaliation, but the flesh simply indented beneath his spear point and then returned to its former shape and inaction.

They looked at each other with shocked hope, and Janice began to cry soundlessly, not even realizing the tears were falling. The sight of her harrowed distress sent him to her, and Steve clasped her to him and murmured words of love, hope, and reassurance till they joined into formless murmurings of comfort.

He held her until the ache left his chest and she stopped trembling, then after a smile and a long look into her eyes, he turned to Dan. He was also smiling as if the sun had just come up instead of it beginning to set. He reached out, carefully avoiding Dan's damaged arm, and hugged his friend's right shoulder.

"You saved our asses, mate," he said, finding sudden tears in his eyes and the heavy weight of his emotions at the back of his throat. He stood back, looking Dan in the eyes; Dan nodded back at him with a world of shared terror and hard-won survival in his haunted expression.

"Thank you, Dan," and he meant it as much as anything he had ever said in his life.

"Well, it was my pleasure, to be honest," Dan said, making them both smile at the joking manner. But his expression quickly clouded again, and his brow creased.

"But we should thank Jonnie. He thought that net up and built it. He saved us. I just turned it on," Dan said thoughtfully, looking at the black skin of the deflated and defeated monster.

"I don't think I'll ever stop thanking Jonnie for as long as I live, mate, nor Brainy. We wouldn't be here if it wasn't for both of them, and we won't ever forget it," Steve said with emotion and sadness clogging his voice.

Janice joined them and hugged both Dan and Steve.

"Is there any way of getting that thing off this rig?" she asked with angry distaste as she partially hid behind Steve's shoulder looking at the depleted corpse.

"I don't think we're going to shift this sack of crap off here anytime soon," Dan said, toeing one of the sagging limbs and wrinkling his nose at the singed-seaweed reek.

"We could go back in the storeroom. Lock ourselves in till help comes." Her hand trembled on Steve's arm as she whispered in an anxiety-troubled voice beside him.

He looked into her wide eyes, dark and damp, lined with the stress and terror she had gone through. He gathered her into his arms and held her shaking body, till she went limp in his arms again.

"We must stay up top, Janice, in case a ship or another helicopter comes. If we go inside and this rig sinks any farther, we'll be trapped. The canteen block is wrecked. There's nowhere to be safe but here," he said, trying to be soothing and reassuring. "Let's get as far from that stinking monster as we can."

He carried her over to the side of the walkway, trying to give her his most comforting smile, but something seemed to prickle along the nape of his neck and his forehead felt pressured with a splinter of pain behind his eyes that made his head ache from temple to temple.

"How long do you think it will take till someone shows up, Steve?" Dan asked, looking to the skies hopefully.

"I don't fucking know, Dan. Give it a rest, will you? We're fucking knackered here," he snapped, aggravation gathering in his mind; as soon as the pressure was released, he was awash in regret.

"I'm sorry, mate. I seem to be stressed out." He rubbed his temples, trying to knuckle the compression from his skull.

"It's alright. You've been through hell, and I'm surprised you have the energy left to stand." Dan put a concerned hand on Steve's shoulder.

Behind them the splayed and limp arms began to expand, rising and swelling with rippling motions, then with jerks of spasmodic movement, which slowed to actions of returning mobility and control, as limbs begun to curl and sinuously bend. The many arms reduced till they were mainly thin, attaching anchor points, leaving one central limb to swell, engorging its black-flake-covered skin and producing large, white-fleshed sucker cups which bloomed in perfect circles from the flesh of the giant tentacle.

The great mass of flesh hanging from metal and cartilage shared in the engorgement process, renewing its form in shuddering ripples along the length of the soft lozenge-shaped body, as the meat of its form began to refill from some unseen spout of satiation. The transformation of rebuilding continued till the former planes and symmetry of the octagonal-indented skin were regenerated. With its physique reborn, it turned its bulk in a posture of awareness toward the sound of talking voices.

Janice held on tightly around Steve's upper chest, burying her head against him and letting the tightly wrapped emotions inside her give way to a catharsis of emotion. It set free every hurt and dread inside her in a gush of feeling that seemed to break through every control she had, and her relief melted every barrier inside her away. She let emotions flood out of her as she bawled with a howl of released anguish into the warm comfort of Steve's embrace.

"Don't let me go, Steve. Please. Not ever." She could hear the pleading in her voice but didn't care. She had always been strong and independent, but right at that moment, she didn't think she could make it through the next hour without knowing he was with her. She couldn't think of a place outside of his embrace, a landscape not made up of his brown eyes or his long hair mysteriously hiding his face.

"I'll always be holding you, my angel," he murmured into her ear. "Don't be afraid. I'll always protect you."

The smell of the sea and the strong sweet-sour musk of him as she was pressed to him seemed to entwine in her senses. She could feel the muscular strength in his arms and the warm pulse of his body against her and felt she was where she belonged and where she would always be.

Perhaps it was some inner instinct, some sixth sense that broke the boundless pleasure of his hold, which made her lift her head at that precise moment. Perhaps it was the unusual shift in the already stressed metalwork which caused the afflicted rig structure to screech in an oddly discordant way, at odds with the rhythmic metallic complaints caused by the ocean waves' regular action.

Whatever the reason for her prescience, she looked up at just the correct moment, just the correct splinter of time, which, despite her soul-flushed state and numbed spirit, made her eyes widen.

In that exact instant of time, Steve saw the fear blossom in her eyes and pushed her away to spin and face what she saw.

She stumbled back against the side of the walkway and

watched as an enormous black tentacle swirled around Steve's body, engulfing him in its hold.

His unthinking action had pushed her clear of the oncoming reach of the creature, saving her from its grip. The encircling limb began drawing him back toward the massive midnight blackness that had risen up, highlighted by the sinking sun. The creature had been resurrected, reborn in all its awful glory behind them, while they had foolishly congratulated themselves on their victory.

She watched as if the volume had been turned off in her mind as the arm rolled away from her with Steve entwined helplessly in its moving coils.

Dan ran to his aid, using his one good arm to swing his spear, which bounced back ineffectively. He struck again and again till he was brushed aside by one of the more slender black arms. With its prize grasped close to its body, the creature began a slow withdrawal to slide back over the edge.

Janice was on her feet and stumbling toward the retreating shape, following as if she were in a waking nightmare; no emotion or sense came to her thoughts, just a random cacophony of white noise that could easily have been a scream.

She walked like a hollow automaton following indistinct programming as she moved solid locked legs toward the edge and looked down the face of the rig through tubular metal spars and metal rectangles. The creature was ten feet below, falling downward in spastic, short, dropping motions, catching itself and then dropping again. She caught a glimpse of Steve's face, congested purple by the tight grip around his torso, as he was rolled around in the monster's clasp.

The creature continued its staccato and faltering stop-start descent till it reached the waterline, then fell, as if it could no longer support the enormity of its own size, into the top of the surf breaking around the rig.

The creature carried Steve below the waves with it, and Janice felt her heart fall into the waves, too.

Her mind seemed to explode with a black surge and only the thunder of her heart in her ears and the ragged breath in her lungs seemed to penetrate the submerged state of her thoughts. Ideas swam in black despair in her mind and in the sea below. Perhaps she was screaming, she might have felt pain, but only the desperate unconscious effort to reach for Steve was driving her body. With the realization of what she was doing, came the realization of where she was.

She was hung over the edge of the stores block, staring down into the ocean, where, at the surface of the sea, waves rolled in to crash into the oil platform's structure. She was looking down between the crisscross of the derrick's pipes trying to see him. She had no idea who was holding her legs to suspend her upside down like this, but felt if she could only reach out to the water below, she might find Steve within her reach.

With a rough yank she was hauled up to fall flat on her back with a dizzying thump. She found herself lying alongside Dan, who clasped her with his good arm and held her tight.

"He's gone, Janice. Don't make his death mean nothing. He wanted you to live with all his heart and fought to save you until his last breath gave out. Don't waste what he was doing for us."

Dan's voice was broken with effort and emotion, his eyes wet with the agonizing struggle to hold her with his broken arm and with his own loss.

"What? He's gone … Trying to do what?" She screamed, letting disbelief and pain burst from her chest.

"He was trying to save us, Janice. Don't let that mean nothing," Dan shouted desperately, gripping her more tightly, as if he feared she may attempt to launch herself from the building once more.

She shuddered in his grip; a dark void felt as if it was opening up inside her as her cold tears splattered down onto her arms. She looked despairingly down to the unbroken waves below as the loss hit her like a hacking blow to her soul, which released a keening from within. She howled deep in her throat in an attempt to let the sound release the pressure of the damage which had gathered in her heart and made it feel like it was being unforgivingly compressed between her ribs.

He was dead.

Steve managed to grasp a frantically small breath before he hit the water, despite it feeling like his ribcage was going to cave in beneath the bands of inexorable pressure that were wrapped around his chest and arms. The salt of the seawater and the complexity of creature and limbs in the water confused his vision and made his ability to judge his position impossible, but he sensed the fading of light, and the weight of compression in his eardrums meant that the creature was dragging him deeper.

He attempted to writhe in a desperate attempt to free himself from the creature's coils, but his struggles were futile against the massive encompassing tentacle that was wrapped around him. He managed to get a hand to the hip pocket of his overalls and with intense frantic effort to grasp the lock knife there. With effort that seemed to make his head feel like it was about to burst, he opened the knife with one hand, put it in his palm, and then began to force the blade into the creature's flesh.

It had no effect; the blade penetrated but was held tight as if he had jammed it into a stone.

His lungs had begun to burn, and he thrashed more violently against the overwhelming requirement for breath. Darkness filled his head and seemed to yammer between his temples in a cloud at the backs of his eyes.

Just as he felt he could no longer hold back the water from his lungs, he was in a world of light; the purple light of the creature surrounded and absorbed his mind.

He was swimming fast in pitch-black ice-covered seas, chasing behind great creatures that seemed to be constructed of unfathomable radiating symbols, crafted of symmetrically beautiful flowing lines that intersected in changing forms of multifaceted light. They shimmered and blurred rainbow trails behind them as they glided through the water. They were vast beings, deep with lore and wisdom; they were, he knew, Gods. He understood at that moment that he shared the mind of this creature, this organism called Argushell. He knew, as Agrushell knew, that they were both being drawn toward these beings.

With an explosive flare Steve's memories burst forth, expanding each moment of his life into individual bursts of illumination which were absorbed into the ever-expanding rainbow trails. Every instant of his life was encoded into light glyphs and taken up by the rainbows that turned like whirlwind funnels as they absorbed his memories along with a billion alien ones from the creature whose consciousness he shared.

And as the whirlwind tubes connected and vanished into a black hole point of darkness he knew his body's life was spent and only blackness lay behind him. So he floated with another mind as light began to grow; he felt as if he were sitting atop a massive swelling ball of radiance which was forcing itself to reach a nova climax of life ending. This was Agrushell's body coming to its end.

He felt the soft touch of its fragmented feelings as it readied itself to pass in a conflagration that would erase it and any trace of its physical body. He knew that this was part of the way it had been made and part of the purpose it had been given. He learned of and understood the damage that the drilling of the seabed had caused the other, and Agrushell understood how ignorant, and perhaps innocent, he and so many of his kind were. Perhaps they shared forgiveness in the bright moment, before the light became so intense that all thinking ceased. In the final inferno of blue puissance, both minds passed like the flicker of a single flame in the fire.

Dan watched the surface of the sea just like Janice did. He did not watch for a last sign of Steve or for help to arrive, but for the creature's final return. He waited with lead weights in his chest for the last victims of this rig to be taken by the demon below. He saw no hope for their continued survival, no way of gaining escape from the murderous arms as it took them to itself or skewered their bodies like meat for the grill.

He had only prayer in his mind as he begged his absent god to guard his children and wife. In his heart he begged for the waiting to be over and for an end to the dread of what was coming for them.

His hopelessness was left nonplussed when the ocean erupted below them in a white-domed detonation of water, deep filled with a blue luminosity that lifted it upward with massive power, throwing water a hundred feet in the air. The dome of seawater hovered for a second, defying gravity, and then collapsed back into the ocean with a thunderous roar. It reminded him of depth charges he'd seen in war movies.

"I don't believe it," he said. "Did you see that, Janice, did you see?"

Janice's voice seemed far away and spoke with a thin monotone of shattered indifference. "I saw it ... What does it mean?"

Her injured voice poured cold water on his excitement as he remembered the cost she'd already paid.

"I think he found a way to destroy that thing, Janice. I think Steve managed to find a way to save you," he whispered to her, no longing holding her in fear of what she might do but to offer his solicitude for her pain.

Inside, Dan thanked Steve for his rescue.

With a deep puffing out of his cheeks and an ache in his ribcage, he felt tears in his eyes and began to weep that he might see his family again and for the man who had made it possible, a man whom he called a friend, who had died to make it conceivable.

"Thank you, Steve," he said out loud, hoping that his words might be heard, could somehow pass the walls of time and reach him. That he might feel his gratitude as he began to freely weep for the sacrifice of his life for theirs. Janice was weeping too, and he held her close, so she knew he was with her in her loss.

The sun started to set in burning dark orange across the ocean before them.

Beneath the waves two creatures cut from Agrushell's same ocean-going dark cloth converged above the remnant of their brother on the ocean floor.

They had traveled from distant planetary trenches at opposite ends of this world where they shared the same collective guardian role that had been given them all, only leaving their responsibility to answer Agrushell's distant call.

They floated above the last remains of their twin flesh, silently still as they hung like black silhouettes in the light-shafted water, till one of the ocean brothers by unspoken agreement glided downward.

The brother reached with one long dark tentacle to scoop up a telescope-sized tube of flesh from the stirred seabed silt. It was a tube of Agrushell's very being, deposited in his final moments; it contained every piece of knowledge, information, and experienced memory of him and his other, stored in the cellular DNA of the cylinder.

The brother subsumed the tube into his flesh and experienced the flash communication of instant recall, feeling every thought and moment the other had experienced in time-blurred micro-speed, while lengthy minutes passed in the macro of real time.

When the full extent of the information contained within Agrushell had been shared, absorbed, and remembered, the two Agrumen shared flash communication between each other as they shared their brother's insights into their enemy and the capabilities of them as a foe. They considered the threat against their kind and the depth of their command to protect.

Distantly, through the echoes of the ocean, they heard more of the light-water killers approaching. They were warned by Agrushell's and by the others stolen memories of the light-water's danger, of those that were called 'human.' They must protect and preserve their duty.

It was instantaneously decided that one would guard the gateways, while the other would take Agrushell's memories through the gate to the boundless waters of their beginnings.

They assessed the potential danger of the remaining creatures on the sinking structure and the amount of time before a multitude of their kind appeared against the compulsion to fulfill their purpose. With agreement they jetted away in opposite directions, becoming deeply and stealthily camouflaged above the seabed.

The fragile humans that they were leaving behind would soon enough be subjects of a greater hunt.

THE END

CHECK OUT OTHER GREAT DEEP SEA THRILLERS

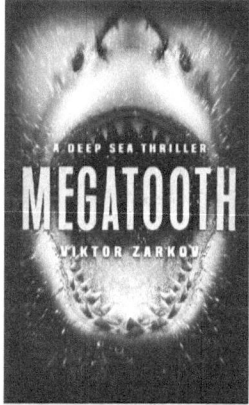

MEGATOOTH
by Viktor Zarkov

When the death rate of sperm whales rises dramatically, a well-respected environmental activist puts together a ragtag team to hit the high seas to investigate the matter. They suspect that the deaths are due to poachers and they are all driven by a need for justice.

Elsewhere, an experimental government vessel is enhancing deep sea mining equipment. They see one of these dead whales up close and personal...and are fairly certain that it wasn't poachers that killed it.

Both of these teams are about to discover that poachers are the least of their worries. There is something hunting the whales...

Something big
Something prehistoric.
Something terrifying.
MEGATOOTH!

BLOOD CRUISE
by Jake Bible

Ben Clow's plans are set. Drop off kids, pick up girlfriend, head to the marina, and hop on best friend's cruiser for a weekend of fun at sea. But Ben's happy plans are about to be changed by a tentacled horror that lurks beneath the waves.

International crime lords! Deep cover black ops agents! A ravenous, bloodsucking monster! A storm of evil and danger conspire to turn Ben Clow's vacation from a fun ocean getaway into a nightmare of a Blood Cruise!

CHECK OUT OTHER GREAT DEEP SEA THRILLERS

SEA RAPTOR
by John J. Rust

From terrorist hunter to monster hunter! Jack Rastun was a decorated U.S. Army Ranger, until an unfortunate incident forced him out of the service. He is soon hired by the Foundation for Undocumented Biological Investigation and given a new mission, to search for cryptids, creatures whose existence has not been proven by mainstream science. Teaming up with the daring and beautiful wildlife photographer Karen Thatcher, they must stop a sea monster's deadly rampage along the Jersey Shore. But that's not the only danger Rastun faces. A group of murderous animal smugglers also want the creature. Rastun must utilize every skill learned from years of fighting, otherwise, his first mission for the FUBI might very well be his last.

OCEAN'S HAMMER
by D.J. Goodman

Something strange is happening in the Sea of Cortez. Whales are beaching for no apparent reason and the local hammerhead shark population, previously believed to be fished to extinction, has suddenly reappeared. Marine biologists Maria Quintero and Kevin Hoyt have come to investigate with a television producer in tow, hoping to get footage that will land them a reality TV show. The plan is to have a stand-off against a notorious illegal shark-fishing captain and then go home.

Things are not going according to plan.

There is something new in the waters of the Sea of Cortez. Something smart. Something huge. Something that has its own plans for Quintero and Hoyt.

CHECK OUT OTHER GREAT DEEP SEA THRILLERS

THEY RISE
by Hunter Shea

Some call them ghost sharks, the oldest and strangest looking creatures in the sea.

Marine biologist Brad Whitley has studied chimaera fish all his life. He thought he knew everything about them. He was wrong. Warming ocean temperatures free legions of prehistoric chimaera fish from their methane ice suspended animation. Now, in a corner of the Bermuda Triangle, the ocean waters run red. The 400 million year old massive killing machines know no mercy, destroying everything in their path. It will take Whitley, his climatologist ex-wife and the entire US Navy to stop them in the bloodiest battle ever seen on the high seas.

SERPENTINE
by Barry Napier

Clarkton Lake is a picturesque vacation spot located in rural Virginia, great for fishing, skiing, and wasting summer days away.

But this summer, something is different. When butchered bodies are discovered in the water and along the muddy banks of Clarkton Lake, what starts out as a typical summer on the lake quickly turns into a nightmare.

This summer, something new lives in the lake...something that was born in the darkest depths of the ocean and accidentally brought to these typically peaceful waters.

It's getting bigger, it's getting smarter...and it's always hungry.

CHECK OUT OTHER GREAT
DEEP SEA THRILLERS

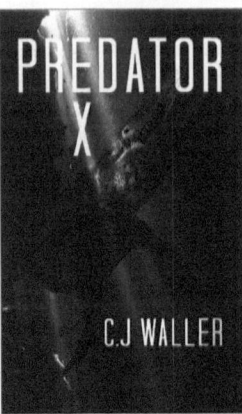

PREDATOR X
by C.J Waller

When deep level oil fracking uncovers a vast subterranean sea, a crack team of cavers and scientists are sent down to investigate. Upon their arrival, they disappear without a trace. A second team, including sedimentologist Dr Megan Stoker, are ordered to seek out Alpha Team and report back their findings. But Alpha team are nowhere to be found – instead, they are faced with something unexpected in the depths. Something ancient. Something huge. Something dangerous. Predator X

DEAD BAIT
by Tim Curran

A husband hell-bent on revenge hunts a Wereshark...A Russian mail order bride with a fishy secret...Crabs with a collective consciousness...A vampire who transforms into a Candiru...Zombie piranha...Bait that will have you crawling out of your skin and more. Drawing on horror, humor with a helping of dark fantasy and a touch of deviance, these 19 contemporary stories pay homage to the monsters that lurk in the murky waters of our imaginations. If you thought it was safe to go back in the water...Think Again!